THE
PRICE OF LOVE
AND
FREEDOM

James Allan Matte

Published and distributed throughout the World by
J. A. M. PUBLICATIONS
43 Brookside Drive
Williamsville, New York 14221-6915
Tel: (716) 634-6645 – Fax: (716) 634-7204
E-Mail: editor@jampublications.com
Website: URL: http://www.jampublications.com

This novel is a work of fiction.
Names, characters, places, events and incidents are either the product
of the author's imagination or are used fictitiously, and any resemblance
to actual persons, living or dead, businesses, companies, corporations,
organizations, events, or locales is entirely coincidental.

Copyright © 2020 James Allan Matte
All rights reserved.
ISBN- 978-1-7322114-2-1
Library of Congress Control Number: 2020900154
Matte, James Allan
The Price of Love and Freedom

Photo of German Army parading at the Arc de Triomphe-Champs Elysee,
Paris in 1940 on the front cover, courtersy of the German Federal Archives.
Bundsearchv, Bild 1011-751-OP067-34/Kropt/cc-by.sa.
Photo of Jewish couple added to German photo,
historically consistent with contents of novel.

Interior and cover design by: TeaBerryCreative.com
Edited by: John Nash

CONTENTS

DEDICATION

This book is dedicated to the men, women, and children who lost their lives at the hands of the Nazis in the Second World War. May their souls be with God in Heaven, where love and peace are eternal.

PROLOGUE

This fictitious story takes place primarily in Paris, France, during the decade preceding the Second World War, and the invasion and occupation of France by the German Armed Forces in 1940. Certain historical events in Europe during the pre-war years provide an understanding and insight into the actions of world dictators leading into the Second World War.

On 28 July 1921, Adolf Hitler is elected Chairman and Leader of the Nazis.

On 31 October 1922, Benito Mussolini becomes Prime Minister of Italy and leader of the National Fascist Party. Three years later he proclaims himself *Il Duce* (The Leader).

On 18 July 1925, Adolf Hitler's book *Mein Kampf* (My Struggle) an autobiographical manifesto and blueprint of his agenda for a Third Reich is published.

In 1933, Adolf Hitler becomes Chancellor of Germany, and leader of the National Socialist German Workers' Party, known as the Nazi Party. The following year, Hitler establishes himself as dictator with the title of *Fuhrer* (The Leader).

In October 1935, Italy invades Ethiopia.

In October 1936, Nazi Germany and Fascist Italy form the Rome-Berlin Axis treaty.

In November 1936, Japan and Germany sign the Anti-Comintern Pact against the Soviet Union, and Italy joins them the following year.

In March 1938, Hitler annexes Austria into Germany.

In March 1939, German Wehrmacht invades Czechoslovakia.

On 1 September 1939, German Wehrmacht invades Poland.

On 3 September 1939, Britain and France declare war on Germany.

In May 1940, Wehrmacht invades Denmark, Norway, Holland, Luxemburg, and Belgium.

On 10 June 1940, Italy declares war on Britain and France.

On 13 June 1940, German Wehrmacht conquers France, establishing the Occupied Zone (North) and the Free Zone (South).

In August 1940, Italy invades British Somaliland.

On 13 September 1940, Italy invades Egypt.

On 27 September 1940, Germany, Italy and Japan sign the Tripartite Pact.

In June 1941, Germany attacks Soviet Union. Soviet Union declares war on Germany.

On 7 December 1941, Japan attacks Pearl Harbor. United States declares war on Japan.

On 11 December 1941, Germany declares war on the United States.

On 11 December 1941, Italy declares war on the United States.

On 3 September 1943, Italy surrenders to the Allied Forces.

On 6 June 1944, Western Allies (U.S., Britain, Canada) invade Normandy, France.

On 25 August 1944, Paris liberated by French and American Forces.

On 7 May 1945, Germany surrenders to the Allied Forces.

On 2 September 1945, Japan surrenders to the Allied Forces.

CHAPTER I
An eventful meeting aboard *SS Ile de France*

The Infirmerie Notre Dame de Bon Secours was a small hospital in an elongated two-story brick building located on the Avenue Notre-Dame-de-Grace in Montreal, Canada. It was governed by the Congregation of Notre Dame Sisters of Bon Secours, dedicated to the treatment and nursing of mostly indigent patients whose number had grown substantially as a result of the Great Economic Depression in the United States and Canada. The year was 1929, and on the first of May of that year, the Congregation's director, Mother Superior Genevieve, a middle-aged woman, dressed in the traditional black habit and white cap with a frilled border and black veil, sat behind her wooden desk in her small library office, waiting for a visit from young Sister Christiane.

Sister Christiane, daughter of Doctor Francois Laurent, and her mother Bernadette Laurent, a practical nurse, had grown up in a household of medical practice that nurtured her into a nursing career, after graduation with honors from the Universite de Montreal with a Bachelor's degree in Medicine and Health. She was even permitted to assist her father, a surgeon, during surgery, experience that subsequently made her an invaluable member of the medical staff at the Sisters of Bon Secours, where she took her vows of chastity, poverty and obedience at the tender age of twenty-three. Her father, a most religious man, believed that no man was good enough for his daughter, and summarily dismissed as unworthy the only suitor his daughter had shown a serious interest. His disapproval effectively ended her relationship with the young man, who got engaged with another woman shortly thereafter. Her father convinced his daughter Christiane that a life dedicated to Jesus Christ was her only honorable choice, and her submissive mother's silence sealed her fate.

With a subdued knock on the open door to Mother Genevieve's office, stood Sister Christiane, wearing the traditional habit of Bon Secours nurses, waiting for permission to enter.

"Come in, Sister Christiane," said Mother Genevieve, who remained seated. "Please have a seat."

"Thank you, Mother Genevieve."

"Have you ever been to France?" asked Mother Genevieve.

"No Mother, I haven't," replied Sister Christiane with suspicion.

"Well, that is about to change. I have been directed by our Mother Superior Lucille in Paris, to have you reassigned to their hopital de Bon Secours[1] in Paris, immediately," said Mother Genevieve.

"This is so sudden. May I ask why I'm being transferred to Paris, Mother?" asked Christiane with a perplexed look on her angelic face.

"Because of your exceptional education and experience as a physician's assistant in surgical procedures, and your fluency

---

1 Hopital is the French name and spelling for Hospital in English.

in French. The economic depression in the United States and Canada is also being felt in France, and the rest of Europe, with poverty on the rise, and funding for medical care nearly absent. Therefore, we at Bon Secours have to step up to the plate, and deliver the medical care needed for as long as our resources hold out. I know what you're probably thinking… that we here in Montreal are also feeling the effects of the Great Depression. However, our geographic location does not restrict our trade to the United States, and our bank system is extremely stable, with the collapse of only one bank in Canada versus several thousand banks in the United States. So we here in Canada are safe, an ocean away from Europe, but our Sisters in France need our help in providing medical care for the poor victims of this Great Depression," said Mother Genevieve.

"I didn't realize the economic situation in Europe was that ominous. When am I scheduled to leave for Paris?" asked Sister Christiane.

"We have to get you a passport with a current photograph. As soon as we obtain your passport, you will be scheduled for departure aboard the *SS Ile de France*, which departs from New York City, and docks at the Port de Saint-Nazaire, France. From there you will take a train to Paris, and a taxi to the Hopital de Bon Secours. All of your expenses aboard the *SS Ile de France*, including your meals, will be defrayed by us. Nevertheless, you will be given a sum of money for unforeseen expenses and emergencies. I highly recommend that you take this time before your passport arrives to visit your parents, because it may be a long time before you see them again, depending on the duration of this economic depression in France," said Mother Genevieve.

"Thank you for being so thorough in your explanation of my forthcoming voyage and duties. I will do my best to serve God, and the Congregation of Hopital de Bon Secours, wherever you send me," replied Sister Christiane.

"That's the spirit that will serve you well during those hours, when all seems hopeless and doomed for disaster. Keep the Faith, Sister Christiane, and God be with you, always," said Mother Genevieve, ending the interview.

The following day, Sister Christiane visited her parents for dinner at their large home on the Boulevard Saint Joseph in Montreal.

Present at the dinner table was her father, Doctor Francois Laurent, and her mother Bernadette Laurent. No other relatives had been invited to this dinner because her father wanted a private meeting with his daughter prior to her departure for France.

"Well, at least they're sending you aboard the *SS Ile de France*, which is a modern passenger ship. However, I suspect you'll be traveling as a third-class passenger, since Sisters and Nuns have taken vows of poverty. But I'm going to call Mother Genevieve, and offer, no, insist on defraying the cost of raising you to at least a second-class passenger, if not first class. I'm not going to have my daughter traveling in conditions less than second-class," said Francois Laurent.

"Father, please don't do that, I implore you. I've taken those vows of poverty very seriously. I'll be nursing people of all faiths and economic status, possibly under horrible conditions that could lead to a revolution. That's the life I've chosen, Father, and you must respect and accept my decision to serve God, which you yourself have strongly encouraged," said Christiane.

Doctor Laurent, remained silent in order to avoid a disagreement with his daughter and only child, on the eve of her overseas assignment that might last several years. However, he did not abandon his desire to elevate his daughter's passenger status on the *SS Ile de France*.

Sister Christiane, wearing a black cape over her traditional black habit, and carrying one suitcase, exited the taxi that had brought her to the Manhattan harbor, where the *SS Ile de France* was docked. She stood for a moment staring at the huge transatlantic vessel and its three gigantic stacks protruding from its deck, with the sudden realization that this magnificent ship was going to be her mobile home for the next week. She joined the line of passengers having their boarding passes checked by a ship representative before walking up the wide inclined plank onto the ship's first deck. She was then informed by the second Ship Officer that her passenger ticket had been upgraded to second-class; therefore, she was directed to the second class deck where she found her room, number 214. The first thing she noticed was the single bed instead of a bunk, and a stuffed chair facing a three-drawer dresser with overhead mirror. She marveled at the small bathroom which managed to include a bathtub with overhead shower. A slim wall closet provided enough room for her limited wardrobe. All in all, she was very pleased with her accommodations, and glad her father had ignored her wishes and upgraded her cabin.

After unpacking and settling in, she decided to inspect the rest of the ocean-liner, and its dining room in particular, which did not disappoint her. In fact, the dining room included three decks requiring a grand staircase at its entrance. She also observed a grand foyer open to four decks. As she traveled through the ship, she came across an elegant gymnasium, but her interest was most satisfied with the discovery of a chapel in the neo-gothic style. After selecting a pew where she kneeled in prayer, she noticed a Jesuit priest wearing a black cassock tied with a cincture, kneeling in a pew facing the statue of the Virgin Mary. After a few minutes, the Jesuit priest stood up and walked up the aisle towards the exit, but not without a conspicuous glance at Christiane, now facing the altar, and the only other person in the chapel.

Christiane returned to her cabin, and wrote a letter to her parents, thanking her father for the cabin upgrade, and giving him and her mother a description of the ship, and its luxurious art-deco interior. She then noticed the movement of the ship from the dock signaling its departure across the Atlantic Ocean to the Port de Saint-Nazaire, France. This encouraged her to leave the cabin, and go up on deck to view the scenery and experience the seagoing atmosphere shared by other passengers also enjoying the seascape. Standing next to the port side railing, looking out into the vast sea, she hadn't noticed the approach of the Jesuit priest, who quietly stood next to her, also facing the sea.

"The vastness of the sea makes one feel so insignificant, yet appreciative of the therapeutic effect it has on one's soul," said the Jesuit who did not receive a reply.

"I'm sorry, Sister. I'm Father Andre. I saw you in the Chapel, and thought that since we appear to be the only clergy on this ship, it might interest you to join me for dinner this evening."

Christiane turned her head facing Father Andre in response to his invitation.

"Please excuse my inattention. I was completely mesmerized by the sea. I'm Sister Christiane with the Congregation de Bon Secours. You're probably right, that we are the only two members of the clergy on this ship. I therefore accept your kind invitation for dinner, Father," replied Christiane. "I gather from your habit that you are a Jesuit."

"Yes, I'm a Jesuit priest and a physician," replied Father Andre, momentarily stunned by her large, inviting blue eyes and angelic face, whose heavenly voice soothed his sensibilities and stirred his heart. "I'm a member of the Society of Jesus in New York City, temporarily assigned to a Christian Abbey in Paris, where they need a doctor with my specialty in cardiology, and it so happens I'm fluent in French," said Father Andre, wanting to impress her with further conversation.

"That's interesting, especially since I'm a nurse and physician's assistant in surgical operations. I'm also fluent in French, being from Montreal, Canada," said Christiane, who found

Father Andre's demeanor gentle and sensitive. She also found his scholarly appearance reassuring rather than intimidating.

"From Montreal. What a coincidence. My mother is from Montreal. That's why I'm fluent in French. I'm sure you're familiar with the Saint Joseph Oratory at the Cote des Neige, on the back side of Mount Royal, which is the largest basilica in the world dedicated to Saint Joseph," said Father Andre.

"Of course. Everyone in Montreal is familiar with Saint Joseph Oratory. What is your mother's name, may I ask?"

"Jeanne Cartier is her maiden name," answered Father Andre.

"But you live in New York City. Are you American?"

"Yes I am. My father is also a medical doctor from New York, who met my mother in Montreal during a medical convention. But I thought your accent, when you speak English, had a familiar ring, then it dawned on me that it reminded me of my mother who has a similar accent when she speaks English. It's your French Canadian accent. So we do have something in common besides religion," said Father Andre.

"I guess we do. It's a small world after all," replied Christiane, now feeling an unanticipated closeness to Father Andre that pleased her, in spite of its potential threat to her vows of chastity and celibacy.

"So where are you going to be working as a nurse?" asked Father Andre.

"At the Hopital de Bon Secours in Paris," replied Christiane, "and you?"

"At the Abbey of Saint-Germain-des-Pres in Paris," replied Father Andre.

"If I know my French history, isn't that Abbey of the Benedictine order?" asked Christiane.

"Yes, it is. However, you must understand that Saint Ignatius of Loyola designed his *company of Jesus* or *Jesuits*, to be available to go anywhere they're needed at a moment's notice, regardless of the Christian denomination, especially for us medical doctors. Therefore, we are welcomed by the Benedictines, and I'm sure by the Sisters of Hopital de Bon Secours," said Father Andre.

"I did some reading about the various religious orders in France, and Paris in particular, and I learned that the Benedictines are anchored mostly to their specific abbeys, and committed to their local community and its needs. I can see why they would welcome you, Father, being a physician, and surely in short supply," said Christiane whose smooth, mellow voice contained a subliminal hint of pride for the doctor.

"Well, my medical services may be called upon by the Hopital de Bon Secours, in which case I will ask for your assistance," said Father Andre with definite intentions.

"Hopefully, I will be available," replied Christiane.

The dining room with its art-deco interior, gave it a regal atmosphere that ran counter to the vows of poverty taken by Father Andre and Sister Christiane, sitting near the center of the dining room, in full view of the entire dining room patrons. Neither one wanted to express their impulsive guilt to the other, for fear of spoiling their appetite. However, Father

Andre realized that if he felt guilty, so would Sister Christiane; therefore, he decided to diffuse the issue.

"You know, Sister Christiane, we may never experience this lavish event again, and I always say, when in Rome, do as the Romans do. So let's enjoy this feast while it lasts, because I suspect that the way the world is heading in Europe, with the economic depression, and its resultant social and political impact, the seeds of war are very real, which could have us soon begging for crumbs and possibly our lives," said Father Andre.

"So you think war is inevitable?" asked Christiane.

"Well, you have Benito Mussolini, Prime Minister of the National Fascist Party in Italy. Then you have Adolf Hitler, who is Chairman and leader of the National Socialist German Worker's Party, also known as the Nazi Party, and author of *Mein Kampf,* an anti-semitic book that blames the Jews for all of Germany's problems, and predicts Germany's rise to power over its neighbors. In my view, that's a recipe for war on a grand scale," said Father Andre.

"Yes, but just because Hitler wrote a book doesn't mean that what he says will become fact," said Sister Christiane, who thought Father Andre was perhaps an alarmist.

"We Jesuits travel extensively, and are well aware of the political unrest that is seething in Europe. Mark my words, Germany will violate the Versailles Treaty and build up its military. It will threaten its neighbors including France with military invasion, unless its neighbors steadfastly resist Germany's expansion. Mussolini the Fascist has illusions of grandeur as the new Roman Emperor. I'm afraid that we are facing terrible times ahead. I'm here on a temporary assignment, and expect to return to New York within a year. But you, on the other hand, may be here when Europe catches fire, and you won't have any means of escape. I know you have taken an oath to serve mankind regardless of the danger," said Father Andre, looking into her large blue eyes and angelic face that had unsuspectedly captured his heart. Never before had a woman ever aroused his libido and feelings of love, but here he was, a Jesuit priest, who had taken vows of chastity, now experiencing feelings of passionate love for a Religious Sister, who had also taken a vow of chastity. He found himself in an impossible situation, but nevertheless felt a need to protect her from unspeakable harm in the hands of Nazis if she remained in France.

"Sister Christiane, I know this may sounds strange, coming from a Jesuit priest, but believe me, the vows you've taken do not require that you remain in France, nor do they forbid you from returning to Montreal. I just hate the thought of you being subjected to the cruelty of the Nazis, who will surely find their way into France, because I believe France is sleeping at the wheel of complacency. I'm not saying you should leave now, but don't delay beyond next year, otherwise it may be too late. I hope I'm still around to help you if you should need assistance in that regard."

"Father Andre. I'm flabbergasted at your suggestion I should leave my assigned post in Paris, because of possible danger from an as yet unlikely, undeclared war with Germany," replied Christiane, who then realized that Father Andre's plea

11

was apparently an emotional one, totally unexpected from a Jesuit priest. She now looked at him more as a man than as a priest, and saw the sensitivity in his brown eyes that seemed to beg her understanding of the emotional dilemma he was suffering. She felt a bond had formed between them with the revelation his mother was a French Canadian from Montreal, which somehow connected them ancestorioly. Had she not been an avowed Sister, she thought, she would have liked to have met his French Canadian mother, which generated thoughts of a deeper relationship she quickly dismissed as untenable.

"I'm so sorry if I offended you, Sister Christiane. I am merely relating the facts as I see them, and I am truly concerned about your safety, inasmuch as my mother would consider you, a Montrealer, a member of the family, with which I would most enthusiastically agree. So, it would greatly relieve my anxiety about your safety, if you would agree to stay in touch with me during your tour of duty in Paris. Would you do that for me, please?"

"Well, when you put it that way, Father Andre, how can I refuse such a kind and sincere request. Yes, I'll do my best to keep in touch with you," said Christiane, knowing she would do so, even if he hadn't made such a plea because she had grown very fond of him, in spite of their brief encounter.

That night, each in their separate cabins, with vivid images of each other in their minds, they attempted to fall asleep. Their thoughts revealed a deep affection for each other that could easily lead to love, and the resulting problems that would ensue if not curtailed.

The following day, they met for lunch, and then dinner, each not able to curtail their desire to be together during this short voyage, that offered them an opportunity for intimate privacy that might never occur again.

Each night, alone in their cabins, their thoughts and desires increased in intensity to a point that by the fifth day of their cruise, they silently realized they had fallen in love for the first time in their young lives, in spite of their sincere attempts to restrain those intimate feelings, that could lead to a violation of their vows of chastity. Each day, they visited the Chapel and prayed for guidance and the strength to resist temptation. However, their night's reverie, overwhelmed with the power of love, released uncontrolled emotions that could only be satisfied by the declaration of love for each other and its consummation.

That Saturday, the day before their arrival at the Port de Saint-Nazaire, Father Andre and Sister Christiane ate dinner together in the ship's elegant dining room, knowing it was to be their last dinner together on board this ship of romance.

"I don't think we're ever going to have this opportunity to be alone again, Christiane," said Father Andre, deliberately omitting her religious title of *Sister*. "I will cherish these past seven days for the rest of my life."

"You must not use such intimate words to describe our friendship, Father Andre. We're both committed to our vows of chastity and devotion to Jesus our savior. Believe me, you're not alone resisting the temptations offered in this voyage, but this is a test of our faith and devotion to God," said Sister Christiane.

"I am also a human being, whose need for love transcends all other emotions, especially when that love is for a woman whose beauty has captured my heart," said Father Andre, looking into her deep blue eyes that plead for mercy and understanding of her impossible position as a Sister devoted to Jesus.

"I wish we'd met under different circumstances, Father Andre. But as things are, I'm afraid that this most enjoyable dinner, will have to be our last one, for obvious reasons. Tomorrow, we'll be disembarking this sumptuous ship for the treatment of impoverished patients in different medical facilities, with possibly no future contact. So, I would like to thank you for the kindness you've shown me on this wonderful voyage and wish you much success and happiness in your work at the Abbey. I must now bid you goodbye, Father Andre, and return to my cabin, where I have things to do before retiring for the night," said Sister Christiane, now standing up from the table, causing Father Andre to also stand.

"Please allow me to escort you to your cabin, Sister Christiane," said Father Andre.

"No thank you, Father. I think it's better if I return to my cabin alone," replied Sister Christiane, who turned and started walking towards the dining room exit without his escort, while Father Andre stood frozen with a lump in his throat, watching her disappear from his life, possibly forever.

Inside her cabin, Sister Christiane removed her habit, and after using the bathroom, got ready for bed wearing only panties and brassiere, when she heard a knock on the door to her cabin. She got up and put on a robe, then stood near the door wondering whether she should open it, when she heard another knock on the door.

"Who's there?" asked Sister Christiane.

"It's me, Father Andre."

"It's late, Father, what do you want?"

"I need to talk to you. It's important," replied Father Andre.

"Can it wait 'till tomorrow morning?" asked Sister Christiane.

"No, it can't wait 'till tomorrow, and what I have to say can't be said through this door, so please let me in, Christiane," said Father Andre in a pleading voice.

Sister Christiane made sure her robe was securely tied, then unlocked the door, and opened it just wide enough to talk to him, but he gently moved forward causing her to back up, allowing him to close the door behind him. Not wearing his Jesuit habit, but slacks, short-sleeve shirt and sandals, Andre stared at Christiane, surprised she was wearing only a white linen robe with her short blond hair fully exposed. He suddenly felt an irresistible urge to embrace her, which he did, kissing her lips with a fervor that Christiane couldn't resist. He slipped his right hand inside her robe and quickly felt the smoothness of the skin on her tear-drop shaped cheeks of her tender derriege, arousing his libido into an erection. The smallness of the cabin with the bed immediately behind Christiane, she felt emotionally and physically captive to Andre's forceful embrace. He moved forward; they both landed on the bed with Christiane under him, her robe now open, revealing her full breasts and young figure. Aroused with great passion, Andre unbuttoned his trousers exposing his penis.

"Andre, please, we can't do this," said Christiane pleadingly, when suddenly she felt his penis entering her vagina, causing her to surrender and join Andre's erotic pleasure and gratification.

Having ejaculated and now physically spent, Andre turned on his side facing her in silence, waiting for Christiane to say something that would ease his guilt, but she remained quiet staring at the ceiling for a minute or two, and then turned her head towards Andre.

"Andre, you must leave and forget this ever happened. We must never meet again, as I will ask for a transfer where you will not find me," said Christiane. "I will pray for our souls, and ask forgiveness for the sin we've just committed."

Andre got up from the bed fastening his trousers and tightening his belt, then turned towards Christiane who had covered herself.

"I will never forget you, and what happened this evening will occupy my mind whenever I think of love, and what could have been, had we not been members of the clergy," replied Andre. "But I will honor your request and avoid any contact."

Andre opened the cabin door, turned around, and without saying a word, closed the door behind him. His sad face with tormented heart was the last image she held in memory of him. Christiane dropped to her knees, and prayed to God for forgiveness and moral strength.

Back in his cabin, Father Andre, undressed to take a shower, when he noticed blood on his penis and also on his white shorts. He then realized he had taken Sister Christiane's virginity, increasing his guilt tenfold. He got on his knees asking God for forgiveness, with the promise he would never see her again. He knew he couldn't remain in Paris, hence he would ask for a transfer to another European country at the earliest opportunity.

That Sunday, the disembarking passengers from the *SS Isle de France* sought transportation to their various destinations. The majority aimed for Paris, known as the City of Light, because it had become the center of enlightenment, due to its higher education and avant-guard philosophy. But it was also because it was one of the first cities to use street lights during the 19th Century's Great Exhibition.

Sister Christiane, dressed in her black habit, carrying her only suitcase, stood on the first deck, waiting to disembark, when she saw Father Andre, also dressed in his Jesuit habit, standing in line to board a bus, most likely destined for Paris or perhaps the train station several miles from the Port de Saint-Nazaire. She waited for him to get on the bus, then she disembarked the ship, hopeful there would be other transportation to Paris that would not bring her in contact with Father Andre.

Standing on the dock, looking so very much alone, anxious and vulnerable, she saw a large black automobile driven by a chauffeur pull up in front of her and stop. A woman dressed expensively, opened one of the four doors to the vehicle, and called out to Sister Christiane.

"Sister, we're going to Paris. If that's your destination, would you like to ride with us," she asked in French.

"Are you sure you have enough room for me, Madam?" asked Sister Christiane, in French.

"Yes, we do, and I would love your company on this long drive to Paris," replied the woman in French.

"I'm Sister Christiane of the Congregation de Bon Secours, and I gratefully accept your kind invitation," said Sister Christiane.

"I'm Madame Claire Beaumont, and this is my daughter Madeleine," then turning to her chauffeur, "Alain, please put Sister Christiane's suitcase in the trunk."

"Well, Sister Christiane, come on in and have a seat," said Madame Beaumont. "My daughter will be entering school in Paris, so we had to return from New York City in time for her matriculation."

"Alright, Alain, you may leave for Paris," commanded Madame Beaumont.

During the drive to Paris encompassing several hours, Madame Beaumont developed an unusually close relationship with Sister Christiane, whose trustworthiness ensured discretion.

"So, you're from Montreal, Canada. I presume you also speak English?" said Madame Beaumont in French.

"Yes, I do, and you?" asked Sister Christiane.

"I'm married to an American, a New York lawyer, so we have two homes, one in Long Island, New York and the other in Paris where I was born and raised," replied Madame Beaumont in perfect English.

"Really! So you're a French citizen and your husband is American. Is your daughter Madeleine an American or French citizen?" asked Sister Christiane.

"I was born in New York City, but I spent most of my summers in Paris and its environs, so I'm fluent in French," said Madeleine, entering into the conversation.

"So, now you're entering a secondary school for girls in Paris, then?" said Sister Christiane.

"Yes, the Lycee Fenelon," replied Madeleine proudly.

"That's a fine school with a great reputation," said Sister Christiane.

"My daughter is a straight 'A' student," added Madame Beaumont. "She wants to become a doctor of medicine."

"I'm sure you'll attain your goal, Madeleine, and become an exceptional doctor," said Sister Christiane, whose encouragement lifted Madeleine's spirit and liking for Sister Christiane.

"So you're going to be working as a nurse at the Hopital de Bon Secours, then," said Madame Beaumont.

"Yes, I've been trained and have experience assisting surgeons in medical operations," said Sister Christiane.

"I'm sure you will be a welcomed addition to their medical staff," said Madame Beaumont.

"I'm looking forward to visiting the various historical places in Paris, and the museums of art and science," said Sister Christiane.

"Yes, there are plenty of places for you to visit, including the Louvre museum, which should be at the top of your list," said Madame Beaumont.

"I've done a lot of research about the attractions Paris has to offer, and I'm sure the list is endless," said Sister Christiane.

"It's the City of Light, a place of enlightenment for intellectually motivated people," said Madame Beaumont.

"If you are interested, I would be glad to be your guide one day when you have the time. Here's my card with my telephone number. Please consider this a sincere invitation, Sister Christiane."

"Thank you, Madame Beaumont, for your kind invitation, which I will keep in mind when an opportunity occurs. But your position and responsibilities must leave you with little time to act as a guide for someone you just met," said Sister Christiane.

"My dear Sister Christiane. You underestimate your wonderful persona, which I find most refreshing in a world of mendacity and treachery. I'm a quick study about the people I meet, and you rank very high on my list of people I wish to associate with," said Madame Beaumont. "I hope you'll consider me as your friend, especially if you are in need, and please call me Claire."

"Well, I hope the weather will always be fair, but if it should get bad, I will always be available to meet your needs, Claire," replied Christiane.

Sister Christiane was delivered by Madame Claire Beaumont directly to the hopital de Bon Secours, and because of Sister Christiane's religious habit, they parted with a warm handshake, with Claire's reminder of her invitation.

CHAPTER II
Birth of illegitimate child named Jacques

Sister Christiane, holding her suitcase, stood facing the three-story building bearing a plaque on the wall next to the entrance identifying it as the Hopital de Bon Secours. As she entered the hospital, she noticed no one in the hall to greet her, so she slowly made her way down the hall until she came to an open doorway where a sister was sitting behind a wooden desk reviewing papers. Upon seeing Sister Christiane, she invited her inside, and seeing her suitcase, guessed she was the nurse they were expecting from Montreal, Canada.

"You must be Sister Christiane from Montreal. I'm Mother Superior Lucille," she said in French.

"Yes, you are correct, Mother Superior," answered Christiane.

"You must be tired after such a long voyage. We have a room reserved for you next door, where our other sisters reside. Let me escort you to your new lodgings, then we can have a long talk about our mission, and your duties as one of our nurses at Bon Secours," said Mother Lucille, continuing in French, her native language, and perhaps lacking fluency in English.

In the meantime, Father Andre reported for duty at the Christian Abbey in Paris, where he received the most unwelcome news from the Father Provincial.

"Father Andre, I have been directed by the Superior General in Rome, to inform you that you have been reassigned to our Christian Abbey in Madrid, Spain. I received those orders while you were in transit on the *SS Ile de France*," said Father Joseph.

"Was a reason given for my transfer to Madrid?" asked Father Andre.

"There is much unrest in Spain, especially in Madrid, as a result of the economic depression, which is causing incendiary social and political conditions that may result in a revolution and civil war. The need for doctors and nurses in Spain is critical, and your particular medical expertise as a surgeon is greatly needed. Here in Paris, we have several doctors in private practice that donate their time to our Catholic hospitals, which adequately supplements our medical staff," said Father Joseph.

"When am I to leave for Madrid?" asked Father Andre, remembering his Jesuit oath of obedience.

"Tomorrow. Therefore, get a good night's rest, and then tomorrow you'll be taking a train to Madrid. Here's a letter of introduction and directions to the Abbey," said Father Joseph.

That evening, Father Andre, knelt on the side of his military style bed and prayed to Jesus, asking him if his transfer to Madrid was his punishment for seducing Sister Christiane and taking her virginity. He pleaded with Jesus not to punish Sister Christiane, who was simply a victim of his lust. Father Andre remained knelt in prayer for the longest time, hopeful that his request to save Sister Christiane from responsibility and punishment would be granted.

The following day, riding on the train to Madrid, Spain, Father Andre, realized he would probably never see Sister Christiane again, and that thought was most difficult to accept, but obligatory in accordance with his Jesuit vows.

It was mid-July when Sister Christiane started suffering from morning sickness, and suspected she was pregnant. By the end of the month her suspicions were confirmed, and she debated whether she should make contact with Father Andre, not realizing he had been reassigned to Madrid, Spain. However, after much thought, she decided that he was in no position to help her, and no good would come by informing him of her pregnancy. She would hide her pregnancy with the wearing of her loose habit for as long as possible, while praying for an answer to her dilemma. Being a Catholic who took her vows seriously, the thought of an abortion never occurred to her, inasmuch as it was considered by the Catholic Church a mortal sin. Each night, she prayed to the Virgin Mary for guidance without any answers forthcoming. Finally, in her seventh month of pregnancy, when her gain in weight became difficult to explain, she decided to reveal her condition to Mother Lucille.

"Mother Lucille, I have a most difficult confession to make, and I feel so ashamed," said Sister Christiane, with tears flowing down her cheeks.

"I know the reason for your shame, and waited for you to find the moral strength to confide in me," said Mother Lucille.

"When did you realize I was pregnant?" asked Sister Christiane, wiping the tears from her face.

"Last month. The question is, who is the father of your unborn child?" asked Mother Lucille.

"I would rather not say. He doesn't know, and he's in no position to help me," replied Sister Christiane.

"Are you sure about that? After all, as the father, he has a right to know," said Mother Lucille.

"It's not that simple, Mother Lucille. I've made up my mind that he must never know, as it would destroy his life. I bear all responsibility for my actions, and I will obey the decision of the Congregation of the Sisters of Bon Secours regarding the disposition of the child, which I'm sure will be in the best interest of the child, under these circumstances," said Sister Christiane.

"I think you know that the child will be placed in our orphanage for eventual adoption by approved parents," said Mother Lucile.

"I ask only that I be allowed to see my child before you take him or her away, and that I may give the child its first name," said Sister Christiane.

"We usually wouldn't allow you to see the child in order to facilitate your separation, but in this instance, I will make an exception, and also allow you to name the child," said Mother Lucille, who had developed a special fondness for Sister Christiane.

"If it's a boy, I would like to name him Jacques, and if it's a girl, Jacqueline," said Sister Christiane.

On the 10th of March 1930, Doctor Aaron Cohen, assisted by two nurses in the operating room at the Hopital de Bon

Secours, recognized Sister Christiane, lying on her back ready to give birth. She had assisted him as a nurse on at least two occasions, and he was clearly flabbergasted at the situation before him. Knowing she had taken the vows of chastity and celibacy, he wondered who was the father of her, as yet, unborn child. He also realized that he had been sworn to secrecy about his role as a physician at the Hopital de Bon Secours, hence asked no questions, and delivered a healthy baby boy. He also noticed, as did the mother, that the child had a small birthmark on his right shoulder in the form of a butterfly.

As the baby was placed in Christiane's welcoming arms, she said to him, "Your name is Jacques, for the whole world to know."

CHAPTER III
The adoption of Jacques by a Jewish couple

That evening, Doctor Cohen was having dinner with his wife Anna at their home in the northeast section of Paris, known as the 17th Arrondissement, when he told his wife about his delivery of a child born out of wedlock. Although he had been sworn to secrecy by the Administrator of the Hopital de Bon Secours, he didn't feel it included his wife, who shared his deepest secrets, especially in this particular instance.

"Anna, darling, when you learned last month from your pediatrician that you could not bear children, you mentioned you were open to adoption. Well, today I delivered a beautiful boy whose mother is a Sister and nurse at the Hopital de Bon Secours. She's obliged to surrender her child to their orphanage for adoption. No doubt she'll be immediately transferred to a faraway place to hide her indiscretion. I think that you'll fall in love with that child once you see him, and you have my total support if you wish to adopt him."

"Do you know who the father is?" asked Anna.

"No, I don't, and I don't think anyone knows, except the mother," replied Doctor Cohen.

"That must be so difficult for her to give up her baby," said Anna.

"Yes, I'm sure it was, but she did name her child *Jacques*, in front of me and the nursing staff, for the record," said Doctor Cohen. "So what do you think? Are you interested??

"Yes, I am very much interested. When can I see the baby?" asked Anna.

"The sooner the better, in case someone else sees him, and decides to adopt him. I have to be in Chartres tomorrow, but this Saturday I will be free to go with you to the orphanage," said Doctor Cohen.

"Yes, Saturday will be fine," replied Anna.

The next day, Mother Lucille visited Sister Christiane at the hospital where she was recovering from childbirth.

"I see that you have recovered well from your childbirth, Sister Christiane. I want you to know that Jacques is doing well and is being well-cared for by the nurses. Eventually, he'll be placed in our orphanage, and hopefully will be adopted by suitable parents. Now, I hope you'll understand that under the circumstances, you cannot remain here in Paris. Mother Superior has reassigned you to the Hopital de Bon Secours in the City of Brussels, Belgium. You are to leave in three days by train to Brussels," said Mother Lucille.

"Yes, I do understand, and I thank you for your kindness. I will be ready for my departure on Friday, Mother Lucille," replied Sister Christiane obediently.

That Thursday, Sister Christiane, decided she had to see Father Andre one last time, before she left for Brussels.

Upon arrival at the Christian Abbey of Saint-Germain-des-Pres, she met with the Jesuit priest administrator, who advised her that Father Andre had been reassigned to Madrid, Spain, shortly after his arrival in Paris, and no further information was available.

Sister Christiane left the Abbey somewhat relieved, that fate had decided for her not to inform Father Andre of the birth of their son Jacques, soon to be adopted by unknown parents. She walked nonchalantly on the streets of Paris, enjoying its wonderful allure, knowing she might never see this City of Light again.

Upon arrival at the Hopital de Bon Secours in Brussels, Sister Christiane buried herself in her work as a nurse, as a remedy for her feelings of guilt and anxiety over what she felt was abandonment of her newborn child. Of course, Mother Superior Blanche had already been informed of the reason for Sister Christiane's transfer to Belgium, but did not reveal that knowledge to the other members of the Hopital de Bon Secours.

In the meantime, that Saturday Doctor Cohen and his wife Anna visited the Bon Secours Orphanage, and after identifying himself and his wife to the sister in charge and explaining their intentions to adopt a child, they were invited to have a seat for their initial interview.

"I'm Mother Dominique, in charge of the orphanage. I am pleased that you considered our orphanage in looking to adopt a child, Doctor Cohen. Are you looking for a boy or a girl, and what age is your preference?"

"May I present my wife Anna," said Doctor Aaron Cohen.

"I'm very pleased to meet you, Missus Cohen. Your husband has been most generous with his time and skill as a physician at our hospital. I understand that you are a registered nurse," said Mother Dominique.

"Yes, I am, but I have relinquished that work in favor of teaching the piano which has become a passionate vocation," replied Anna.

"My wife is understating her talent. She was invited to give a piano recital at the Grande Salle of the Royal Academy of music in Paris," said Doctor Cohen proudly.

"That's very commendable, and I'm sure a most positive influence on the child you're adopting. At the present time we have more than a dozen babies, and several boys and girls varying in age, that are housed in an adjacent building. Are you looking for a newborn baby, an infant, or toddler? We also have some preschoolers, but I don't think that's what you're looking for," said Mother Dominique.

"My wife and I have discussed this, and we feel that the younger the baby, the better he or she will assimilate and accept us as parents. As far as gender is concerned, we'll leave that to providence as we get acquainted with the babies in your care," said Doctor Cohen. "One other thing, Mother Dominique. We are of the Jewish faith, and since your orphanage is part of the Congregation of the Sisters of Bon Secours, a Catholic organization, does that disqualify us?"

"No, it does not, especially since you have served as a medical doctor for the Hopital de Bon Secours. I am sure that the child you adopt will be well-cared for, and very fortunate to have parents of your social status. Let's visit the ward where the newborn and infants are located," said Mother Dominique.

"I think we can skip the newborns. We prefer to look at the infants and toddlers," said Doctor Cohen.

"Very well, then. They would be in wards two and three. Let's start with the infants in ward two," said Mother Dominique.

The ward was filled with infants from one week to twelve months old. Doctor Cohen watched his wife Anna inspecting each infant without comment, until she came upon the fifth infant, whom she just recognized from his birthmark on his left shoulder as Jacques. She looked at her husband, and then queried Mother Dominique.

"May I pick him up?" asked Anna.

"Yes, of course," replied Mother Dominique.

Anna held the infant, a boy, in her arms with tenderness and a smile of acceptance, as he touched her face with his tiny little hands that begged her to take him with her, which melted her heart. She indicated to her husband she had made her choice.

"I must tell you that the mother of this infant insisted on naming him *Jacques* as a condition of his release to us," said Mother Dominique. "I hope you'll honor her request."

Doctor Cohen looked at his wife with a strange smile, then together they replied, "the name *Jacques* is fine with us. Actually we love that name."

"Are you sure you don't want to look at the other infants and toddlers?" asked Mother Dominique.

"No, we're sure, Jacques is our first and only choice," said Doctor Cohen quickly.

"When can we take him home?" asked Anna.

"Since we already have your credentials and residence on file, Doctor Cohen, we should be able to complete the adoption within the next day or two, and then Jacques will be yours to take home," said Mother Dominique.

"That's just wonderful. Thank you so much for helping us find our baby boy," said Anna excitedly.

Once outside the orphanage, Doctor Cohen turned to his wife. "That birthmark made it easy for you to identify him, and I'm sure you'll agree, he's a beautiful baby boy."

"Yes, he certainly is, and I'm going to love him as if I gave him birth," replied Anna.

Two days later, Jacques was officially adopted by Aaron and Anna Cohen on the 2d of August 1930, and given the name Jacques Cohen.

CHAPTER IV
Jacques' Childhood Years in Paris

Doctor Cohen was highly respected by his medical colleagues at the Hopital Hotel-Dieu in Paris, his first medical residency, in addition to his voluntary service at the Bon Secours Hospital. His wife Anna was an accomplished pianist who gave piano lessons to selected students at their large home in the 17th Arrondissement of Paris. She wasted no time in exposing Jacques to music and the piano in particular, and at the early age of two, she had him enrolled in nursery school. His progress was so rapid that he was able to start his first year of 'Cours Moyen' or 4th grade Elementary school at age seven, in the year 1937. However, it was at one of those evenings the following year when the Cohens invited several of their friends over for cocktails, that Jacques' real talent was truly discovered. One of their guests was Francois Montagnant, the director of the Paris Music Hall orchestra, and his wife. Also in attendance, was the celebrated opera singer Marie Bellevue, who had retained her maiden name for professional reasons.

The Cohen residence was quite large, containing an entertainment room with a hanging crystal chandelier, and a grand piano that served also as the room where Anna Cohen gave piano lessons. This was an opportunity for Anna Cohen to show off her star pupil and Jacques' talents as a pianist. She asked her son to play Claude Debussy's "Clair de Lune," a romantic piano piece from the Third movement of the *Suite Bergamasque*. Sitting upright, a bit taller than expected for an eight-year old boy, Jacques faced the keyboard of this grand piano with a calmness that got everyone's attention as they waited for him to play the first notes of this famous piece.

Jacques began by slowly moving his hands towards the keyboard, softly touching the keys, creating a dreamy atmosphere of a folk song into a melody of love that a boy of his age could not possibly know and understand, yet whose mind through his fingers, transmitted the most beautiful rendition of Claude Debussy's musical poem, with a sensitivity that held the audience's breath and Director Montagnant's curiosity about this young man, whose talent merited a much larger audience.

"Look at his fingers, barely touching the keys, as they flow across the keyboard with such delicate yet firm command," said Anna to her husband standing next to her.

"I didn't know he could play that well. Do we have a prodigy on our hands?" asked Aaron Cohen.

"I believe we have, Aaron, but you've been too busy at the hospital to take notice, my dear," replied Anna.

"Well, I've got to do something about that, don't I?" said Aaron Cohen.

"I think the wheels of fortune for our young son are already turning, if I interpret our Director friend's reaction to Jacques performance correctly," said Anna, looking in the direction of Francois Montagnant, who had joined the other guests clapping their hands in approval of Jacques' performance. Jacques stood up and bowed before the small audience, then joined his parents, at which time Francois Montagnant and his wife Marie approached them.

"Congratulations, young man," said Montagnant. "Your recital was excellent, and far exceeds a boy of your age."

"Thank you, Monsieur. My mother should be given credit for my recital. I owe my talent to her wonderful teaching," replied Jacques.

"My son is not used to complimentary reviews of his skill as a pianist," said Anna.

"Well, I noted a sensitivity in his performance of that piece of music that is nothing short of extraordinary, especially for a boy of his age. I would like to hear him play other pieces of music, but I don't expect him to have yet learnt more difficult musical works from artists such as Tchaikovski and Rachmaninoff, which would then merit a recital at the Paris Music Hall or Opera House," said Montagnant.

"Would you like Jacques to play Tchaikoovsky's *Swan Lake* for you?" asked Anna with a confident smile.

"You mean he's made that much progress already?" asked a surprised Montagnant.

"Jacques…would you like to play *Swan Lake* for Monsieur Montagnant and his wife Marie?" asked Anna, who wanted them to know the breath of her son's repertoire, and that his artistry was self-driven.

"Oui, Maman," replied Jacques who excused himself and walked back to the piano, and without hesitation, started playing the introduction to Swan Lake without using any sheets of music.

"You mean he's put to memory the entire musical piece," asked Montagnant.

"Jacques can memorize and play an entire piece of music after hearing it only once, but of course they are not of the length of Tchaikovsky's Piano Concerto Number One. He fell in love with *Swan Lake,* and therefore mastered it in record time, as you will now see and appreciate," said Anna with pride.

Again, the audience, although a small and friendly one, marveled at this young boy's absolute command of the grand piano's keyboard, whose melodious sound had mesmerized everyone in attendance.

"Madame Cohen, you have done a spectacular job of training your son, whom I believe is ready for advanced training with one of the masters available here in Paris, through the Paris Music Hall. I would also like to discuss the possibility of your son performing at one of our concerts at the Paris Music Hall, which would introduce him to the world of music that Paris does best," said Montagnant.

"I appreciate your kind offer, Mister Montagnant, believe me, but I think that Jacques needs another year before he gives live performances before a critical crowd," said Anna.

"I agree with my wife, Francois," said Aaron Cohen. "Jacques needs at least another year before he is subjected to the whims of critics, which can devastate a young boy's confidence, but be largely ignored by a slightly older boy."

"I do see your point which is well taken. But whenever you feel your son is ready for the Paris Music Hall, please let me know, and I'll make the necessary arrangements for his first recital," said Montagnant.

CHAPTER V
The Invasion of Belgium by Nazi Germany

It was in March 1938 that Sister Christiane, who was well settled in at the Hopital de Bon Secours in Brussels, Belgium, received a letter from Father Andre, that had been posted from Madrid, Spain to the Bon Secours Hospital in Paris, and forwarded to her in Brussels. The letter had been in transit over one month. In the privacy of her small room at the convent where the sisters resided, she read the two-page handwritten letter describing the horrible conditions in Spain, where the civil war was in full bloom between the Nationalists aided by Fascist Italy and Nazi Germany, and the Republicans aided by the Soviet Union and volunteer forces from Europe and America. Father Andre expressed his undying love for her, and stated that if he thought Christiane would abdicate her vows of celibacy, and leave the Congregation of Sisters of Bon Secours, he would do the same, and leave the Society of Jesus in order to marry her. But alas, he was not hopeful she would ever entertain such a drastic change of life unless her love for him was as strong and deep as his own. His parting words were that he had never envisioned the degree of cruelty he witnessed these last few months in Spain, and as a doctor, he was losing his faith in the decency of humanity.

Sister Christiane read the letter again, especially that part about his willingness to abandon the Society of Jesus in order to marry her. It got her thinking about *Jacques* and the fact that

Father Andre was not aware he had fathered a son. My God, she thought, if they got married, they could then find their son *Jacques*, not realizing he had been adopted. She allowed the idea to ferment in her mind, not knowing if Father Andre was still at the return address on the envelope, in a civil war where people are constantly in transit. However, in May 1940, Christiane, along with the people of Belgium, soon experienced the tragedies of war, when Nazi Germany invaded the country through which it entered France and defeated the French Army. In June of that year, the French Government departed Paris, leaving it an open city for the Germans to occupy, its horrified citizens feeling betrayed by their military leaders, whose army was twice the size of the Germans.

The horror of the German occupation of Belgium became personally dreadful to Sister Christiane when she learned that her very close friend, Sister Bernadette, was one of the 140 civilian victims deliberately killed by German Wehrmacht troops in the church at Meigem, some 35 miles from Brussels. Apparently the massacre was in retaliation for the Belgium army's resistance in the villages of Vinkt and Meigem. This event had a devastating effect on her morale and reason for being there, away from her home in Montreal, Canada, where civilization was still intact. Father Andre's offer of marriage suddenly became a reality that promised a secure family life, with the son she should never have abandoned. Being a Sister and not a nun made it somewhat easier to abdicate her vows and leave the Congregation of Sisters of Bon Secours.

Sister Christiane explained with great difficulty to Mother Blanche, her reason for leaving the Congregation of Sisters, citing the traumatic effect of the recent massacre and death of Sister Bernadette, and her desire to return to Montreal.

"I just can't find myself capable of nursing any of those Boche soldiers. They're nothing but murderers. They even pulled out some of our wounded Belgium soldiers from their beds and shot them. I'm sorry, Mother Blanche, God may forgive them, but I can't. That's why I must leave, find my son, and go back to Montreal, where civilization still exists," said Christiane.

"I'm sorry you feel that way, Sister Christiane. But you must realize that traveling with a Canadian passport in Belgium and France will result in your arrest and detention in a concentration camp, because Canada is at war with Germany," said Mother Blanche. "Instead, why don't you just take a leave of absence, and travel as a Sister of Bon Secours, which provides you with acceptable identification for travel through Belgium and France."

"I hadn't thought of that. I guess my Canadian passport would send me to a German concentration camp. Alright then, how much time will you give me to find my son?"

"Well, actually, I don't expect you to remain with us after you've found your son, whom you intend to take home to Montreal," replied Mother Blanche.

"Your kindness and understanding are truly admirable. I shall never forget your assistance, and my son will surely be appreciative of your life-saving support," said Christiane.

"You will need some funds for your long and arduous journey, will you not?" said Mother Blanche.

"I have money left over from my voyage from Montreal to Paris given to me by my father. So, I'll be alright, Mother Blanche," replied Christiane.

"Very well, then, I wish you God speed and a safe and successful journey," said Mother Blanche.

However, Sister Christiane first planned on visiting Father Andre in Madrid, Spain, in response to his explosive letter. Upon arrival at the Christian Abbey in Madrid, she was invited for an interview with Father Sebastian.

"I'm from Montreal, Canada, and a good friend of Father Andre, whom I last met on the *SS Ile de France*, in our journey to Paris, where I was assigned as a nurse at the Hopital de Bon Secours," said Sister Christiane. "I hope he's still assigned to this Abbey."

"I'm afraid I have some bad news, Sister Christiane. Father Andre was killed during a bombing raid two weeks ago," said Father Sebastian. "I'm very sorry."

"Oh, My God!" exclaimed Christiane, "I can't believe this is happening." She suddenly felt so very much alone and helpless.

"Would you like some water?" asked Father Sebastian, seeing her turn pale, fearing she might faint.

"No thank you, Father. I must go," she replied, and slowly walked to the entrance door, and left the premises without saying another word.

Christiane found a modest hotel room to get some rest and think about the next step she must take to find her son, whom she would take home to Montreal. Lying on her bed looking up at the ceiling, she wondered if Father Andre's death was God's punishment for seducing and impregnating her. And she wondered if God was simultaneously punishing her for failing to resist his advances and abandoning her son. She got out of bed and knelt in prayer, asking for forgiveness, with the promise she would do whatever it took to find her son and raise him as a Christian.

A week went by before it became known to Father Sebastian at the Christian Abbey in Madrid that Father Andre had not been in the building that had been bombed, and he had in fact joined a group of American volunteer fighters for the Republican Army seeking a doctor for their wounded.

Back at the Abbey, Father Andre learned from Father Sebastian that Sister Christiane from the Congregation de Bon Secours, whom he had met on the *SS Ile de France*, had visited the Abbey looking for him, and she was told he had died in a bombing raid. Father Sebastian could not recall if she gave her name, but Father Andre knew it was Christiane from the given description.

"Did she say where she was going from here?" asked Father Andre.

"No, but she was visibly upset at the news of your reported death," replied Father Sebastian.

Father Andre decided to write Christiane another letter to the only address he had in Paris, to let her know he was alive and well, and for her to send him a reply with her reason for her visit to Madrid.

When Father Andre's letter arrived at the Hopital de Bon Secours in Paris, it was forwarded to Sister Christiane's assigned Hopital de Bon Secours in Brussels, Belgium, where it lay unanswered.

CHAPTER VI
The German Invasion of Paris and Internment of Jews

Upon learning of the French Army's defeat by the German Wehrmacht in Northern France and its panzer-led blitzkrieg advancement towards Paris, the French government departed Paris on 10 June 1940, declaring it an 'open city' for the Germans to enter and occupy.

The first sign of the Germans' arrival was the entry on 13 June 1940 of several small gray-green military trucks with two speakers facing opposite directions mounted on their roofs. They loudly announced in French the German Wehrmacht's occupation of Paris and demanded the surrender of all private arms and ammunition from its citizens. It further threatened Parisians with the death penalty for any acts of aggression against the German occupiers.

One of those trucks stationed itself across the street facing the Hospital Hotel-Dieu, where Doctor Aaron Cohen worked and had just completed a surgical operation. He found several nurses and staff in the hallway talking amongst themselves excitedly about the loud German announcement coming from the street. One of Cohen's medical colleagues, Doctor Michel LeGrand, approached him.

"The German army has just occupied Paris, Aaron. You should have accepted that position with St. Bartholomew's Hospital in London. Now it's too late, my friend," said LeGrand.

"I was born and raised here in Paris, and so was my wife Anna. I don't think the Germans will bother French doctors, who may well be needed for them too," replied Cohen.

"That may be true, Aaron, but if their treatment of Jews in Germany is any indication, you may not be as safe as you think. If there's any chance of you leaving France, take it my friend, because the clouds of Nazi persecution of Jews will soon engulf all of Paris," said LeGrand.

Outside the hospital, a crowd of Parisians, including some of the hospital staff, stared at the German officer with microphone in hand, spewing his warning of the impending occupation of Paris. Two German officers stood by, watching the crowd that had gathered around them.

"Look at them," said one officer, "they're like sheared sheep. They gave us Paris without a fight."

Several women and some men silently shed tears of sadness at the realization their country and Paris were now going to be governed by Nazi Germany, their historical enemy. There was also hatred in the eyes of many Parisians for these German invaders who dared impose their fascist rules on the peace-loving French.

The next day, 14 June 1940, the Wehrmacht entered Paris in full force, with swiftness and military precision, occupying the various buildings that had previously served the French Government, the result of meticulous planning, which was evident from the posting of street signs in German, directing the enormous military traffic.

The German emblem bearing a black swastika within a white circle on a red flag was immediately unfurled at the top of the Eiffel Tower in the middle of Paris, and all prominent buildings within the city were adorned with the conqueror's flag of dominance over the City of Light, now darkened by its humiliating defeat.

Parisians were in shock at the defeat of their French army and their Government's abandonment of Paris, leaving them in such a vulnerable position under complete control of Nazi Germany and its fascist regime. Unknown to the French people, the German Army's general staff had obtained through their intelligence agents with the cooperation of many French officials with anti-Semitic feelings the names, addresses, occupations and bank accounts of affluent Jews in Paris. The German general staff also had identified for seizure businesses and property owned by Jews who were destined for subsequent internment upon the occupation of Paris. They even had the location of every bordello in Paris with a select few reserved for German officers. The City of Lights as Paris was known, would soon find its lights extinguished by a waterfall of lies, atrocities, and collaborative treachery that would shock even some German military personnel still in possession of moral standards.

On 22 June 1940, Adolf Hitler sought to further humiliate France by insisting on signing the document of capitulation of France in the same railway carriage used when Germany surrendered in 1918. This was perhaps the most demeaning action taken by Germany against France.

With all the commotion taking place in the environs of Paris, Aaron Cohen left the hospital earlier than usual to be with his wife and their adopted son Jacques at their home in the northeast section of Paris.

"Oh! Aaron, I just got a call from Yvonne LeGrand about the Germans taking over Paris. She said her husband at the hospital heard the Germans announcing their occupation of Paris."

"Yes, I was there, but we shouldn't jump to conclusions about their occupation of Paris. It's a big city, and they'll need the help of the French police to keep order, and the various government agencies that make the city function. Otherwise it would be chaos and a poor example to other countries they wish to surrender cooperatively. I think that as a physician the Germans will find me useful and leave us alone," said Aaron Cohen.

"I hope you're right, Aaron, because I heard stories of how they treated Jews in Germany, closing their shops, stripping them of citizenship and employment rights, and forbidding them to marry Aryans. Yesterday, one of my students told me her mother's sister who resides in Berlin, wrote to her at least once a week, but stopped writing a month ago. She hasn't answered her mother's letters, which makes her mother think her sister and her husband have been sent to an internment camp for Jews. I'm worried, Aaron, maybe you should have accepted that offer to work at a hospital in London," said Anna.

"I can understand your worry, Anna, but this is France, not Germany. The Germans would need the full cooperation of the French police, and its affiliates, to enforce such drastic actions against the Jewish population in Paris," said Aaron.

"I'm also thinking of our son Jacques, and what would happen to him, if the Germans enforce the persecution of Jews," said Anna.

"Jacques is not Jewish. He's a gentile born of a Catholic mother, therefore exempt from such persecution," said Aaron.

"The Germans wouldn't know that. They would readily assume that our son is Jewish, and we have no proof to the contrary," replied Anna.

"Perhaps you're right, but before we go into a panic, let's just wait and see what happens next, Anna. I will make some discreet inquiries, and find out what options are open to us," said Aaron.

Jacques returned home from school and apparently hadn't heard of the Nazi occupation yet, and his parents decided to avoid the subject during dinner or afterwards, believing he didn't need to be burdened with their unsupported fears, which might never materialize.

However, Aaron decided to camouflage a small hidden room in the attic above the third floor for use by Jacques in case the Gestapo or the French Police came to evict them for transport to a concentration camp for Jews. Aaron showed Anna the hidden room he had provisioned with a large jug of water, several cans of sardines and cheese. He also provided a flashlight, a small mattress with pillow and two blankets.

"Is that enough food for Jacques?" asked Anna.

"He's not to stay in there very long. Just enough to escape the eviction, then when the coast is clear, leave the house, and go directly to the Hopital Hotel-Dieu to find Doctor Michel LeGrand. He's to give Michel this letter explaining Jacques' ethnicity as a gentile and the circumstances of his birth. The letter further spells out the assistance needed in hiding Jacques from the Germans and the French Police by unofficially adopting him into his family," said Aaron.

"What makes you think he would do this for us?" asked Anna.

"Michel and I grew up in the same neighborhood and graduated from medical school together. We've been very close friends, and as you know, his wife Yvonne adores Jacques for his musical talent as a young pianist. I have no doubt as to his loyalty and willing assistance in protecting Jacques from the Nazis. In addition, I've included a money order in the amount of one hundred thousand francs, which we certainly won't need if we're incarcerated," said Aaron.

"Do you think we should tell Jacques of his adoption from the Bon Secours Orphanage and the fact he's not Jewish but the son of a Catholic nurse?" asked Anna.

"Yes, I think we should do that before he gives that letter to Michel LeGrand. Let's face it, Anna, our chance of survival once interned in a concentration camp is very small," said Aaron.

"But there's no rush right now in telling him of his true parentage. Let' wait a while and see how the Germans are going to handle the Jewish population in Paris," said Anna.

"I suppose you're right, Anna. We'll wait a while, but if things get threatening, we'll have to act fast, and secure Jacques in a safe place like the attic, or if time permits, get him directly into Michel's custody for safekeeping until the war ends, and hopefully France is free again," said Aaron.

CHAPTER VII
French Collaboration with Nazi Government

Inside Nazi Headquarters in the Hotel Meurice, a luxurious five-star, eight-story building on the Rue de Rivoli in the 1st Arrondissement of Paris, requisitioned by German authorities, Colonel Otto Knochenbach, the Senior Commander of the Scherheits Polizei (Security Police) in Paris, waited in his office on the third floor for the arrival of Pierre Lavoie, Prime Minister of Paris and Roger Lamaison, Chief of the Prefecture in Paris.

Colonel Knochenbach took his orders directly from Field Marshal Wilhelm Keitel, Chief of the Armed Forces High Command in Berlin. In a tailored uniform decorated with several rows of ribbons attesting to his military experience and bravery, a tall, slim, dark haired man in his late thirties, sporting a slim mustache, Knochenbach looked at his watch.

"Hans, where the devil is that Prime Minister and his Chief of Police? Weren't they supposed to be here a 0900?" asked Knochenbach of his assistant, Major Hans Hoffman.

"They're only 10 minutes late, sir. You know how those Frenchmen are. Punctuality is not one of their virtues," replied Hoffman.

"Apparently the only virtue they have is in their cuisine," said Knochenbach.

There was a sudden knock on the door, which was then opened enough for Knochenbach's clerk to announce that his two guests had arrived.

"Very well, Rolf, you can send them in," said Major Hoffman standing near the office door.

The French Prime Minister, a portly, middle-aged man of average height with a receding hair line prudently entered the large office with his Chief of Prefecture immediately behind him.

Colonel Knochenbach stood up and walked around his large, highly polished wooden desk to greet them.

"It's a pleasure seeing you again Mister Prime Minister," said Knochenbach, shaking his hand. He then looked at the Chief of the Prefecture.

"May I introduce Roger Lamaison, our Chief of the Prefecture of Paris, who is responsible for the administration and enforcement of the law in Paris," said Pierre Lavoie.

"Enchante de vous connaitre (a pleasure to meet you)" said Knochenbach in French, in an attempt to establish a fertile association with Lamaison, to whom he would be delegating an enormous task in the fulfillment of the final solution of the Jewish problem in Paris and its environs.

Roger Lamaison, a robust man of average height in his late thirties, was a career policeman who climbed the ranks to his present position through politics as well as police proficiency. He was also fluent in German, having grown up in the Alsace Loraine region of France, on the border with Germany. Even though Knochenbach had never met Lamaison, he had a full dossier of him on his desk and realized that people from the Alsace Lorraine region were very empathic towards the Germans. He was hopeful this would enhance Lamaison's cooperation with German authorities in the enforcement of laws imposed by the Third Reich on Parisians.

"Please be seated, gentlemen, as we have much to discuss, which may take us well into lunch," said Knochenbach, who then sat behind his desk and opened a folder containing several papers.

"I have asked you gentlemen here because there are several conditions in the Armistice Agreement between the German High Command of the Armed Forces and French Plenipotentiaries that need to be implemented and enforced.

The first one is the establishment of a curfew from nine o'clock in the evening until five o'clock in the morning," said Knochenbach.

"I don't know that a curfew in the city of Paris can be enforced," replied Roger Lamaison.

"According to Article III of the Armistice, in the occupied parts of France, the German Reich exercises all rights of an occupying power. The French Government obligates itself to support with every means, the regulations resulting from the exercise of these rights, and to carry them out with the aid of French administration. You are therefore obligated to establish and enforce a curfew as directed by the Third Reich," said Knochenbach.

"What will we do with those who violate the curfew?" asked Lamaison.

"Arrest and turn them over to the Gestapo for interrogation," replied Knochenbach.

"I'm sure this curfew was directed by your high command in Berlin," said Pierre Lavoie. "However, Parisians are used to their freedom of movement, and a curfew may well stir a resistance movement that could turn into a rebellion that our police would be unable to contain."

"We've implemented a curfew in other occupied countries without any difficulty, and it had a significant effect on curbing anti-German activities. I expect the French police to implement and enforce this curfew immediately, and I need your assurance that this curfew will be posted throughout Paris tomorrow and in effect in all of Paris within 48 hours of posting," said Knochenbach.

Lavoie looked at Lamaison for assurance it could be done, and when Lamaison nodded in subdued agreement, Lavoie turned his attention back to Knochenbach.

"I guess the Armistice Agreement obligates us to enforce German regulations, so you have our promise of support in establishing a curfew in all of Paris," replied Lavoie.

"Excellent. Now the second condition is the rationing of food, tobacco, and coal. Our administration has a model for such rationing, and Major Klaus Mayer, whose office is on the second floor, will assist you in developing your rationing system," said Knochenbach. "Any questions?"

"No, I expected that," replied Lavoie.

"Good. The third condition is one that has the highest priority, and must be enforced without delay. All Jews in Paris must be identified and compelled to wear the yellow Star of David Badge on their outer garment. The inscription of 'Juif' (Jew) in black letters on a yellow Star of David will be worn either on the left-breast side of their outer garment or else on an arm band. We do have an extensive list of prominent Jews residing in Paris which will be made available to you. But we will need your full cooperation in identifying all Jews residing in Paris. Will that be a problem?" asked Knochenbach.

"No sir, I don't see that as a problem. Do you Roger?" asked Lavoie.

"Frankly I'm not fond of Jews and will gladly carry out any regulations that restrict their influence in Paris," replied Lamaison.

"Well, I'm glad we agree on the resolution of this problem. In that regard, our Headquarters wants you to void the license of Jews to practice medicine, the law, education, real estate, and the license to drive a vehicle," said Knochenbach.

"Does that include medical doctors and judges," asked Lavoie.

"Yes, it does, no exceptions," replied Knochenbach.

"I hope you'll provide us with some technical and legal assistance in executing these laws," said Lavoie.

"I understand its immediate ramifications, and you'll get all the support you need for this important solution to the Jewish problem," replied Knochenbach, pleased with the cooperation of his French collaborators.

"Is there anything else that you wish us to do to satisfy the requirements of the Armistice Agreement?" asked Lavoie.

"Actually, I'm glad you asked that question, Monsieur Lavoie. I truly appreciate your cooperation and that of Chief Lamaison. You may be sure that we Germans know how to reward those who assist us in the administration of occupation regulations. In that regard, once all Jews in Paris have been identified, we will first start the roundup of Jews in the lower class Arrondissements and then progress to the affluent sections of Paris. These Jews will be confined at the Drancy Internment Camp for later deportation to Auschwitz and other extermination camps," said Knochenbach, staring at Lavoie and Lamaison for their reaction to this coldblooded solution to the Jewish problem.

When neither Frenchmen voiced an objection, nor displayed any facial expression of rejection to the idea of Jewish extermination, Knochenbach realized these two Frenchmen shared the Third Reich's anti-Semitism, and he should show his appreciation with a reward for their cooperation.

"Gentlemen, now that we've established a cooperative partnership in the administration of regulations in Paris, I feel that you deserve special consideration for youselves and family. Henceforth your fuel and food rations will be unlimited. Also, in the event you should have any problems with our administration, you may contact me directly," said Knochenbach.

"Thank you, Colonel Knochenbach. We appreciate your kind generosity. We will keep you informed of our progress in the implementation of the regulations we discussed on a daily basis," said Lavoie, speaking for Lamaison as well.

"If you run into any problems, please don't hesitate to call me, as these matters are most important to our High Command in Berlin," said Knochenbach, ending the meeting.

CHAPTER VIII
Expulsion of Jacques Cohen from French School

It was early morning when Jacques entered l'Ecole de Montparsant where he was matriculated in the first year of Cours Moyen. As he entered the classroom, he was immediately instructed by the teacher, a middle-aged woman, to report to the school principal. With a puzzled look on his face, Jacques obediently left the classroom, and upon arrival at the principal's office, was told to have a seat in the waiting room. After more than ten minutes, the secretary finally took notice of Jacques.

"You may go in now, the principal will see you," said the secretary, opening the door for him to enter.

Sitting behind his desk, the principal, a middle-aged man sporting a thin mustache and wearing a suit, white shirt and red tie, motioned for Jacques to approach the large desk.

"Sit down, Jacques. Your family name is Cohen, is that correct?" asked the Principal.

"Yes sir, it is," replied Jacques.

"You do attend the synagogue with your parents each Saturday, is that correct?" asked the principal.

"Yes sir," replied Jacques, wondering why he was being asked all these personal questions, even at his young age.

"So you and your family are Jewish, it that correct?" asked the principal.

"Yes sir," replied Jacques.

"Well, I'm afraid young man that being Jewish disqualifies you from attending this school, effective immediately, by order of the Prefect of Police. Here is an official notice of your ineligibility to attend this school, which you must give to your parents," said the principal, handing the notice to Jacques.

"I don't understand, sir. Am I being expelled from school because I'm Jewish?" asked Jacques.

"Yes, that's correct. Those are my orders. You must now leave the school, and return home to your parents with this letter," said the principal.

Jacques left the school premises in bewilderment, and quickly went home to tell his mother of his expulsion.

Anna Cohen read the notice while Jacques looked on for a possible answer.

"Maman, I don't understand. I didn't do anything wrong. Why am I being expelled?" asked Jacques

"You're being expelled because you have a Jewish family name, Jacques. Not for anything you did wrong. I think it's time for me to explain certain things to you, but we'll have to wait for your father to come home, then everything will be explained to you. OK?" said Anna.

"Alright, Maman. But does that mean I won't be going back to school?" asked Jacques.

"Not to that school, but let's wait for your father, Jacques," replied Anna, not knowing the answer herself to that question.

CHAPTER IX
Enforcement of anti-Jewish laws in Paris

It was mid-afternoon when Doctor Aaron Cohen entered his residence, a two-story brick house in the affluent 17th arrondissement of Paris, surprised to find his son Jacques home so early from school.

"Oh! Aaron, I'm so glad you came home early, because Jacques has been expelled from school," said Anna.

"Really, why?" asked Aaron.

"Because he's Jewish. The School Principal told Jacques that he was being expelled by order of the Prefect of Police because he's Jewish," replied Anna, with Jacques standing next to his mother.

"I think it's time for us to have a serious talk, Jacques," said Aaron in a compassionate voice. "Let's go into the living room."

"What I am about to tell you Jacques, is the hardest and most difficult thing I have ever had to do. However, no one ever anticipated the occupation of France, and Paris in particular, by the Nazis. The Germans have ordered the French Administration and the Police to enforce laws that persecute Jews. As a result, Jewish people in Paris will now have to wear a yellow Star of David badge on the breast side of their outer garment identifying them as Jews. Jews will no longer be able to practice medicine, law, and other professions, and their children will no longer be able to attend French schools, which is why you were expelled today, Jacques," said Aaron, now turning his attention to his wife, whose facial expression demanded an explanation.

"Is that why you're home early?" asked Anna.

"Yes, my medical license has been revoked, and the hospital had to release me," replied Aaron.

"Oh! My God, what's going to happen to us now?" said Anna, forgetting the presence of Jacques witnessing the dramatic revelations of his father.

"Well, we'll have to prepare for the worst and hope for the best. The first thing for us to do is to get Jacques into a secure place where the Nazis won't be able to have access to him," said Aaron to Anna, with Jacques listening attentively.

Aaron then turned to Jacques. "You know Jacques, that Anna and I love you very much; you're our only son, and what I am about to reveal to you is the truth. You are not Jewish. I was the doctor who delivered you at the Hopital de Bon Secours. Your mother was a Sister and nurse who got pregnant by having a very brief affair with a man whose identity was never revealed to me. Being a Sister, member of the clergy, and an unwed mother, she was not allowed to keep you, and you were immediately put up for adoption. When I delivered you from your mother, I knew that Anna would fall in love with you, and we adopted you as our son, and in accordance with the law, you were given our last name of Cohen, which identified you as a Jew. However, your mother, whom we only knew as Sister Christiane from Montreal, Canada, was Catholic, and we can presume your father was also Catholic, which makes you a non-Jew. Nevertheless, the Germans and the French

Police won't believe us, and we don't have any proof because the adoption papers don't reveal the mother's identification and religion. Therefore, I have written a letter to my friend Doctor Michel LeGrand, explaining your situation, and I have asked him to take you into his family and shelter you. I have also enclosed a money order made out to his name for a very large sum of money for his service. Now, listen carefully, Jacques. You must no longer use the name Cohen. From now on your last name is LeGrand, Jacques LeGrand, and you're a Catholic, not a Jew. I'm placing this letter in your hiding place in the attic. I expect that when the French Police start rounding up Jews in this arrondissement, they'll come for us too, and when that happens, you must hide in the attic, and be very quiet until they have left the house and gone from the neighborhood. Then when it's quiet and safe, you are to take this letter, and go directly to the Hospital Hotel Dieu, and find Doctor LeGrand. You must not show or give this letter to anyone, and I mean no one but to Doctor LeGrand. Stay with him until he has read the letter and accepted the money order. He will then know what to do, and I expect he'll take you to his home, and from there to a safe place in the country," said Aaron, looking into Jacques' teary eyes absorbing the dreadful news.

"Is my real mother's name Christiane?" asked Jacques.

"Yes, but we don't know her family name, because these Bon Secours sisters are only known by their first name, preceded by the title of Sister denoting their rank within the religious order," replied Aaron.

"You can still call me 'Maman' Jacques. You'll always be our loving son," said Anna.

Jacques threw himself into Anna's arms. "I hate those Nazis. Why doesn't God stop them?"

"He will, through the efforts of his earthly disciples, but it takes time for good people to assemble and organize into a force that can defeat the Nazis," replied Aaron. "In the meantime, we must do whatever it takes to protect ourselves, and you in particular, Jacques."

"What if Doctor LeGrand is not at the hospital when I get there, what will I do?" asked Jacques.

"On the envelope, is the street address where Doctor LeGrand resides in Paris. If he's not at the hospital when you get there, find out when he will return, and if it's more than an hour, leave the hospital and make your way to his residence. If he's not at his residence, ask to speak to his wife Yvonne, and explain to her that you were sent there by your parents to speak to him personally about a matter of extreme importance. But do not tell or show her the letter. That is only for the eyes and hands of Doctor LeGrand," said Aaron.

"His wife Yvonne, knows Jacques, and was always impressed with his musical talent. Why can't he show her the letter? Don't you trust her?" asked Anna.

"It's not a question of trust, Anna. Her husband Michel knows our situation better than his wife, and I just don't want to leave this initial meeting, requiring such an important decision, to anyone other than Doctor LeGrand, who will have all the necessary information and resources to protect Jacques, that's all," replied Aaron, looking at his wife for her to read between the lines of his comment for the benefit of their son.

"Oh! Alright. Listen to your father, Jacques, he knows best," said Anna.

It wasn't long before word spread throughout Paris of the French Police raids on dwellings occupied by Jews in the middle and lower class arrondissements. The raids were conducted in the early morning hours, and Jewish occupants were summarily herded into trucks that transported them to Drancy Internment and Deportation Camp located in the northeastern suburb of Paris. It didn't take long for some of the neighbors to invade the now empty dwellings and steal furniture and anything else of value.

At the Cohen house, Aaron sat with his wife Anna to discuss their precarious position without the presence of Jacques, who was in the living room practicing a musical piece on the grand piano.

"The Wehrmacht Occupation Commander has ordered the seizure of all Jewish bank accounts and safety-deposit boxes. Luckily, I withdrew a large sum of money from my account a couple of weeks ago, including the money order for Doctor LeGrand. However, I don't know how long what we have left will last," said Aaron.

"It may not matter, Aaron. The French Police are systematically raiding the dwellings of Jews in the various arrondissements of Paris, and it's just a matter of days or weeks before they raid our neighborhood," replied Anna.

"Yes, you're right, Anna. Our days are numbered," said Aaron.

The very next morning, the Cohens were awakened by the front door bell followed by loud banging demanding entry by the French Police.

"My God, Aaron, they're here, the Police," said Anna to her awakened husband.

"I must get Jacques dressed and into the attic quickly," said Aaron.

Into the next bedroom, Aaron got Jacques to dress and gather essential items previously identified for his use while hiding in the attic.

"Hurry, Jacques," said Aaron with Anna watching.

They both embraced Jacques, knowing that this might be the last time they would ever see their son again. Reluctantly, they urged Jacques to climb the pull-down staircase into the attic.

"Goodbye Jacques, we love you," said Anna, holding back tears, as Jacques hurriedly pulled up the staircase closing the attic entry. Jacques opened the wall panel and entered his hideout, closing the panel behind him, and barring it with a wooden plank across two metal hooks that secured the entry panel. He sat there in the dark, quietly listening for any sound of entry into the attic, wondering what would happen to his adopted parents. He kneeled in silent prayer for their safety, suspecting with reason, that he might never see them again. He now feared for his own safety, simultaneously questioning why God would permit such devilish behavior and persecution of Jews. Suddenly his prayer was interrupted by noise from the room below the attic, but to his relief, no one climbed the stairs into the attic.

In the meantime, Aaron ran downstairs to unlock the front door before the police broke it down. The moment he opened the door, the policeman in charge pushed Aaron aside, allowing three other policemen to enter the premises.

"By order of the Prefecture of Police, your house and its contents are being requisitioned by the Wehrmacht Occupation Command," said the senior French Police Officer, who then looked at a list of names in his notebook. "According to my records, there are three occupants in this house. I presume you are Aaron and Anna Cohen."

"Yes, that's correct," answered Aaron.

"Where is your son Jacques?" asked the police officer.

"He's on summer vacation with the Scouts de France in the South of France," replied Aaron.

"Where in the South of France?" demanded the police officer.

"At Montpellier," replied Aaron, thinking of the most distant French town in southern France.

"Very well. You may bring one small suitcase of personal items, that's all, and you have exactly five minutes to change into adequate clothing for your new quarters at Drancy," said the police officer.

Aaron and Anna quickly climbed the stairs to their bedroom on the second floor, followed by two police officers who began searching the house.

"If you don't mind, my wife would like some privacy while she gets dressed," said Aaron to one of the police officers who stood inside the entrance to the bedroom.

The police officer reluctantly allowed Aaron to close the bedroom door.

"You'd better dress warmly, Anna, 'cause I doubt there'll be any heat in those buildings at Drancy."

Anna packed one suitcase with underwear, shirts and toilet articles, as quickly as possible when the bedroom door suddenly opened with the senior police officer standing in the doorway.

"It's time for you to vacate the premises, hurry up," commanded the officer.

Aaron, carrying the small suitcase with Anna behind him, descended the stairs and exited their house to the awaiting truck, which had a portable ladder for entry into the back of the vehicle, already occupied by other Jewish victims of the round-up.

Inside the truck sat a dozen other Jews, and a couple with small children, on wooden benches fastened to both sides of the vehicle. Anna, sitting beside her husband, grabbed his arm and leaning against him, started weeping. Aaron wrapped his arm around her in silent consolation, oblivious to those around him, who no doubt suffered the same fate and emotional distress.

Another couple of Jews were picked up before the truck was deemed full and ready for transport to Drancy, which took about forty-five minutes to arrive at the entry gate to the internment camp guarded by armed French security police. After entry into the camp, the truck eventually stopped before a two-story building. The captive Jews were ordered to exit the truck, escorted into the building, and directed to the first floor of the barracks, where military bunks were lined up with metal lockers behind them against the wall.

"This is your new home. Find yourselves a bunk," said the guard, who then left the barracks.

"My God, Aaron, they're treating us like cattle," said Anna.

"These are military barracks. If I'm not mistaken, there's a latrine at the other end of the barracks. But don't expect any privacy. We'll just have to organize ourselves into some form of civilized living arrangement," said Aaron.

A middle-aged man approached Aaron and Anna.

"Aren't you Doctor Cohen?" he asked.

"Yes I am."

"I'm surprised to find you, a prominent doctor, sharing our unfortunate displacement," said the man. "I'm Alain Dumas and that's my wife Odette sitting on the bed over there with our nine-year old daughter Yvette."

"The French Police are acting on the orders of the Wehrmacht Occupation Command, and they make no professional or economic exceptions of Jews destined for internment," replied Aaron.

"What do you think is going to happen to us?" asked Dumas with a worried look on his face.

"Frankly, they wouldn't have gone this far, if they weren't going to make this a permanent separation from the non-Jewish citizens of Paris. If what happened to Jews in Germany is any indication, I'm afraid the worst is yet to come, and if you can bribe one of these guards into releasing your daughter, now is the time to do it, because you may never get another chance," said Aaron, feeling sorry for the poor man and his daughter.

Dumas, now in thought about Aaron's advice, slowly walked back to his wife and daughter.

"Aaron, our son is most probably safe now, and I doubt we'll need all that money we've hidden inside our clothing. When I look at that poor little girl, my heart goes out to her. Why don't we give them some of our money for them to bribe a guard that could save her life. You know as well as I do, Aaron, that we're destined for extermination in one of the German death camps. I'd like to think we did something to save the life of one Jewish child before we die," said Anna.

"Yes, you're right Anna. Jacques is on his way to a safe place. You've got fifty thousand francs sewed inside the lining of your jacket, and I've got the same amount inside my jacket. Why don't we offer Dumas the money inside my jacket and keep what's in your jacket in case an opportunity occurs to save your life," said Aaron.

"I would never leave you, Aaron. You're my husband and I love you. I'm staying with you for the rest of my life, no matter where they take us. So why don't we give the Dumas all of our money, and hope it's enough to secure their daughter's freedom," said Anna.

"I don't think I've ever loved you so much as I do now. Your kindness overwhelms me, and I consider myself the luckiest and most blessed husband with you, my dearest wife. Have I ever told you how much I adore you?" asked Aaron.

"You just did, my darling," replied Anna. "Let's first find out if they have enough money or jewelry to bribe a guard."

Aaron and Anna together walked over to the Dumas.

"Can we have private talk. It's about your daughter," said Aaron to Alain with his wife and daughter standing beside him.

"Yes, of course. What's it about?" asked Alain Dumas.

Making sure they would not be overheard by the other barracks' inmates, Aaron and Anna stood in the corner of the barracks with Alain and his wife Odette, while their daughter Yvette sat on their bunk wondering what their secret conversation was about.

"We're very concerned about your daughter's safety, and wonder if you ever considered bribing one of the guards into releasing your daughter from Drancy into the general population of Paris, with instructions to find a trusted friend who would care for her," said Aaron.

"Unfortunately, we don't have any money or other resources to bribe a guard. The French Police closed my barber shop, seized my meagre bank account, expelled my daughter from school, and now we're here waiting for the next humiliation," said Alain. "I'm afraid for my daughter, whose innocence prevents her from realizing the perilous situation she's in, with us unable to help her."

"Well, that's what we want to talk to you about. We want to give you one hundred thousand francs which we've hidden in our clothing, for you to use in bribing one of the guards.

Actually, you should use ninety thousand francs to bribe the guard, which is a lot of money, and give the other ten thousand francs to your daughter with instructions to use it for transportation and other essentials needed to find the person you trust who will take care of her," said Aaron.

"My God, you are the angels of mercy I've been praying for," said Odette. "I can hardly believe this is happening."

"Do you know of anyone in Paris or its environs who is not Jewish, therefore not likely to be apprehended, that you trust with the safety of your daughter?" asked Aaron.

"As a matter of fact, we do," replied Alain.

"Odette's sister Lucille married a Catholic, Henri Baudelaire, and she converted to his religion. They own a boulangerie (bakery) in the southern section of Paris, and live in the second story above it. They would take and protect Yvette as if she were their own daughter, and Yvette knows them well, so the adjustment would be easy," said Alain.

"Alright then, when you find a guard you think you can trust to accept the bribe, let us know, and we'll give you the money. Just make sure no one in the barracks sees you with the money," said Aaron.

"Thank you so much. God bless you both. You have no idea how much this means to me and Odette. We'll get moving on this right away because they might soon move us to a place outside of Paris and even France," said Alain.

"You are absolutely right, Alain. You must move quickly," replied Aaron.

Now alone, Aaron confided with his wife Anna. "Strange how things are working out. I feel so much better, now that we've set in motion the means of freeing this young girl from certain death," said Aaron.

"Yes, and I'm proud that you so readily agreed to my suggestion, Aaron. I'm so glad I married you, my dear. I hope that God reserves a place for us to remain together in the after-life," said Anna.

The following day late in the afternoon, Alain accosted Aaron and Anna with promising information.

"I was talking to Etienne Bourdain, who told me he was able to trade his watch for a loaf of bread and some cheese from one of the security guards named Auguste. He said that this guard didn't care for the Germans and their occupation of Paris, but had to follow the orders of his police chief. He said his wife was appalled by this forced roundup of Jews by the French police and thought the Germans should be doing their own dirty work. So he didn't mind helping us as long as it didn't jeopardize his position," said Alain.

"You think then, that this guard, Auguste, will accept a bribe, and help you free your daughter?" asked Aaron.

"Yes, apparently so, according to what Etienne told me," replied Alain.

"Can you point that guard out to me?" asked Aaron.

"Sure, he has the night shift, and comes on duty at 6:30 in the evening," said Alain.

"I think it would be wise if I accompanied you with the money to meet with this guard. That way, he would be less likely to defraud us," said Aaron.

"Perhaps you're right. Besides, it's your money, so you're entitled to make sure he lives up to our arrangement," replied Alain.

"Alright, then. Let's meet this guard right after he comes on duty, and find out if he's willing to help us," said Aaron.

That evening, promptly at 6:30 pm, the guard, Auguste, relieved the day guard, and entered the barracks to survey the premises. As he was leaving the barracks to occupy his outside post, Alain and Aaron, approached him.

"Monsieur Auguste," said Alain, "may we have a word with you, sir."

Police Officer Auguste, a middle-aged man of medium build, looked at these two men, and then responded.

"Yes, what can I do for you," replied Auguste.

"My nine-year-old daughter does not belong here, and I am willing to pay a high price for her removal from this detention center and release into the Paris population, where she can find refuge and safety from the German Occupation Forces," said Alain nervously, knowing the gravity of his request and his possible denunciation.

"Well, now, Mister.........?" said Auguste, stopping for an answer.

"My name is Alain Dumas, and this is my friend Aaron," replied Alain.

"Well, now Mister Dumas, I can understand and sympathize with your dilemma concerning your daughter. I have a daughter of my own. But what you're asking comes with some very high risks. I would need absolute discretion on your part, and a substantial sum of money to offset the risk of being caught. How much are you prepared to pay me for such a dangerous venture?" asked Auguste.

"Ninety thousand francs," said Aaron, "and my name is not important."

"You have the money with you, Monsieur?" asked Auguste, not insistent about Aaron's family name.

"It's in a safe place until we reach an agreement as to the time when the transfer will take place," said Aaron.

"What is your daughter's name, Monsieur Dumas?" asked Auguste.

"Yvette Dumas," replied Alain.

"Where would you want me to deliver your daughter in Paris?" asked Auguste.

"We haven't decided exactly where in Paris yet. However, I can understand your inability to leave your post, and you would probably need an assistant to make the delivery of my daughter to her destination in Paris," said Alain Dumas.

"I would only trust my wife to help me in this venture. I would deliver your daughter to my wife outside the Drancy gate, and she would drive her to any destination within Paris," said Auguste. "Would that be satisfactory?"

"Yes, indeed, that would be perfect," replied Alain Dumas.

"I could arrange to have this done at 6:30 pm tomorrow, at which time you can give me the ninety thousand francs," said Auguste.

"Yes, that arrangement is fine with me," said Alain, looking at Aaron who nodded his head in agreement.

"Good then. You decide where you want your daughter dropped off by my wife tomorrow, I think it's best if your daughter does not carry any luggage that would bring attention to her," said Auguste.

"Yes, I agree. I'll see you then with my daughter tomorrow, and thank you for your kind help," said Alain, who wanted to shake the guard's hand but refrained from doing so, for fear that others in the barracks looking through the windows might find such friendliness with a guard suspicious.

The following day after supper, Yvette Dumas embraced her mother Odette, both teary eyed with the knowledge that this was probably the last time they would see each other.

"Goodbye my darling, God bless and protect you on your journey," said Odette.

"We must leave now, Odette, or we'll be late for our appointment," said Alain with Aaron and Anna standing next to them.

"Here's the money," said Aaron, giving Alain one brown envelope containing ninety thousand francs, and another containing ten thousand francs. "Good luck."

"Thank you, Aaron. I hope all goes well," replied Alain, who then left with his daughter Yvette, now in possession of ten thousand francs, for his rendez-vous with Auguste at the last barracks on that street, next to a seldom-used rear exit gate.

Upon arrival at the entrance to the empty barracks, Auguste immediately asked for the money and quickly counted it, then placed it in the pocket of his jacket.

"We must hurry. My wife is parked outside the rear gate, waiting for your daughter. I have the key to the padlock to that gate. Where do you want my wife to drop off your daughter?" asked Auguste.

"At the Gare Montparnasse," replied Alain, who didn't want Auguste to know his daughter's final destination but knew his brother-in-law Henri Baudelaire's bakery was just a short walk from the Gare Montparnasse.

Auguste unlocked the gate, and after Yvette embraced her father one last time, she walked through its exit, while Alain and Auguste watched her get into the waiting black car, whose passenger door had been opened by Auguste's wife. The car quickly sped off, leaving Alain with a sinking feeling of apprehension, wondering whether his daughter would really find sanctuary at his in-laws for the duration of the war and the occupation of Paris. But as he returned to his barracks to join his wife Odette, calm came over him in the knowledge that his daughter was now free from the clutches of the German Wehrmacht and its internment camp.

Aaron and Anna Cohen wondered if their son Jacques had successfully escaped discovery and apprehension by the French Police in the invasion of their house in the 17th Arrondissement. Unknown to them, Jacques waited until late morning, then quietly exited the attic and house, carrying only his envelope containing a letter and money order made payable to Doctor Michel LeGrand. Jacques was aware of the curfew hours from 9:00pm to 5:00am, therefore felt more secure in his travel through Paris at noontime, when the pedestrian traffic was its busiest for him to mingle, while he walked to the Hopital Hotel Dieu where Doctor LeGrand practiced.

Upon arrival at the Hopital Hotel Dieu, Jacques found it busy with people seeking assistance, but managed to find his way to Doctor LeGrand's office. A nurse was talking to a woman, but upon seeing Jacques, turned her attention to him.

"What can I do for you young man?" asked the nurse.

"I'm looking for Doctor LeGrand?" replied Jacques.

"Do you have an appointment?" asked the nurse.

"No, I don't, but I have a very important message to give him, Ma'am," replied Jacques.

"And what might that message be?" asked the nurse.

"I've been told to give that message only to Doctor LeGrand, Ma'am," replied Jacques.

"Very well, then. I'll see if Doctor LeGrand is available," replied the nurse, who then excused herself with the woman to whom she'd been talking and entered the next room. Shortly thereafter, she returned and instructed Jacques to have a seat, and Doctor LeGrand would see him after he got through with his patient. The nurse then resumed her discussion with the woman, after which they both left the room together leaving Jacques alone for more than twenty minutes.

Finally, the door to the other room opened, and Doctor LeGrand appeared with his patient, an elderly man, wishing him good luck, as the man left the office. LeGrand then gave Jacques a curious look knowing he'd seen him before but not sure of his identity and wondering about the message this young man had for him.

"Aren't you Doctor Cohen's son, Jacques?" asked LeGrand.

"Yes sir, I am," replied Jacques.

"You've grown so much since I last saw you; I hardly recognized you. Well, young man, I understand you have an important message for me?" said Doctor LeGrand.

"Yes, sir, Doctor LeGrand," replied Jacques, handing the doctor an envelope addressed to the Doctor.

Doctor LeGrand opened the sealed envelope and withdrew a folded two-page, handwritten letter, containing a bank money order in the amount of one hundred thousand francs which momentarily startled him. He carefully read the letter, then looked at Jacques with compassionate eyes and a smile on his face, that Jacques found most reassuring.

"Well, Jacques, I guess you're now a member of the LeGrand family," said LeGrand, placing the letter and money order back inside the envelope which he put in his jacket pocket.

"From now on, Jacques, your family name is LeGrand. For your protection, you must forget you ever used the name of Cohen. In fact, we must leave the hospital right now. I'm taking you to my house where my wife Yvonne, who surely remembers your piano recital, will welcome you with open arms," said LeGrand, who then escorted Jacques to his automobile for the ride to his home on the outskirts of Paris.

In the meantime, another round-up of Jews in Paris occurred just after midnight. Several trucks were parked on the street, and French police officers were busy evacuating Jews from their homes, according to a list of Jews the commanding officer carried with him, that had been provided to the French police by Gestapo Headquarters for internment.

As the officer-in-charge stood next to a truck checking the list, a middle-aged Frenchman from one of the houses on that street approached him.

"Sir, may I have a word with you?" asked the Frenchman.

"Yes, what is it?" replied the officer curtly.

"There's a Jewish family living on this street that I don't think you have on your list, sir," said the Frenchman.

"Oh! Yeah! What's his name?" asked the officer.

"His name is Antoine Carpentier, and his wife's name is Josette. They also have a daughter named Margot, and they live in the lower apartment at the end of this street on the left side," said the Frenchman.

"Is that right? What's your name?" asked the police officer.

"I'd rather not say, sir. You know what I mean," replied the Frenchman.

"Yes, I know very well what you mean, but I need your name for our records, sir," said the officer firmly.

"My name is Francois Lazard, sir. I would appreciate it if you would keep my name confidential. I don't want my neighbors to know I cooperated with the police," said Lazard.

"You mean the German Gestapo, don't you," replied the officer. "Your identity will remain confidential. Where do you reside, Monsieur Lazard?"

"Number 73 on this street, sir," replied Lazard nervously.

"Very well, then. Thank you for the information. You may go now," said the officer, dismissing Lazard with obvious disdain, inasmuch as the officer was not sympathetic to the anti-semitic round-up and was merely following the orders of his commanding officer.

One of the police officers who had completed the evacuation of what appeared to be the last family on the list, accosted the officer-in-charge.

"Lieutenant Marchand, sir. I believe we've rounded up all of the Jewish families whose names you gave us," said the officer.

"I've got another family's name, but I'm going to have it checked out first for accuracy before I include it on our list," replied Alfonse Marchand, ending the round-up for that day.

However, Lazard's visit with Officer Marchand did not go unnoticed by some of the neighbors on that street, who wondered what possible reason Lazard would have to solicit a conversation with the officer-in-charge of the Jewish round-up. One of those neighbors was Henri Barbeau, who owned the Boulangerie Parisienne, a well-known bakery frequented by the Germans as well as the French. Officer Marchand was a cousin to Henri Barbeau with whom he and his family frequently had dinner together.

A couple of days later, Officer Marchand visited the bakery and had a personal conversation with his cousin Henri Barbeau.

"I tell you, Henri, this round-up of Jewish families, especially those with small children, is getting to me, and I don't know how long I can do this," said Alfonse Marchand.

"I sympathize with you, Alfonse, but what can you do. Those are your orders, and if you don't follow them, you can end up in a concentration camp yourself, and your family as well," replied Henri Barbeau.

"Yeah, I know. In my latest round-up a couple of days ago, one of the French neighbors denounced another neighbor as being Jewish, who was not on our list of Jews for internment," said Alfonse Marchand.

"Was he correct?" asked Barbeau.

"Actually we checked it out and he was correct," replied Marchand.

"What was his name?" asked Barbeau.

"Antoine Carpentier, with wife Josette and daughter Margot," replied Marchand.

"Oh! I know them. Josette comes here to the bakery almost daily to buy bread and pastries," said Barbeau. "I hope you're not going to add them to your list."

"I thought about it, the risk I mean, in not reporting it, but then, you and I are the only ones that know it, other than Francois Lazard," replied Alfonse Marchand.

"Did you say Francois Lazard?" asked Henri Barbeau.

"Yes, why?" asked Marchand.

"Because he's a Jew," replied Barbeau.

"Are you sure?" said Marchand.

"Yes, I'm sure. Two years ago, he had me bake a cake especially for his son's 13th birthday in celebration of his Bar Mitzvah, a Jewish fête recognizing him as a Minyan having reached manhood," said Barbeau.

"Good God! A Jew denouncing another Jew. I can hardly believe it," replied Marchand.

"Now, he should go on your list, the son-of-a-bitch," replied Barbeau.

"Well, I guess it's a matter of survival. By denouncing another Jew, he thinks it'll hide his own Jewish ancestry," said Marchand.

"It's in these times of duress that we really find out who we really are, and whether we have the courage of our convictions," said Barbeau.

"That's if you even have any convictions," replied Marchand.

"Well, Alfonse, what do you intend to do, my dear cousin?" asked Henri Barbeau.

"I'm not going to include Antoine Carpentier and his wife and daughter on the list of Jews, but I am going to include Francois Lazard," replied Marchand.

"I know how awful Francois Lazard's denounciation is, but should his wife and son be penalized for the sins of the patriarch?" asked Barbeau.

"When you put it that way, Henri, I guess that wouldn't be fair either," said Marchand, "but what's to prevent him from denouncing other Jews?"

"Why don't you pay monsieur Francois Lazard a visit and inform him that you know he's a Jew, and that unless he keeps his mouth shut, he will find himself and his family in Drancy Concentration Camp," said Barbeau.

"That's an excellent idea, and it will insure that Antoine Carpentier and his family are not denounced by him, when I exclude them from the list of Jews," said Marchand. "You know, Henri, you are a very wise man."

"Thank you, dear cousin. How about sharing a café-au-lait and a croissant," said Barbeau.

"With pleasure *mon cousin*," replied Marchand.

It was a bright, sunny day, when Doctor Michel LeGrand, accompanied by Jacques arrived at the LeGrand home, a spacious two-story house in the 16th Arrondissement of Paris.

As they entered the house, Yvonne immediately recognized Jacques, but wondered what brought him to their home with her husband, sensing trouble in the air.

"How are you Jacques," exclaimed Yvonne, looking at her husband for an explanation.

"This will explain everything," replied Michel LeGrand, handing his wife the envelope with the letter and money order.

Yvonne carefully read the letter, noted the amount of money reflected on the money order, then looked at Jacques with a smile.

"Well, Jacques, welcome to your new home. Let me show you to your room upstairs, then I'll give you a tour of the house," said Yvonne, taking Jacques by the hand and leading him to the staircase, while Michel looked on with delight at his wife's ready acceptance of Jacques as a member of the family.

While Jacques was familiarizing himself with the garden in the back yard, Michel had a private talk with his wife.

"You know that Jacques can't stay here, 'cause we can't suddenly have a son. However, my brother Roland, who has a farm in the country with a son and a daughter slightly older than Jacques, is perfect. Jacques could take the part of Roland's other son, also named Jacques, who died a few years ago of pneumonia, and he would be about the same age as Jacques with the same name," said Michel.

"Yes, that would be a perfect match and cover. Luckily, Jacques is a common French name. The sooner we take him to the farm, the safer it is for him and us," replied Yvonne.

The following day, after explaining the reason for his move to Roland LeGrand's farm, and his clandestine adoption as Roland and his wife Madeleine's son, Jacques was driven the one hundred ten kilometers southwest of Paris, not far from the demarcation line separating the Nazi occupied region of France from the southern unoccupied Vichy region.

Jacques was welcomed with open arms, and soon made himself useful working with his newly acquired older brother Etienne and his sister Giselle, only two and one years older, respectively. Jacques found Etienne most friendly and easygoing, while Giselle tended to be bossy, even though she was a year younger than her brother Etienne.

"According to your brother Michel, Jacques' mother was a sister-nurse, who got pregnant by someone whose identity is unknown, except for his mother, of course," said Madeleine. "Do you know where his mother is now, Roland?"

"No I don't. I presume she was immediately transferred to another Hopital de Bon Secours."

"Does Jacques know this?" asked Madeleine.

"Yes he does, and he now knows he's not Jewish, and his adopted Jewish parents were seized from their home, and sent to a Nazi concentration camp. I doubt Jacques will ever see them again," said Roland.

"How awful. That poor boy. I'll love him as if he was our own blood," said Madeleine.

"You are the kindest woman I know, Madeleine. No wonder everyone loves you," replied Roland.

"I hope that includes you," replied Madeleine with a teasing smile.

"Of course, my darling, and now I must get in contact with Gilles Morel, in Chambery, for Jacques' identification card," said Roland.

"Yes, he'll need that right away. You never know when the Nazis make their unannounced visits, looking for downed pilots, resistance members and Jews," said Madeleine.

"Now that the Americans are in this war, I think things are going to change, and those Nazis are going to get what's coming to them, the bastards," said Roland. "By the way, Michel told me that Jacques' mother is from Montreal, Canada."

"Really! So he's half Canadian. I wonder what nationality is his father?" replied Madeleine.

"Who knows. Hopefully we'll eventually meet with his mother, and then perhaps she'll confide in you about Jacques' father," said Roland.

CHAPTER X
Auschwitz, the final destination for the Cohen family

It was a cloudy day that early morning, when all occupants of barracks one through six at Drancy were ordered to grab their belongings and board buses for transportation to the railroad depot at Bobigny, a suburb of Paris, where many windowless cattle wagons awaited them for transportation to Auschwitz Concentration Camp in Poland.

"Where are they taking us, Aaron?" asked Anna, alarmingly.

"I don't know, but we'll find out soon enough," replied Aaron Cohen, suspecting the worst.

A half-hour later, the buses arrived at the Bobigny depot, and its occupants were told to disembark and gather in front of windowless cattle wagons.

"My God, Aaron, they're not going to put us in there, are they?"

"Let's wait and see, Anna. I hope not," replied Aaron.

Several SS guards, assisted by French Policemen, gathered around the crowd of Jews, and began separating them into groups of fifty persons. They were told to take a string tag from nearby baskets and write their name and tie it to their suitcases, including the women's purses, and place them in a large cart, to be loaded into a separate train car, for later retrieval at destination. They were then ordered at the point of rifles to get into the cattle wagons. Those who hesitated were struck with batons into submission, until they boarded the wagons. Two buckets were provided each wagon; one filled with water, the other one empty, to be used as a toilet, but no food, and hardly any room to sit, as they were packed in the wagons like sardines in a can.

Standing in the corner of the wagon train, Aaron held his teary-eyed Anna in his arms, helpless and unable to console her. He'd heard of German concentration camps being erected in Poland from a Doctor Samuel Aschmann, who had left Germany with his wife for migration to Paris, France, resulting in his employment at the Pitie-Salpetriere Hospital. Aaron had met Samuel at a medical conference in Paris, where he was told of the atrocious conditions levied against Jews in Berlin, and their deportation to extermination camps in Poland. Aaron withheld that information from his wife to spare her the worry and agony that would soon enough be upon them.

"Where are they taking us?" asked Anna.

"I presume to another internment camp. We'll know shortly," replied Aaron, who suspected from the way they were being treated as cattle that their destination was not going to be an improvement over Drancy.

The stench from the accumulation of human waste in the provided bucket that served as their only toilet was overwhelming. One of the men pulled out a folded knife and through the slot of the door attempted to unlock it but failed.

The use of the toilet bucket was most humiliating for the women on the train. Anna Cohen resisted its use until it became so painful, she had to ask her husband to bring the bucket to the corner where she could use it, with Aaron

94

standing in front of her to provide some privacy. They had been provided no food, and the sole bucket of water in less than sanitary condition, was avoided by some of the passengers, including the Cohens.

During the night, Aaron and Anna squatted in their corner of the wagon in each other's arms, listening to the continuous clanking of the train's wheels against the tracks, and the occasional whimpering sound of a woman in distress, or a child crying for sustenance and comfort. But then they heard someone recite the most important of all Jewish prayers, "Shema Yisrael Adonai Eloheinu Adonai Echad" (Hear, O Israel: the Lord our God, the Lord is one), which was joined by several other Jews in a chant that, for a brief moment, resurrected their hope that somehow, God would come to their rescue, but then the reality of their abysmal situation tested the faith of the most ardent Jew, who understandably wondered how this could have happened in the first place.

"How could God allow this evil to happen to his people and flourish in France and throughout Europe?" asked Anna.

"Living under these horrible conditions is far more difficult than dying, which is a quick way of joining God in heaven, where love, joy and peace await us. Perhaps that's the reason God is not interfering with Satan's disciples," replied Aaron.

"Yes, perhaps you're right, my darling. Whatever happens, we'll be together 'till the end," said Anna.

The next morning, it was discovered that an elderly man had died during the cold night, and his wife had become nearly catatonic from the loss of her husband and the hopelessness of her situation. Doctor Cohen and Anna made their way to her and attempted to console her, but it became obvious she was beyond help and destined to quickly follow her husband.

Aaron started chanting the Jewish Prayer for the Dead called *El Malei Rachamim,* "God, full of Mercy." He was immediately joined by his wife Anna, and most of the occupants in the wagon, many in tears of sadness, not only for the deceased, but also for their desperate selves.

The next morning, upon arrival at the station facing the entrance to Auschwitz Concentration Camp, the recently widowed woman was found to have joined her husband, where they now could rest together in peace.

The loud noise of the cattle wagon doors being unlocked and opened caused the occupants relief but also anxiety about their fate at this new concentration camp. Ramps were placed at the doors' openings and the prisoners were ordered to vacate the cattle wagons leaving the dead bodies behind for later disposal. There must have been a thousand prisoners gathered together for inspection by SS officers, guards and prisoner functionaries known as Kapos. These Kapos were prisoners themselves who volunteered to work for the Nazis in maintaining order of the prisoners at Auschwitz in return for better treatment, such as the wearing of civilian clothes, a private room within the barracks, and extra food rations.

Amongst the SS Officers conducting the inspection of prisoners were a few medical doctors deciding the fate of each prisoner as to whether they would be used as forced labor or exterminated in the gas chambers. The elderly, the feeble, and children too young to work were separated from the rest and gathered into a group destined for extermination. Those deemed fit for work were gathered into another group to be housed in barracks governed by Kapos, at the direction of SS officers and guards.

Watching the selection process, Aaron Cohen realized that his wife Anna might be selected for extermination, therefore had to act quickly.

"Anna, stay with me, no matter what happens. I'm going to approach that one SS doctor who speaks French, rather than the other SS officers."

"Sir, I'm a doctor and this is my wife, a nurse," said Aaron producing his medical license, although revoked.

The SS doctor looked at the license, then at Aaron.

"Where did you practice medicine, Doctor Cohen?"

"At the Hopital Hotel Dieu in Paris, sir," replied Aaron.

"What was your specialty?" asked the SS doctor.

"I'm a cardiac surgeon, but I also performed other surgery, sir," replied Aaron.

"And your wife, she's a nurse?" asked the SS doctor.

"Yes, she's a registered nurse, and has assisted me in many surgeries, sir," replied Aaron, exaggerating his wife's nursing experience.

"Very well, I'm sure we can find some use for you both," said the SS doctor, handing Aaron a business sized card with his name on it, where he'd written 'medical doctor and nurse'.

"Go over there and join that group of special workers," said the SS doctor.

"Thank you, sir. We really appreciate this," said Aaron.

"Don't thank me yet, doctor, this is not the Hotel Dieu," replied the SS doctor, who understood the meaning of *Hotel Dieu* as *God's Hotel* in English.

With great relief, Aaron and Anna joined the small group of people, mostly men, selected to work hopefully at their specialty at Auschwitz. They were eventually escorted by SS guards and Kapos through the main gate of Auschwitz to a brick barracks, unlike the majority of other barracks made of wood. Aaron and Anna were among 90 other inmates housed in a barracks intended for 40 prisoners. To accommodate that number of prisoners, three tiered bunks in 30 spaces were provided, on a come first basis. The bunks had straw mattresses, one thin blanket and no pillow. The more aggressive prisoners hurriedly selected their bunk of choice, while others quietly walked through the barracks in search of an unoccupied bunk. Aaron made sure he found two lower bunks side by side for him and his wife, located at the other end of the barracks. The Kapo, wearing a Lagerpolizist (camp policeman) armband, had a private room on the right side at the entrance to the barracks opposite the washroom and latrine.

"Alright. I want all prisoners to stand in front of their bunk in the aisle," yelled the Kapo.

As the prisoners stood in line in the aisle, the Kapo walked to the center, then facing them, identified himself.

"My name is Frederic Moineau. I'm in charge of this barracks, and you will address me as Monsieur Moineau. You are here at the pleasure of the Third Reich, and I have been given authority and discretion over your pitiful lives, while you are assigned to this barracks. I expect full obedience from you at all times."

Moineau then started walking up the aisle carrying a swagger stick, inspecting each prisoner with a severe look of disdain on his face. He stopped in front of a woman in her late twenties standing next to her husband of the same age.

"What's your name?" asked Moineau.

"Margo, Monsieur."

"What's your last name," he asked brusquely.

"Weinstein, Monsieur," replied Margo.

"An attractive Jew. I'm sure I'll find something useful for you to do," said Moineau, with a sardonic smile that intimidated her and angered her husband Nathan standing next to her, but unable to vent his anger at Moineau's coercive sexual promise.

Moineau continued his inspection, and upon facing Anna Cohen, he stopped, then looked at Aaron standing next to her.

"You have a very attractive wife, Doctor Cohen. Yes, I was given your name by Doctor Schmeling, who was apparently impressed with your credentials. But here in this barracks, you and your wife are just prisoners of the Third Reich and submissive to my orders and obedient to my requests, or else you suffer severe consequences, and that goes for all prisoners in this barracks," said Moineau, as he looked squarely into Anna's eyes with a look that sent shivers down her spine, eliciting a sadistic smile from Moineau, who then turned and walked back to his room without further comment.

"My God, Aaron, that man is evil personified," said Anna, still shaken from Moineau's words.

"Don't worry, Anna, I won't let him touch or hurt you, I promise," replied Aaron.

Later that morning, inside the Auschwitz Security Office, Frederic Moineau stood at attention in front of Major Hans Bach, Deputy Commandant, being instructed about his duties as Kapo of barracks Number 7.

"The prisoners in barracks 7 are professionals whose services are needed at the Farben synthetic and petroleum plant, with the exception of Doctor Cohen and his wife, whose medical services will be used at our medical facility under the supervision of Doctor Gerhard Gruber. Therefore, in order to maintain their full cooperation, these prisoners will not have their heads shaved, but they will be tattooed with a serial number for identification, sometime next week. Do you have any questions?" asked Major Bach.

"No sir," replied Moineau, a Jewish prisoner himself, most thankful for his position as a prisoner functionary also known as a Kapo, that excluded him from the harsh treatment suffered by most prisoners.

That evening, just before 2100 hours, when the barracks lights went out, Monsieur Moineau stepped out of his room and walked up to the bunk occupied by Margo Weinstein.

"Come with me," ordered Moineau, pointing his finger at Margo.

Margo looked at her husband Nathan with fear in her eyes. Nathan got out of his bunk and stood facing Moineau.

"What do you want with my wife, Monsieur Moineau?" asked Nathan firmly.

"You dare question me," said Moineau, striking Nathan repeatedly in the face and his head with his swagger stick until he fell on his knees. Margo stepped in between them with her hands raised for Moineau to stop.

"I'll go with you. Please don't hit my husband anymore," pleaded Margo with tears streaming down her face.

"Come with me now," ordered Moineau, grabbing her by the arm, and then shoving her forward towards his room.

Screams and then cries could be heard coming from inside Moineau's room, and then silence.

"My God, Aaron, he's raping that poor woman," said Anna. "I'm afraid he may come for me next."

"Unlike her husband Nathan, I'm a medical doctor, who knows how to take lives as well as save them. So don't worry, my darling, that bastard will never touch you," said Aaron in a most confident voice that Anna found reassuring.

Aaron, along with his wife Anna, quietly walked over to Nathan now lying on his lower bunk. Upon seeing Aaron and Anna, he gave a faint smile, but it was obvious he was in pain.

"I'm a doctor. Let me see if there's anything I can do for you," said Aaron, who then lit a match to better see Nathan's facial injuries.

"Anna, can you quietly go into the latrine and bring back a wet towel or rag so I can wipe off the blood from his face," said Aaron.

"I see you've got a couple of lumps on the left side of your head, but the cuts on you face are superficial, and after I wipe off the blood, you should look if not feel better. Give it a few days for it to heal," said Aaron.

"Thank you doctor. Is my wife still with Monsieur Moineau?" asked Nathan.

"I'm afraid so," replied Aaron, now being joined by Anna who started wiping the blood off Nathan's face with a wet, dirty towel.

"That's the best I could find in the latrine," said Anna, referring to the dirty towel.

"It'll have to do," replied Aaron.

"Somehow, I feel better. Thank you for your kindness," said Nathan.

Returning to their bunk, Aaron and Anna heard the door to the Kapo's room open, and then Margo in a disheveled state exited the room, with the door abruptly closing behind her. The barracks lights were out, but some light entered through the windows, allowing her to slowly navigate towards her bunk and awaiting husband, who upon seeing her, found the strength to rise from his bunk and hold her in his arms, as she was about to faint. Anna immediately went over to help Margo, with Aaron right behind her, knowing that Anna, as a nurse, was best equipped to assist Margo, who most probably had been sexually assaulted and raped.

Margo was now lying on her back in the lower bunk normally used by her husband. When Nathan approached her,

Margo turned her head away in underserved shame. Her subdued sobbing was tearing Nathan's heart.

"That bastard raped my wife, I'm going to kill him for this," said Nathan.

"I'm a nurse. Please let me talk to her, and see what can be done to ease her suffering," said Anna.

"Do you want me to examine her for evidence of rape?" asked Aaron of Nathan.

"No, that won't be necessary. My wife's condition is enough evidence for me," replied Nathan.

"Margo, this is Anna, I'm a nurse. Let me help you through this traumatic event. Perhaps I can find a way to ease your pain."

Margo slowly turned her head, and upon seeing Anna's face, stopped sobbing. Anna took her left hand in hers, then placed her other hand over it with tender strokes meant to soothe her and gain her trust.

"As a nurse, I've treated several women who were sexually assaulted, and the one thing you must not do, is blame yourself. You were sexually assaulted by a sadistic man who will eventually be punished for his crime. In the meantime, Margo, allow your mind and body to heal with the knowledge that God is near you, and knows of your suffering, and will not allow it to continue for long," said Anna, not realizing the prophecy of her last statement.

Two evenings later, the barracks lights were about to be extinguished, when Monsieur Moineau came out of his room, walked up the aisle, and stopped in front of the cubicle, where Anna and Aaron were bunked opposite each other.

"It's time for you, Anna Cohen, to visit me," said Moineau, pointing his finger at her.

Aaron immediately rose from his bunk and walked up to Moineau.

"I know what you have in mind, Monsieur Moineau, but I have something far more valuable and rewarding that would set you up for life," said Aaron.

"And what might that be?" asked Moineau, aroused by Aaron's daring offer.

"I don't think it's wise to discuss this in front of the other prisoners. Why don't we go to your room for privacy," said Aaron.

"Alright, but it better be good, doctor," replied Moineau, leading the way to his room.

Moineau allowed Aaron to enter the room first, then closed the door behind him.

"So, what are you offering, diamonds, gold, or paper money?" asked Moineau.

"Gold is too heavy and bulky to hide, and paper money may become worthless if the winds of war change. But diamonds are a man's best friend," said Aaron slowly advancing towards Moineau, now smiling at the mention of diamonds.

"And where are those diamonds hidden?" asked Moineau.

Aaron moved his right hand as if reaching from inside his shirt pocket, but then stiffened his right hand like a spear which he drove directly into Moineau's throat severing his windpipe. Moineau's eyes momentarily froze as he gasped for air, and then collapsed to the ground dead. Aaron felt only relief at ridding this world of a monster. Knowing what he had to do next, he didn't find it necessary to hide Moineau's body over or under his bunk. He simply left the room, locking the door behind him, and walked back to his bunk to join his wife, whose questioning eyes wondered what had transpired in Moineau's room.

Making sure his conversation was out of earshot of the nearby prisoners, Aaron whispered in Anna's ear.

"I killed the bastard, so he won't bother anyone else. However, we now have no choice but to leave this hellhole called Auschwitz, and I've come prepared for that eventuality," said Aaron, pulling out a stainless steel capsule which he unscrewed at its center, revealing two purple pills.

"These are cyanide pills. You won't feel a thing, and it won't take but a few seconds, then you'll be free from this house of horror and join me in a world of peace and love for all of eternity," said Aaron.

"Oh! My God, Aaron. I love you, and I'll go anywhere with you, darling," replied Anna.

"Let's lie down together in my bunk and take our cyanide pill together at the same time while in each other's arms," said Aaron.

Now lying down together, Aaron gave Anna one of the cyanide pills.

"Are you ready, darling?" asked Aaron.

"Yes, darling, I am," replied Anna.

"Let's do it. Heaven, here we come," said Aaron, ingesting the cyanide pill one second after watching Anna ingest her pill.

The following morning, no one sounded reveille because Monsieur Moineau was permanently indisposed. The prisoners in Barracks 7 wondered what had happened to their Kapo. Some of them went into the latrine to ready themselves for the day's travail, while others remained in their bunk to take advantage of this restful period. More than an hour transpired before SS Lieutenant Dieter Hofer, entered the barracks to find out why its Kapo had not held roll call of the prisoners that morning.

"Where's Monsieur Moineau?" asked Lieutenant Hofer of the prisoners bunked near the barracks' entrance and the Kapo's room.

"We haven't seen him, sir. I don't think he ever came out of his room, sir," said one of the prisoners.

Lieutenant Hofer knocked on the door to Moineau's room several times and got no answer. He tried the door knob and found the door locked. The lieutenant stepped back, and then with his right foot hit the wooden door hard, successfully opening it. Inside the room he found Moineau dead from an obvious homicide. He immediately ordered all prisoners to fall into the middle aisle, and stand at attention.

He then deliberately walked up the aisle looking question-ably at each prisoner until he reached the end of barracks, at which time he noticed Aaron and Anna Cohen lying together on the same lower bunk with their eyes dead open. He walked over, and with his swagger stick hit each of them in the face in anger, then turned and walked back into the middle aisle.

"Does anyone know who those two dead people are?" asked Lieutenant Hofer, aware these prisoners had not yet been tattooed with identification numbers.

"Yes, sir. They are Doctor Cohen and his wife Anna," said one of the prisoners who bunked in the same cubicle.

"Does anyone know who visited your Monsieur Moineau in his room last night?" asked Hofer.

When no one answered, Lieutenant Hofer walked slowly back down the aisle staring into the faces of each prisoner for an answer, and when none came, he gave his response.

"Very well, then. I will hold all of you responsible for his death," said Hofer, who then left the barracks.

Lieutenant Dieter Hofer immediately reported the loss of two prisoners and one Kapo in barracks 7, to Major Hans Bach, the Deputy Commandant at the Auschwitz Security Office.

"You'd better get Doctor Schmidt over to barracks 7, to determine the cause of death, in particular that of Doctor Cohen and his wife. Are you sure Frederic Moineau was killed by one of the prisoners?" asked Major Bach.

"Who else could have done it, and it had to be someone strong enough to collapse his throat," replied Hofer.

"So, you did examine Moineau, then," asked Major Bach.

"Yes, to satisfy myself he was dead, and from the looks of him, it appeared his windpipe had been severely crushed," replied Hofer.

"Well, we know that Kapos are hated by the prisoners, so it comes as no surprise that once in a while, one of them will be angry enough to kill his tormentor," said Major Bach.

"I asked them to reveal the name of the prisoner who visited Moineau in his room last night, and when no one came forward, I told them I would hold all of them responsible for his death. I recommend they all be sent to crematorium bunker 2 for extermination, sir," said Hofer.

"I agree, and it will make room for the trainload of new prisoners scheduled to arrive in a couple of days," replied Major Bach. "So, get a squad of Sonderkommandos to assist you in the extermination, but not before Doctor Schmidt has had a chance to determine the cause of death of those three prisoners, Doctor Cohen and his wife in particular."

A couple of hours later, Doctor Schmidt reported his findings to Major Bach.

"Doctor Cohen and his wife Anna died of cyanide poisoning. I found this stainless-steel capsule that must have contained the cyanide pills on the floor near his bunk. An ingenuous way to hide it. When searched, all he had to do was swallow it, and retrieve it with a bowel movement. Being of stainless steel, the capsule would resist acidic corrosion. They clearly committed suicide. However, Frederic Moineau was killed by a severe blow to his windpipe that suffocated him to death. Someone with combat or medical training, I would guess," said Doctor Schmidt.

"Maybe it was Doctor Cohen, and that's why he committed suicide with his wife," replied Major Bach.

"Perhaps, but this required someone with the audacity and strength of a soldier," said Doctor Schmidt.

"Well, it doesn't matter, because I'm having them all sent to Bunker 2 crematorium," replied Major Bach with finality.

Lieutenant Dieter Hofer, wearing his Luger pistol, arrived at barracks 7, with a squad of Sonderkommandos, Jewish prisoners assigned specifically to assist SS Officers in the extermination of Jewish prisoners, hence armed only with batons. He ordered all prisoners to fall out of the barracks, and in formation for roll call, leaving the three deceased prisoners inside the barracks for later retrieval and disposal.

Most of the Sonderkommandos stationed themselves behind and to the side of the formation, insuring no one tried to run away. Lieutenant Hofer stood in front of the formation ready to explain the reason for their assembly in a manner designed to hide their true fate until it was too late.

"You are going to march a short distance to a sanitation building where you will be disinfected, and then bathe with shower. Afterwards you will be tattooed for identification, and then you will be ready for assignment to the Farben synthetic rubber and petroleum plant," said Lieutenant Hofer.

Hofer then ordered the SonderKommandos to march the prisoners to Bunker 2 crematorium. Upon arrival, the prisoners were herded into a specially constructed barracks connected to Bunker 2 crematorium, where they were ordered to remove all their clothing and hang it up on numbered wall hooks for subsequent retrieval after they had showered. Amongst them were Nathan Weinstein and his wife Margo, still recovering from her rape.

"I can't disrobe in front of all these men," said Margo to her husband Nathan.

"If you don't, they'll just beat you 'till you do. Just stay close to me, and I'll cover you as much as possible," said Nathan, who then watched Margo remove her clothes, which Nathan hung on wall hook number 33, next to his hook number 34 with his clothing. When they had completed their own undressing, they heard large swing doors being opened by two Sonderkommandos at the other end of the building that led into Bunker 2 containing the overhead showers.

As they were herded into the bunker, Nathan noticed several metal round columns, whose sides were perforated with holes that rose from the cement floor to the ceiling. He noticed there were some towels hanging from wall hooks, a cosmetic deceit facilitating its real purpose. Suddenly the swing doors were closed and locked, and then the lights went out.

"What's happening?" asked Margo of her husband.

"I don't know, but I don't like it," replied Nathan.

On the roof of the building, an SS Officer, and a Health Service Officer, carrying canisters of Zyklon B gas pellets, donned gas masks, then poured the contents down the perforated columns inside the bunker. As soon as the pellets hit the open air, they became lethal, and the gas pushed through the columns' perforated holes into the bunker killing the victims with diabolical efficiency.

The prisoners attempted to flee from the columns' deadly fumes with nowhere to go but on top of each other in a panic of screams and horrifying cries.

Nathan had pulled Margo away into a corner of the bunker where he held her in his arms, knowing he had little time left to console his wife.

"Darling, they don't know it yet, but they're liberating us from this evil world, and God is waiting for us where we'll have peace and love for eternity. So, kiss me darling, before we go to sleep in a better world," said Nathan in an embrace with Margo that ended with them both lying on the ground still holding each other.

Fifteen minutes later, electric ventilators evacuated the gas from the bunker allowing Sonderkommandos, wearing gas masks, to remove the bodies, where they could be flooded with water hoses before their hair was shaved off for commercial use, and gold teeth removed for subsequent melting into bullion for the enrichment of the Third Reich.

CHAPTER XI
Christiane's recruitment into the French Resistance

Sister Christiane, in an effort to find her son Jacques, made her way by train from Madrid, Spain to Paris, having to travel north through the French Free Zone to the Demarcation Line separating the Free Zone from the Occupied Zone which included Paris. Feeling protected by the wearing of her religious habit, Sister Christiane sat quietly in a window seat in one of the mid-section cars reserved for civilian passengers, while cars in the forward section were occupied by German military personnel. The last car was used exclusively for the transport of detainees for trial or internment.

A man in his mid-thirties, wearing a gray wool jacket over an open light-blue shirt and dark trousers, sat in the seat next to Christiane and struck up a conversation.

"How are you this fine day, Sister?" he said. "My name is Jean-Guy Lambert."

"I'm doing fine, Monsieur Lambert," replied Christiane, a bit suspicious of his direct approach, wondering if perhaps he was a German Gestapo agent.

"Please excuse my forwardness. It's just that my sister Marie was a nun in the Augustinian Order and a nurse, and you remind me of her," said Lambert.

"I'm Sister Christiane. You spoke of your sister in the past tense?" said Christiane as a question.

"Yes unfortunately. She was assigned to a hospital in Warsaw, Poland, and when she insisted on treating Polish patients before German patients, she was summarily shot," said Lambert.

"I am so sorry to hear that. I'm sure she's now in a safe place with Jesus, and surrounded by Angels," said Sister Christiane.

Lambert looked around quickly to see who was sitting within hear shot, before he vented his true feelings.

"Now I have two reasons for hating the Germans," said Lambert in a low voice.

"You must know that hate will hurt you far more than the hateful. I will say a prayer for you and your sister, Monsieur Lambert."

"Thank you Sister Christiane. Where are you heading?"

"Paris," replied Christiane.

"You know that Paris is in the Occupied Zone. I hope your identification papers are in order. They look for any excuse to detain people, especially women, even nuns," said Lambert.

Christiane remained silent, leaving her safety in God's hands. It wasn't long before a French Policeman, accompanied by a man dressed in a suit, white shirt and black tie, came into their train, and started checking passengers' identification.

"The man in the suit is from the SS Gestapo," whispered Lambert to Christiane.

"Your papers, please," said the policemen with the Gestapo looking on.

Lambert pulled out his identification booklet, which the policeman examined then returned to him. When Sister

Christiane produced her identification, the Gestapo man took it from the policeman.

"Your papers show you to be from the Hopital de Bon Secours in Brussels, Belgium. What is your destination, Sister Christiane, if that is your real name?" asked the Gestapo.

"That is my real name, Monsieur, and my destination is Paris," replied Christiane.

"And what is your purpose for going to Paris, may I ask?"

"To visit the Hopital de Bon Secours in Paris, where I was previously assigned," replied Christiane.

"Your papers do not authorize you to travel through France, and certainly not into the Occupied Zone. Furthermore, you would not be the first resistance fighter to disguise herself with a nun's habit in order to travel into the Occupied Zone. I am therefore placing you under arrest until we have ascertained your identity and reason for travel to Paris. Please stand in the aisle and come with us," ordered the Gestapo man.

Lambert stood up and stepped back to allow Sister Christiane to step into the aisle. Christiane started walking behind the policeman with the Gestapo right behind her, not realizing that Lambert and another man were walking right behind them. As the policeman entered the enclosed section that separates the trains, he turned to see if Sister Christiane was behind him. Once the three of them were inside that section, the policeman turned to unlock and open the door to the detainee train when suddenly Lambert and his friend pushed themselves into the compartment, and using pistols with silencers, killed both the policeman and the Gestapo man. Ignoring Sister Christiane's momentary shock, they opened the side door and threw the two bodies off the train.

"Sister Christiane, this is Marcel. We're from the Maquis, French Resistance. You are in grave danger, and must come with us. The train will stop in about fifteen minutes for the exchange of passengers, and that's when we'll leave. You'll be safe, you have my guarantee," said Lambert as they remained in that in-between trains section, until the train stopped, then disembarked and left the train station, boarding a car that had been waiting for them.

"The next train stop would have been the checkpoint at the demarcation Line of the Occupied Zone. Philipp here followed the train so we could to disembark at the stop before that checkpoint. You see, Sister Christiane, we were warned by Father Andre in Madrid, Spain that you might attempt to enter France, and most likely the Occupied Zone to Paris," said Lambert, with a smile. "You were mistakenly told he had died, weren't you?"

"Yes. Oh! God. Thank you," exclaimed Christiane.

"So we had two teams, each boarding a different train traveling north from Madrid into France, and with divine help and amazing luck, Marcel and I got on the same train you did, and being the only Sister on board, I sat next to you to make sure you were in fact Sister Christiane. And there you have it," said Lambert.

"God moves in mysterious ways. I just wished there hadn't been a need to kill those two men," said Christiane.

"I wouldn't feel sorry for them, Sister. Do you have any idea where these people they detain end up?" asked Marcel.

"Where do they end up?" asked Christiane.

"Concentration camps like Treblinka and Sobitor in Poland. They're nothing more than death camps," said Marcel.

"I understand from Father Andre that you are a nurse. We in the Maquis can sure use your nursing experience, Sister Christiane," said Lambert.

"If I can be of any help, I'm at your service," replied Sister Christiane.

"I hope you won't mind if we ask you to wear ordinary clothes that won't identify you as a member of the clergy. We will provide you with new identity papers that are fail-proof," said Lambert.

Once inside the black, four-door Citroen automobile, Christiane wondered where they were taking her, and how she was going to make contact with Father Andre.

"Where are you taking me?" asked Christiane.

"To a farm in the free zone bordering the perimeter of the occupied zone. This provides us with freedom of movement, yet secretive access to the occupied zone," replied Lambert.

"How long a drive is that? I may have to use a bathroom," said Christiane.

"It's about an hour's drive, but there's a café about five kilometers from here, where we can stop for a brief moment. We know the proprietor," replied Lambert.

"Thank you, Monsieur Lambert, I feel safer already," replied Christiane.

"Please call me Jean-Guy, and I'll drop the Sister title from your name, now that you're part of the Maquisards Resistance, also known as Maquis," replied Lambert.

Christiane remained silent, weighing her new identity and comrades, realizing she had no choice in the matter, considering the life-threatening situation that brought her to this French resistance group.

The Lemagne family farm in Chambery, where Christiane was being taken was located about five hundred and seventy kilometers southeast of Paris, in the unoccupied zone under the Vichy government. It was also the center for the French Resistance with a subterranean facility under their large barn that included a cache of arms and explosives. The large house had a basement that extended beyond its perimeter, to house surgical and medical recovery rooms. When needed, Doctor LeGrand would leave the Hotel Dieu Hospital, and visit the Lemagne farm to attend to the wounded, some of them resistance fighters, others downed pilots, who eventually were secretly transported to Spain or a southern port for shipment to England. The risks were immense, but now that England was receiving aid from America, the French Resistance felt a surge of encouragement with the sudden increase of weapons, and other munitions from England, through night flights at prearranged landing zones by the Resistance. It was also where Jean-Guy Lambert and Marcel Levasseur of the Maquis French Resistance were taking Sister Christiane for her own safety, and expected assistance as a nurse to the French Resistance.

Upon arrival at the Lemagne farm, Christiane was led inside a large two-story house, and was immediately met by Charles Lemagne, a tall, muscular, middle-age man, dressed in work clothes, and his wife Monique, wearing her auburn hair in an elegant chignon. She was dressed in a short-sleeve shirt and slacks that complimented her well-developed figure.

"I would like to introduce you to Sister Christiane, who was about to be abducted by the Gestapo on the train, just before we reached the checkpoint at the demarcation line of the occupied zone," said Jean-Guy Lambert. "She is also a nurse."

"A nurse...you are doubly welcomed Sister Christiane," said Charles. "We can certainly use your medical skills. In case you haven't been told, you are now at the center of the Maquis French Resistance. Your discretion as well as your skills as a nurse are much needed. I hope you will stay with us in our fight against the Nazis, and their occupation of our beloved country."

"I too have personal reasons for wanting the defeat of the Nazis, Monsieur. I will gladly assist you in helping your wounded," replied Christiane. "If it's not too much trouble, I would like to change into regular clothes that won't identify me as a member of the clergy."

"That's no trouble at all. You're about my size. I'll lend you some clothes," said Monique.

"If you don't mind, please call me Christiane and dispense with the sister title."

"Of course, that makes sense since you're going to be here incognito with new papers showing you as my younger sister," said Monique.

"That's fine with me, as long as I retain my first name," replied Christiane.

"Well, let's get you settled into your new home. I'll show you your room upstairs," said Monique, leaving the men downstairs to discuss the fact that Jean-Guy and Marcel had to kill the French policeman, and the Gestapo agent on the train.

During dinner that evening, the Lemagne family that included their two sons Julien and Maurice, as well as Jean-Guy Lambert and Marcel Levasseur, freely discussed the recent activities of the French resistance in the presence of Christiane, who had quickly become part of the family and the resistance movement.

"May I ask where exactly you met Father Andre?" asked Christiane.

"He contacted us through one of our agents in a bistro in Madrid. He wanted us to find you, to let you know he was alive, and seeking to join you," said Jean-Guy Lambert.

"Father Andre is a medical doctor and surgeon who could be of great assistance to you," said Christiane, who wanted Andre to join her in finding their son Jacques.

"Really. We could certainly use his medical expertise, especially with you at his side. This would free Doctor LeGrand from coming here, at great risk to his safety, as well as ours," said Charles. "Where can we find him?"

"The last I heard, Father Andre was assigned to the Christian Abbey in Madrid," replied Christiane.

"We'll have someone contact him, and tell him of your whereabouts, and offer to safely bring him here to join us," said Charles.

"This is great news. To have a doctor and nurse here to tend to our wounded is fantastic. After dinner, I'll show you our modest medical facility in the cellar, where Doctor LeGrand conducted his surgery without a nurse other than Monique to assist him," said Charles.

CHAPTER XII
The Reunion of Father Andre and Sister Christiane

Upon his return from a visit to the Christian Abbey in Madrid, Spain, Gregoire Barnier, a member of the Maquis, reported his findings to Charles Lemagne, whom Christiane soon learned, was one of the leaders of the Maquis French Resistance in the unoccupied section of France with more than a hundred members.

"Well, Gregoire, did you locate Father Andre?" asked Charles.

"No, I didn't. Apparently he hadn't been told that Christiane had been transferred to the Hopital de Bon Secours in Brussels, Belgium, therefore made his way to Paris, and the Bon Secours hospital there," replied Gregoire.

"Obviously, when he got there, he must have found out about her transfer to Belgium, and probably made his way there, only to find her gone with no leads to her whereabouts," said Charles.

"What do you suggest we do now, sir?" asked Gregoire.

"Let's put the word out to all members, including our associates in the occupied section and Paris, to be on the lookout for Father Andre, a medical doctor, and a person of importance to the French Resistance. Once located, he's to be told only that the person he is seeking is in the unoccupied zone, and waiting for his arrival, which should motivate him to be escorted to our location," said Charles.

"Consider it done, sir," replied Gregoire.

Charles Lemagne then informed Christiane of their unsuccessful attempt to locate Father Andre.

"We're putting out an alert to all our agents throughout France for his location and transportation here," said Charles. "Do you have any idea where he may have gone or where he may be now?"

"Other than the Hopital de Bon Secours in Paris, and the Bon Secours in Brussels, I haven't the faintest idea where he might be," replied Christiane.

"Well, hopefully something will turn up. We've got a lot of eyes and ears out there looking for him," said Charles in a confident voice.

"I hope so," replied Christiane.

Later that evening, Christiane decided she must confide her delicate situation involving Father Andre and their son Jacques with Charles' wife Monique, before Father Andre's arrival there. She intended to tell Father Andre he was the father of a boy named Jacques, and she expected him to help her find him. Christiane had developed a close relationship with Monique, who as an ally, would be in a sympathetic position to explain Christiane's situation to her husband Charles.

"There is something I must tell you in confidence, Monique. It must not be told to anyone else, except your husband," said Christiane in an uncertain voice that spelled caution.

"Whatever it is, Sister Christiane, you have my solemn promise, I will not violate your trust in my confidentiality," replied Monique.

"Father Andre and I met on the *SS Ile de France* passenger ship from New York to the Port de Saint-Nazaire, and we fell in love resulting in an indiscretion on the last day of our voyage. A couple of months later I discovered I was pregnant. I also learned that shortly after his arrival in Paris, Father Andre was transferred somewhere in Spain without knowing he was the father of my unborn child. As a member of the Congregation of the Sisters of Bon Secours, I was not allowed to keep the child, a boy, who was immediately placed in the Bon Secours Orphanage for adoption. I was permitted to see my son briefly, and named him Jacques. I was then transferred to the Bon Secours Hospital in Brussels, Belgium. Father Andre wrote me a letter reaffirming his love and offering to leave the Jesuits in order to marry me. I have already informed the Mother Superior of Bon Secours in Brussels of my intention to leave the congregation in order to find my son Jacques and bring him back to Montreal, my home and country, hopefully with Andre as my husband. As you can see, when Father Andre does arrive here, I will have to tell him about Jacques, and together we will find him, and bring him with us to America," said Christiane.

"My God. That is quite a story. Listen Christiane, I will do whatever I can to help you find your son. Don't worry. We'll find him," said Monique in an empathic voice that was most reassuring to Christiane, who had been uncertain about revealing her dilemma to anyone, including Monique.

That night, as Monique and Charles retired to the bedroom, she related Christiane's story to her husband.

"Good Lord. Looking at her in that habit, I would never have guessed she could get involved in a love affair, especially with a Jesuit priest. Did she say how old their son would now be?" asked Charles.

"Yes, she said he was born in March 1930, so he'd now be eleven years old," replied Monique. "But she doesn't know who adopted her son, and the Bon Secours Orphanage will not reveal that information."

"Well, these are exceptional circumstances in times of war, where the rules can be broken. We'll see about that," said Charles encouragingly.

Several days later, Father Andre's unsuccessful attempt to find Christiane left him no choice but to return to the Christian Abbey in Madrid. He was immediately informed by Father Sebastian that an agent of the French Resistance was looking for him with the information he was seeking. He was further told that he should contact a man named Albert Moulet at the El Toraro Café on the Calle de Avendano in Madrid. Father Andre wasted no time, and wearing civilian clothes with his habit and crucifix packed in a small suitcase, he left the Abbey for his rendez-vous with Moulet.

At the El Toraro Café, Father Andre told the apparent proprietor he was looking for Albert Moulet, and after identifying himself, he was led back into the kitchen and out the back door into the alley, where he was directed to the house whose back yard faced the café.

"You will find Albert Moulet in that house over there," said the proprietor, pointing to the house.

Father Andre opened the wooden gate, and walked through the small yard, then climbed the few wooden stairs to the porch leading to the back door. Father Andre knocked on the door, and when no one answered, he knocked again, then heard a faint noise of someone approaching from the side of the house.

"Who are you looking for, mister?" asked the young man, wearing a loose jacket that hid a revolver.

"I'm looking for Albert Moulet."

"And who might you be?" asked the man, advancing closer to Father Andre.

"I'm Father Andre from the Christian Abbey. A message was left for me to contact Albert Moulet," replied Father Andre.

"Do you have some form of identification?" asked the man.

"Yes, I have," said Father Andre, producing his Spanish and Jesuit I.D. Cards.

"I'm glad you could make it, father. We can't be too careful, you know," said the man, who then led him inside the house, and offered him a cup of coffee which he accepted.

"Sister Christiane has joined the Maquis Resistance, and is located in Chambery, about 570 kilometers southwest of Paris. I will drive you there, if you're ready to make the trip," said Moulet.

"That's wonderful news. Yes, I'm ready to leave when you are," replied Father Andre.

Upon arrival at the Lemagne farm in Chambery , Father Andre, still dressed in civilian clothes, carrying a small suitcase containing his Jesuit habit, exited the automobile, and escorted by Albert Moulet, walked towards the farm house where two men were sitting on the porch. One of them immediately went into the house to alert Charles Lemagne of Father Andre's arrival.

"Monique, would you go fetch Christiane. Father Andre is here," said Charles, who then went onto the porch to greet his guest.

"Welcome to our humble home, Father Andre," said Charles.

"Thank you for inviting me," replied Andre, looking for Christiane.

"If you're looking for Christiane, my wife went to fetch her. She's been busy refurbishing our medical room in anticipation of your arrival," said Charles, who then escorted Andre into the house.

"I see you're not wearing your Jesuit habit," said Charles.

"No, I don't think it wise to advertise my Jesuit connection under these circumstances," replied Andre.

"I completely agree with you, therefore if you don't mind, we'll refrain from addressing you as Father," said Charles. "In fact, we're going to provide you with false papers of identification, as we have with Christiane, in case we should be visited by the Gestapo, or while you're in transit somewhere."

"Yes, I agree. Unless you feel that it is perilous, I do wish you would retain my full name of Andre Duval on the false papers."

"No, it wouldn't be unsafe. We'll use your full name," replied Charles.

At that moment, Christiane emerged from the cellar and upon seeing Andre, walked up to him, and dismissing the presence of onlookers, embraced him.

"Oh! God. It's so good to find you alive and well," said Christiane.

"I'm sorry for the mix-up, but now that I've found you, all is well," replied Andre with a broad smile of contentment, now that he'd found his love.

"I've got so much to tell you, Andre. Charles and Monique have lodged us in their guest house on the other side of the barn," said Christiane.

"Why don't you take Andre to the guest house for him to settle in, then when you're done, come back here for a discussion about your role as doctor and nurse with the French Resistance," said Charles.

"That's an excellent idea," replied Christiane who immediately grabbed Andre's arm leading him out the front door carrying his suitcase.

The one-story guest house, made of wood with a weather worn look, had two bedrooms. Christiane had cleaned up the place, and given it a feminine, cheerful appearance with flowers and plants. It also had a stone fireplace.

"I hope you like it here, Andre. I tried to make it comfortable for us while we're here, which I hope won't be too long, because I have plans for us, which I will now explain to you," said Christiane, pointing to a sofa for him to sit with her.

"I hope your plans for us are permanent," replied Andre.

"First of all, Andre, after I read your letter, I surmised you intended to leave the Jesuit congregation in order to marry me, and hoped I would do the same because you love me. Is that correct?"

"Yes, it is, Christiane. I will do whatever is necessary to win your hand in marriage," replied Andre.

"Well, my dear Andre, hold on to your hat, because what I'm about to tell you will floor you. You are the father of my son Jacques, who should be eleven years old now," said Christiane observing his reaction to this unexpected news.

"You mean our *SS Ile de France* love affair resulted in your pregnancy?" said Andre with a look of incredulity.

"That's right, Andre. When I discovered I was pregnant, I first tried to hide it, but then I tried to contact you, but you had already been transferred to Spain, so I decided not to burden you with my problem and had the child which I named Jacques. However, because of my status as a member of the clergy, I was not permitted to keep him, so he was placed in the Bon Secours Orphanage, and adopted by persons unknown," said Christiane.

"My God, I can't believe it. I'm the father of a boy whose whereabouts are unknown," replied Andre, looking into Christiane's eyes for her to see and feel his guilt and empathy.

"Yes, but now that you're here, Andre, together, and with the assistance and resources of the Maquis Resistance, we'll find our son, and then the three of us can return to America," said Christiane.

"You said his name is Jacques, no last name?" asked Andre.

"That's right. But when he was adopted, he automatically was given the last name of his adopting parents. I was enroute to Paris to visit the Bon Secours Orphanage to find out who adopted Jacques, when the Gestapo and a French policeman arrested me on the train to Paris. Fortunately for me, two members of the Maquis were also on the train and rescued me from the Gestapo and brought me here," said Christiane.

"Wow! That's quite a story to tell Jacques when he grows up," said Andre.

"Yes, but I'm sure we'll have other interesting stories to tell him from our experience as members of the French Resistance. I believe you know why the Maquis went through so much trouble to bring you here. Being a physician makes you a most desirable guest," said Christiane.

"I guessed that much, but there's always a price for everything," replied Andre.

"I have been busy fixing things downstairs in their makeshift operating room, so that the conditions will be sanitary. Apparently Doctor Legrand from the Hopital Hotel Dieu, who has been coming here to do surgery, left a full complement of surgical instruments, so he wouldn't have to carry them each time he came here. According to Monsieur Lemagne, our being here will relieve Doctor LeGrand of that dangerous responsibility," said Christiane.

"Let's go downstairs and look at what we have to work with," said Andre.

CHAPTER XIII
Jacques' initiation into the French Resistance

Some one hundred and ten kilometers southwest of Paris, on a farm near Orleans, owned by Roland LeGrand, brother of Doctor Michel LeGrand, Jacques quickly immersed himself into the family chores with his newly acquired brother Etienne and sister Giselle. A couple of weeks later he received his counterfeit identification papers making him part of the LeGrand family. Soon, he learned that he would also participate in the clandestine operations of the Maquis Resistance with his brother and sister as couriers and they would do other tasks that required vigilance.

Jacques proved to be a quick study, and most useful to the Maquis, who found him to be intuitive, and resourceful in times of danger, which endeared him to Giselle, his adopted sister, to Etienne's amusement.

Roland decided it was time to train James in the use of handguns not only for his own protection, but also for that of his colleagues when the occasion demanded it. Etienne and Giselle were already trained in the use of small arms, and it was at their suggestion that Jacques was given the same training. The three of them called themselves 'Les Trois Mousquetaires' (The Three Musketeers) after Alexandre Dumas' historical adventure novel of 1844.

As a result of Jacques' exposure to adult members of the Maquis, he learned of the Nazis' concentration camp at

Drancy, where Jews were being incarcerated for subsequent transportation to death camps at Auschwitz, and other death camps in Poland. He then realized that any hope of ever seeing his adoption parents Aaron and Anna Cohen again were non-existent, which instilled a hatred for the Nazis that his religious upbringing could not subdue.

It was on one of those Maquis missions that required the three musketeers go into the village of Creteil, a commune in the southeastern suburbs of Paris, where they were tasked with the taking of photographs of anyone dressed in civilian clothes entering and exiting the three-story house occupied by the Gestapo. The building faced a park with trees, shrubs, and an abandoned wooden house at its center, where Jacques and Giselle, were to station themselves, and take pictures with a telephoto-lens camera through one of its broken windows while Etienne perused the rear of the Gestapo house to find a safe place to conduct his surveillance. The Maquis leaders felt that Jacques and Giselle's presence in the park would not be conspicuous due to their young age. Nevertheless, Roland LeGrand gave Jacques a Walther PP double-action, semi-automatic blowback pistol, with an 8-round detachable magazine with 7.65mm ammunition, acquired from a dead SS officer. The pistol was small enough to be concealed with its holster on the inside of his trousers held by his belt at the hip. Roland felt this precaution necessary in view of the danger Jacques and Giselle would be exposed to, and the absolute requirement never to be captured which was instilled in them when they were briefed prior to their mission.

More than an hour transpired with several photos taken of visitors to the Gestapo house, while Colonel Jurgen Gottlieb, SS Inspector from Berlin, dressed impeccably in his SS uniform, wearing the traditional Luger pistol, took his daily walk through the park. As he approached the apparently abandoned one-story house, he heard voices from inside, and decided to quietly investigate its source. Jacques was facing the open window with Giselle standing beside him when they suddenly became aware that someone was standing behind them.

"What are you doing here?" asked Colonel Gottlieb in French with a pronounced German accent.

"Nothing, just talking to my girlfriend," replied Jacques, trying to hide his camera behind him.

"What are you hiding behind you?" asked the Colonel now pointing his pistol at them.

Reluctantly, Jacques brought the camera within view. "I was just taking pictures of the birds, sir," replied Jacques.

"Don't lie to me. Let me see the camera," said the Colonel.

"This is an expensive camera, with telephoto lens," said Colonel Gottlieb, now looking through the window, which provided a clear view of the entrance to the Gestapo house.

"You are both under arrest for espionage," said the Colonel, motioning with his pistol for them to exit the house.

At this point, Jacques realized that once inside the Gestapo building, they would undoubtedly be tortured. He couldn't stand the thought of them torturing Giselle, and decided he must act now or never. Colonel Gottlieb made the mistake of underestimating the dangerousness of these youngsters by not frisking them for weapons. In a sudden swift move, Jacques turned, and in a quick draw of his already chamber loaded Walther, fired his pistol point blank into the chest of Colonel Gottlieb, who fell dead at his feet.

"C'mon Giselle, let's get out of here fast," said Jacques, running out of the house and park in the opposite direction of the Gestapo house, where they merged with the population, figuring Etienne would somehow find his way back to the farm.

"My God, Jacques, I never thought we'd have to shoot anyone," said Giselle, a bit shaken from the incident.

"I had no choice, Giselle. There's no way I would let those Nazis' take you into their house of horror," said Jacques.

"I appreciate that, Jacques. I know you did what you had to do. I'm glad you were able to save the camera. I think it will identify some of the collaborators the Maquis has been trying to find," said Giselle.

"Yeah! That's another reason I couldn't let them take us inside that Gestapo house," replied Jacques who had suddenly grown into a premature adult.

Upon arrival at the farm, Jacques and Giselle were happy to see Etienne had made it safely back, and upon hearing Jacques had killed a Gestapo agent, he developed a heightened respect for this young man, two-years his junior.

After the camera negatives were developed, Roland LeGrand had a meeting with three of his Maquis associates.

"According to the description of the German officer Jacques shot, it appears he was a field grade officer of the Gestapo. There's going to be serious reprisals resulting from this by the

Nazis. We'd better have Jacques, Giselle and Etienne stay close to the farm for the next few weeks," said Roland LeGrand.

"I think it would be wise to destroy that Walther pistol. If Jacques or anyone of us were found with that pistol, it could be matched through ballistics to the bullet that killed that SS Colonel," said Paul Benoit, a trusted confederate.

"I agree. Do you realize who was in those photos taken by Jacques?" said Francois Lucier, one of the leaders in the Maquis.

"Yes, Daniel Weber, the bank manager at the Banque de France. The photos show him entering and leaving the Gestapo house with a briefcase. The question is, what was in the briefcase," asked Roland rhetorically.

"I'll bet he's been providing the Gestapo with the names of anyone withdrawing large sums of money, or closing their bank account, which would indicate their plan to secretly leave France," said Pierre Lacotte, a Maquis associate.

"How do you think the Nazis got the names and bank accounts of affluent Jews in Paris, which they forfeited," said Lucier.

"I think we should pick up Monsieur Weber and bring him to our house at 16 Rue Saint Denis for interrogation," said Roland LeGrand.

"I totally agree, and I think that if our suspicions are correct, he should be disposed of in the usual fashion, never to be found," said Lacotte.

"Yes, but we also have another pressing matter," said Roland LeGrand. "Claudette Beaufort. As we are the only ones privy to her affiliation with the Maquis, Claudette has been regularly escorted by Major Hans Hoffman, Deputy to Colonel Knochenbach, SS Occupation Commander of Paris, and in that capacity, she has provided us with invaluable information. She sent a brief message to one of our associates last night, warning us that the Gestapo has been ordered to put a surveillance on all doctors, and surgeons in particular, who may lead them to the hideout of the French Resistance they service. Therefore, we must alert Doctors we've used in the past to refrain from contacting us in any manner, and stay away from the farm until further notice. I will see to it that my brother Michel is notified and told we now have a physician and a nurse on site," said Roland LeGrand.

"I think Claudette is playing with fire, dating that Nazi Major. I hate to think what they'll do to her if they ever find out she's a member of the Maquis," said Lucier.

"She's a big girl. She knows the dangers, and can quit anytime she wants. After the war, I will make sure her courage and patriotism are recognized and rewarded," said Roland LeGrand.

"Yeah! If she survives," replied Lucier, who had amorous aspirations for her.

"How is Jacques dealing with the fact he shot a man to death?" asked Pierre Lacotte.

"My wife Madeleine has been talking to him, and she's convinced that Jacques has not been traumatized by it, mostly because he feels justified by the deadly threat the Gestapo officer posed to Giselle and the fact that his adopted parents were victims of the Nazis," said Roland LeGrand.

"You would never think that an eleven-year old boy who can play the piano with the sensitivity of a master pianist could shoot a field-grade Gestapo officer in cold blood," said Lacotte.

"I think 'cold blood' is inappropriate, Pierre. He simply had to act quickly and deliberately in order to save Giselle and himself, as well as the film, that's all," replied Roland LeGrand.

"I think Jacques is going to grow up as a strong leader in whatever field of endeavor he chooses," said Lucier.

At that moment, the meeting was interrupted by another member of the Maquis with the published news that Colonel Jurgen Gottlieb, SS Inspector from Headquarters in Berlin had been assassinated in the children's park across from Gestapo Headquarters in the Village of Creteil.

"Good God, there's going to be hell to pay for this," said Lacotte. "I think we ought to lay low for a while."

"On the contrary, we shall strike at a location where they store their munitions. That will divert their attention to more important matters than the death of a single officer, even if he is a Colonel from Berlin," said Roland LeGrand. "However, I think Jacques must not be exposed to any further potential violence that would harden his feelings and respect for human life, in view of his tender age. So, I'm going to keep him on the farm for the time being."

"That's an excellent idea, he's just a boy," said Lucier.

However, the following week, a French police informant notified the Maquis that the Gestapo received information from a park maintenance man that on the day the SS Colonel was killed, he saw a young boy and girl run out of the house where the SS Colonel was found dead. At the time, the maintenance man merely thought the two teenagers were just being playful, but upon reading about the SS Colonel's death, realized the importance of what he saw and reported it to the Gestapo. An all-out alert for the apprehension of the two teenagers by the Gestapo with a reward was posted throughout Paris and its environs.

Sitting at the dinner table in their farm house, Roland LeGrand and his wife Madeleine waited until the children had finished eating their dinner and gone outside, before discussing the immediate future of Jacques and Giselle.

"We've got to get Jacques and Giselle far away from this farm and Paris, until the search for them by the Gestapo is over," said Madeleine.

"Yes, I agree. I've been thinking about that, and I've come to the conclusion that the only safe place to send them would be to my cousin Fernand Bouchard and his wife Laurette in Haute-Vienne, Limousin," said Roland.

"That's quite a distance to travel, and they'd be so far away," replied Madeleine, concerned about Giselle, her only daughter.

"It's only about 250 kilometers from here, and they'll be with family, near wonderful Lake Vassiviere, where they can fish and canoe to their heart's content. It will be a delightful experience for them," replied Roland.

"I suppose you're right, Roland, but who will drive them there?" asked Madeleine.

"As a cautionary measure, I will have two of our Maquisards drive them there, just in case they should run into the Gestapo, or some policeman anxious to collect the reward," said Roland.

"Yes, that's a good idea. When do you want them to leave?"

"Tomorrow morning. The sooner the better," replied Roland.

"Let's call the kids in and explain the reason for sending them to live with your cousin in Limousin," said Madeleine.

The following morning, after a sumptuous breakfast, Jacques and Giselle, having packed two small suitcases of clothes, excitedly boarded the back seat of the four-door black sedan, driven by Jean-Claude Lavigne with his associate Alain Lucroy, sitting in the front passenger seat. Both men were armed with pistols and extra ammunition, but Lucroy also had a British Sten gun with 9mm ammunition from a 32-round box magazine. Roland had chosen these two veteran Maquisards at the insistence of his wife Madeleine, who cherished these two children, having embraced Jacques as one of her own sons. Roland deliberated, but then decided in favor of giving Jacques his cherished Beretta M-1935 single-action, semi-automatic blowback pistol, with an 8-round detachable magazine of .32 ACP ammunition, plus an additional 24 rounds if needed. Roland was confident about Jacques' understanding of the responsibility that went with the acceptance of this pistol, in spite of his young age.

During the trip, Jacques wore the Beretta concealed under his waistband with the top of its handle covered by his shirt and jacket, without the knowledge of Giselle and the two Maquisards. Giselle, sitting next to Jacques, felt a sense of belonging as if she had known him since early childhood. Saving her life enhanced her feelings for him beyond the contrived sibling relationship for his protection from the Gestapo. She fantasized that someday she would marry him, and there was plenty of time for her to win his heart.

More than an hour had passed, and they were now traveling on a road that had a deep escarpment to its right, when suddenly they heard a loud noise coming from the rear of their sedan, and the clatter of riding on a blown tire.

"Merde!" exclaimed Jean-Claude Lavigne, the driver, bringing the sedan to a stop alongside the road, and exiting the vehicle to assess the damage with Alain Lucroy following him.

"Well, it's just a flat tire," said Lucroy.

"I hope it's the only flat tire we get, because we only have one spare," replied Lavigne, who then opened the trunk, and after removing the luggage, pulled out the spare tire and the lug wrench.

"You might as well get out and stretch your legs," said Lucroy to Jacques and Giselle.

Jacques and Giselle walked around the sedan and stood in back of it to watch Lavigne and Lucroy jack up the rear of the vehicle to remove the damaged tire, when they heard a four-door black sedan approaching, then slow down as it reached them. Inside the vehicle on the passenger side was SS Major Hermann Engels, wearing a black leather overcoat; a uniformed French gendarme named Marc Barrriere was driving.

"I find it strange that a young boy and girl should be driven by two men, obviously not a family excursion," said Major Engels.

"I think you have a point, sir, and in view of the notice we received to be on the lookout for a young boy and girl suspected in the death of Colonel Jurgen Gottlieb, I think we should check their papers and destination," replied Barriere.

"If these teenagers are the ones we're looking for, then we can assume those two men are from the French Resistance and armed. So be alert," said Major Engels, as they exited their sedan and started walking towards the impaired automobile, and the two men attending it.

"Jean-Claude, we've got company," said Alain turning towards the two advancing men.

Jean-Claude, holding the log wrench, turned, and in the process, inadvertently revealed the handle of his pistol sticking out of his waistband, causing Major Engels and Barriere to draw their pistols.

"Get your hands up and turn around," yelled Engels, pointing his pistol at them. "Alright, now place your hands on top of the car. Barriere, frisk them and remove their weapons."

While the German officer and French Gendarme were busy arresting the two maquisards, Jacques and Giselle, standing at the rear of the vehicle, were temporarily ignored. Jacques quickly realized immediate action was required, or else they would all end up in a German concentration camp. There was no time to waste. Jacques momentarily turned his back to the action, pulled out his Beretta, loaded a round into the chamber cocking the hammer, then turned around and aimed his pistol at the Major with the gendarme standing next to him.

"Don't move and drop your weapons," said Jacques.

"You must be insane pointing this toy gun at me, boy," said the Major, turning towards Jacques with gun in hand.

Jacques immediately fired two bullets into the chest of the Major, and another two rounds into the chest of the gendarme, who had hesitated one second too long.

Both men fell to the ground mortally wounded, to the relief of Jean-Claude and Alain, staring at the two bodies visibly dead. Turning their attention to Jacques, they watched him calmly replace his pistol inside its holster in his waistband, then turn to Giselle, "it's alright now, you're safe."

"Oh! Jacques, I'm so glad you were armed. Again, thank you for saving my life," said Giselle.

Jean-Claude and Alain walked up to Jacques with renewed respect for this young man whom they no longer looked upon as a boy.

"That was quick thinking and shooting, Jacques. You sure saved the day. We're now going to have to get rid of the bodies," said Jean-Claude.

"Let's put the two bodies inside their car, and drive the car over the escarpment," said Alain.

"Good idea," replied Jean-Claude.

Having placed both bodies inside the sedan, they then turned on the engine, drove the car to the edge of the escarpment, and with the engine still running, put the car in forward gear, propelling the car over the cliff onto the rocks below into an explosion incinerating its contents.

"Well, that takes care of that. Let's get out of here," said Jean-Claude.

"I think we'd better take the side roads for the next hour, because this main road may soon be the focus of a search for us," said Alain.

As they sat in the back seat, Jacques pulled out his Beretta pistol and removed its cartridge. He then inserted four new rounds in the magazine, which he replaced in his Beretta, again concealing it inside his waistband, while Giselle watched silently, hoping he would not have to use it again.

The remaining journey went without any eventful incident. They arrived at the large three-story house of Fernand and Laurette Bouchard, on a hill overlooking Lake Vassivierre, in Haute-Vienne, Limousin.

Fernand was an engineer by trade, now retired and enjoying a life of leisure with his wife Laurette, a retired music teacher and accomplished pianist. Their son Jean, a captain in the French Army, lost his life when the Wehrmacht forces came through the Ardennes forest and surprised the French Army with its blitzkrieg offensive. Their daughter, Michelle, engaged to Rene Balland, a doctor and general practitioner, still resided with her parents in this beautiful location, where memories of her childhood and teenage years were now unfortunately dampened by the Nazi occupation of her country. Limousin's geographic location was in the unoccupied free zone governed by Vichy, which operated under the dictatorship of the

Wehrmacht. However, they were not far from Switzerland and Spain, both neutral countries, with several avenues of escape.

Jacques and Giselle were received by Fernand and Laurette with joyful delight and an invitation for Jean-Claude and Alain to stay the night and return to the LeGrand farm up north the following day which they readily accepted, especially when a grand family dinner had been planned to celebrate the children's arrival.

After being shown their individual bedrooms on the second floor of the spacious house, Jacques and Giselle were given a tour of the rest of the house, including the large living room which had a grand piano as its centerpiece. Jacques was immediately attracted to it, especially since he had not had occasion to practice his gifted musical talent, but made no attempt to test its sound, leaving it to another time when alone.

The sumptuous dinner, cooked by Laurette with help from Michelle, lived up to the expectations of French cuisine. It was attended by the hosts, Fernand and Laurette Bouchard, her daughter Michelle and her fiancé Rene Balland, their very close friend Albert Auclair and his wife Josette, Jean-Claude Lavigny and Alain Lucroy, and lastly but not least, their guests of honor, Jacques and Giselle LeGrand.

Several days passed, allowing Jacques and Giselle to explore their surroundings, including the small beach at the bottom of the hill on the shore of Lake Vassiviere. Laurette provided Giselle and Jacques with bathing suits, and the use of a row boat which they enjoyed daily, even though the water was cold that time of year.

Then one evening, when Fernand and Laurette were sitting on the outside porch with Giselle telling them about her life with her parents at the farm, they heard the sound of their piano playing the melody 'Tristesse' (Sadness) composed by Frederic Chopin.

"That's Chopin's 'Tristesse' one of his Etudes," said Laurette, recognizing the famous melody from her years as a music teacher and pianist. "Who's that playing?" she asked.

"That must be Jacques. I heard him once playing 'Clair de Lune' by Claude Debussy at the farm on our old piano," said Giselle.

"Let's not disturb him while he's playing. I love this melody, and he plays it so well," said Laurette.

When the melody ended, Laurette and Giselle got up and went into the house and living room, where they found Jacques looking through some of the music sheets that lay on the side of the piano.

"Where did you learn to play the piano, young man?" asked Laurette.

"My mother Anna was a piano teacher, and she taught me everything I know," said Jacques.

"Well, I'm a retired piano teacher, and I must tell you that she did an excellent job with you. You played Chopin's 'Tristesse' better than any pupil I ever had, including professionals I've known and heard. Could you play me another one of your favorite melodies?" asked Laurette, who was now joined by her husband Fernand, whose curiosity got the better of him.

"Perhaps you'd like to hear something more powerful, such as Sergey Rachmaninov's piano concerto number 2 in C minor?" asked Jacques.

"That's a very difficult piece of music, Jacques. Perhaps you'd like to play something less demanding?" asked Laurette.

"Rachmaninov's concerto is one of my favorites," replied Jacques with a smile, as he then started playing it.

The music grew more powerful as it progressed through its stages. Jacques seemed possessed by the melody, as if he was born to play it. Fernand was captivated by the force of the music while Laurette sat transfixed with tears in her eyes as she listened to this superb rendition of Rachmaninov's phenomenal concerto by this young boy who had just turned twelve. Giselle, sitting in a padded chair, watched Jacques with wonderment at his musical talent, questioning whether she could measure up to him as he grew older and more proficient with great demand for his talent. She realized she was in love with him, and it hurt because she feared losing him to someone who had more to offer.

Jacques finally ended the piano concerto, and sat motionless for a minute, as if coming out of a trance, then turned towards his small audience and smiled.

"Jacques, that was marvelous, simply marvelous, the way you played that concerto," said Laurette, enthusiastically.

"My boy, you have definitely found your niche as a pianist," said Fernand.

Jacques looked at Giselle who had remained silent.

"I hope you liked it, Giselle, it's probably Rachmoninov's favorite composition, and my favorite too," said Jacques.

"Yes, I loved the way you played it, Jacques. I really did," replied Giselle apologetically.

"Well, next time I'll play Claude Debussy's 'Reverie' for you. It has a calming influence on its listeners," replied Jacques, who then left the piano to join them.

The following day, Jacques and Giselle went down to the Vassiviere beach where the Bouchard's row boat was beached.

"Before we go boating, let me ask you: Do you know how to swim?" asked Jacques.

"Yes, but not very well. There's not much opportunity where I live on the farm," replied Giselle.

"That's alright, I learned at the swimming pool in school," said Jacques.

"Where was that, in Paris?" asked Giselle.

"Yes, that's right," replied Jacques.

Giselle sat in the row boat facing Jacques, manning the oars. She thought he was bigger than his age, more like a fifteen year old, probably due to the largesse of his parents, most likely his father whom he never knew. The fact she was a year older than Jacques, in her mind, made his advanced maturity most acceptable. She wondered where he acquired his prodigious musical talent. His adopted mother, a music teacher, may have guided him, but he had to have the talent to begin with, in order to develop into such an extraordinary pianist at such a young age. He seemed to be in touch with the composers when he played their melodies, as if he had temporarily traversed into another world. She looked at him, rowing slowly and quietly, seemingly in peace with the calmness of the lake with the bright sun warming the air on that unusually cool day.

"Tell me, Jacques, where do you get your inspiration when you play Chopin's 'Tristesse' or Rachmaninov's piano concerto?" asked Giselle.

"I guess it's the music itself that is so profoundly beautiful. It takes over my mind and heart to a height beyond this world," replied Jacques.

"You mean it takes you into another world," said Giselle.

"I mean, it's as if the composer's spirit somehow took over my mind and body to play his music, and I'm merely an instrument at his disposal," replied Jacques.

"I envy you, Jacques, because that talent enables you to escape the reality of this hateful world wherever a piano is available," said Giselle.

"Perhaps, but it's only a temporary relief," replied Jacques.

"I think the United States and Russia, now in the war on our side, will make a big difference, and Germany and Italy will be defeated sooner than you think," said Giselle.

"I certainly hope you're right, Giselle, 'cause I can't see how we can endure much more of this Nazi occupation without a revolution," replied Jacques.

"When is the last time you went to church?" asked Giselle.

"Why do you ask?" said Jacques

"Because I believe that prayer is the only thing that will save us from this Nazi tyranny," replied Giselle.

"Well, I was raised as a Jew, and the Nazis made sure there aren't any active synagogues in France, at least none that I know of?" replied Jacques.

"But my father told me you're not a Jew, only your adopted parents were, so why don't you come to church with me next Sunday?" said Giselle.

"Sure, why not. I was made to understand that we all pray to the same God," replied Jacques.

Giselle then explained the basic tenets of the Catholic Church, and what to expect during Mass on Sunday.

Sitting on the back porch of the Bouchard residence, Jacques was using a pair of binoculars to survey the area when he suddenly caught the image of a uniformed SS Captain standing on the terrace of the house east of the Bouchard residence. The Captain had emerged from the house to better appreciate the view of the beach, and was followed by a blond haired woman dressed in shorts and a polo shirt. She placed her arm over his shoulder in an intimate gesture, obviously an invited guest, not an intruder.

At that moment, Michelle entered the patio with Giselle, and asked Jacques if he'd found anything interesting.

"Yes, I have. Are you aware that your next door neighbor is having an SS Captain in uniform as her guest?" asked Jacques.

"Yes, we know. They're the Muller's. Their daughter, Ingrid, has been living with an SS Captain, Johan Scholl, in Limoges, and they visit her parents occasionally. Ingrid's father, Franz Wagner, is German, and his wife Adele is French, so guess who dominates that relationship. My father told me to avoid them, 'cause he doesn't trust them," said Michelle.

"Under those circumstances, I can understand why," replied Jacques.

"What circumstances?" asked Michelle.

"C'mon Michelle. I'm not blind. Your father is one of the leaders of the French Resistance. But don't worry, your secret is safe with me," replied Jacques with a laugh.

"You don't miss much, do you," said Michelle.

"You have to be alert, with all the treachery that's going on with the Nazis, and their French collaborators ready to betray you," replied Jacques.

"Yes, I guess you're right, Jacques, and I'm sure my parents don't doubt your loyalty. You've proven that at least three times," said Michelle, referring to the three men he shot to death.

"How about going fishing tomorrow morning, Giselle?" asked Jacques, turning his attention to Giselle.

"OK! We can use lures instead of live bait. It's easier and less messy," said Giselle, not particularly fond of handling worms.

"Yeah! That's alright with me. By the way, Michelle, what's in that shed at the bottom of the hill against the beach?" asked Jacques.

"Oh! Just a speed boat, but my father seldom uses it. Probably needs repair," said Michelle.

"You think your father would let me use that motorcycle he has in the garage. It sounds like fun," said Jacques.

"Do you know how to drive one," asked Michelle.

"I've never driven one, but I know how to ride a bicycle, so it shouldn't be difficult to learn. Then Giselle and I can go riding together because it's a two-seater," said Jacques.

"Why don't you ask my father. He likes you, so I'm sure he'll let you ride it, as long as you don't go too far. Remember, you're still in Nazi controlled country, and they're still looking for you and Giselle," said Michelle.

"Yeah! I know. I'll ask him after dinner this evening," said Jacques.

That evening, Fernand Bouchard volunteered to teach Jacques to drive the motorcycle and also do the maintenance on it. He realized there may come a time when the motorcycle may be the only means for Jacques and Giselle to escape the clutches of the Gestapo. Within a week, Jacques was able to drive the motorcycle with enough confidence to have Giselle ride on the seat behind him, to the satisfaction of Fernand, a strict master. However, Jacques was restricted to the side roads within the Limousin area. Nevertheless, he always carried concealed his Beretta .32 ACP pistol whenever he ventured off the farm.

The year was 1942, when for the first time in his life; Jacques celebrated Christmas by attending midnight mass with Giselle and the Bouchard family at the Cathedrale Saint-Etienne de Limoges. The music and the practiced children's choir impressed Jacques immensely. The church was packed to the limit with worshipers, which lent an air of peace and hope, at a time when France was occupied by an army of atheistic murderers of Jews and other ethnic groups deemed unfit for existence under the Nazi regime.

Spring had arrived with sunshine, and blooming flowers, in the garden of the Bouchard family house on the hillside overlooking Lake Vassiviere. It was on one of those full moon evenings that Fernand Bouchard and Alain Auclair, one of his most trusted confederates, went down to the recessed wooden shed, off the beach on the Lake below, and unlocked the swing doors to the shed, revealing a 21-foot speed boat equipped with ship-to-shore radio, sitting on a two-wheel trailer.

"What time are we supposed to rendez-vous with the aircraft?" asked Auclair.

"2300 hours at these coordinates," said Bouchard, showing him the map.

"It gives us a full hour, and it's only about three kilometers from here, so we've got time," said Auclair.

"Yes, but I'd rather get there early than be late because the pilot is not going to wait around if he doesn't get a response from us that we're ready to receive his package," replied Bouchard.

"You mean one of DeGaulle's Free French Marins Commandos," said Auclair.

"Yes, and he comes with special qualifications that will be most helpful to us," said Bouchard without further explanation.

The two men pulled the trailer with boat out of the shed and turned it around so the trailer's rear wheels would hit the water first. Once the trailer was sufficiently submerged to float the boat, Bouchard slid the boat off the trailer, took the front line from the bow, and sank the attached spike in the sand to keep the boat from floating away. He then went back and locked the doors to the shed, then wiped the tire tracks in the hard sand leading to the water. Satisfied he had erased evidence of the boat launching, Bouchard went to the boat, throwing the spike and line into the bow. He then turned the boat around for the bow to face the open lake.

"OK! Albert, get in the boat. I'm going to give the boat a push forward, and then as soon as I get in, start the engine," said Bouchard.

Albert Auclair, who had driven the speedboat several times before, pushed the starter button, and the inboard engine immediately went into action, moving them forward, out into the open lake, within view of their curious neighbor Franz Wagner, whose daughter was intimately involved with SS Captain Johan Scholl.

Upon arrival at the specified coordinates on the lake, Bouchard had Auclair slow the engine to a crawl to keep it within those coordinates, while waiting for the arrival of the British aircraft transporting their French commando.

At 2250 hours, they heard the sound of the aircraft approaching, then the radio call from the aircraft commander.

"Calling JBL, this is BKW,"

"This is JBL, we're ready for package,"

"Package will be lit upon impact. Confirm receipt,"

"Will do, Roger," replied Bouchard.

The French Commando jumped from the aircraft with a black parachute that made him almost invisible until he hit the lake water and turned on a blue flashing light for them to find him which they did after more than ten minutes. While Bouchard helped the commando board the boat, Auclair attached a small iron wheel to the parachute line which sunk it, leaving no evidence of his arrival.

"I'm Fernand Bouchard, and this is my colleague Albert Auclair of the French Resistance. Welcome to France."

"I'm commander Jean-Guy Boivin, Premier Bataillon de Fusiliers-Marins Commandos at your service."

Unknown to Bouchard and Auclair, their boat launch was immediately reported to the Gestapo by Franz Wagner who had been spying on them for some time.

Jacques and Giselle had decided to walk on the beach on such a lovely evening, but as they started to descend the hill, they noticed a group of armed SS officers accompanied by Franz Wagner, on the beach in front of the shed, talking.

Jacques and Giselle ducked behind some bushes and watched one of the SS officers giving orders to his men to hide behind the shed and bushes, then saying something to Wagner who saluted the officer and then returned to his house.

"Let's get back to the house and warn Missus Bouchard right away," said Jacques.

Inside the Bouchard house, Giselle excitedly told Laurette Bouchard what they had witnessed, and Jacques confirmed the Gestapo was lying in wait for the return of her husband and Albert Auclair.

"It is most important that I call Fernand right away," said Laurette, now walking into the home office of her husband, where she moved a large bookshelf on hinges revealing a ship-to-shore radio and a Paraset spy shortwave radio. In view of this revelation, she had to suspect her telephone and even her radio communications may have been compromised by the Gestapo, hence she would have to use code to warn her husband of the impending danger.

"This is songbird calling porpoise," said Laurette repeatedly until she finally received a response from her husband.

"This is porpoise, the weather is fine. Caught one fish." replied Bouchard.

"We have company from neighbor, one fish won't be enough. Advise you catch at least a dozen more for our friendly guests," said Laurette.

"Got the message. Fishing not good this evening. Make excuse with guests, and join me at Pointe B," replied Bouchard, who understood he was not to return to the beach and his house that night, and for Resistance members to be alerted, and have someone meet him at Pointe B, a code for Plage de Nergout on the coast of Lake Vassiviere.

"Roger that. See you at Pointe B," replied Laurette.

Now turning her attention to Jacques and Giselle, she drew open a desk drawer and pulled out a Ruby self-loading pistol of World War One vintage, with a .32 ACP cartridge and 9-shot capacity, unusual for that period.

"Here Giselle, you just may be needing that where you're going," said Laurette, handing her the pistol. "I know you're familiar with guns."

"Where am I going," asked Giselle, surprised by Laurette's statement.

"You and Jacques must leave here at once, because the Gestapo may raid this house at any moment. That radio message I sent to Fernand was to warn him that he must not return with the Free French Commando he picked up after he parachuted on the lake. Instead he's going to take the Commando to Plage de Nergout, where he will be met by a team of French Resistance fighters who'll take him to a safe place, where he'll be able to complete his mission. That's where you and Giselle come in. I want you to take this very important letter which I'm about to write to Ernest Latreille. He lives in the village of Oradour-sur-Glane with his wife Danielle and their two sons Roger and Jean-Pierre," said Laurette.

"Isn't that village near here?" asked Giselle.

"Yes, I'm going to give you a map of the village, and I'm going to mark the exact location of the Latreille residence, which is a two-story brick-and-stone house on the outskirts of the village. You're to give Ernest this letter and also explain to him what I've told you, and he's to immediately go to the Plage-de-Nergout to pick up my husband, Albert Auclair, and the French Commando and bring them back to his house. But unfortunately, that's just the beginning of your trip. Here's a map of France, with all of the back roads which you must take to avoid the main thoroughfares used by the Nazis and French police," said Laurette, with a pause.

"Yes, you must return home, Giselle, to the LeGrand farm with Jacques because it's no longer safe for you to remain here. I will miss you both terribly, and I had hoped that you, Jacques, would remain here to be my pupil long after the war was over because I believe your musical talent will take you the Palais Garnier Opera House in Paris. Maybe someday we'll meet again. I hope so. In the meantime, I wish you both safe passage to your destination," said Laurette, handing Jacques French paper currency.

"That's for any unexpected expenses you might incur on your way to the LeGrand Farm," said Laurette.

"Thank you, but it shouldn't take us more than a few hours to get to the farm," replied Jacques.

"You never know what you're going to run into. Better safe than sorry," replied Laurette.

"Giselle, my dear. Look after Jacques. He needs you more than he realizes," said Laurette, knowing how Giselle adored him.

Laurette quickly wrote the letter to Ernest Latreille, and addressed the envelope which she did not seal, and gave it to Jacques.

"I presume your motorcycle is full of gas, and you've got your identification papers in case you're stopped," said Laurette.

"Yes, the motorcycle has a full tank of gas, and I'm armed with my papers, and ready to go, and so is Giselle, but where are you going to go?" asked Jacques.

"First, I'm going to Limousin to warn Michelle, who's at Rene Balland's apartment; then I'll join my husband at the Latreilles in Oradour-sur-Glane," replied Laurette.

Laurette hugged the two of them. "Go quickly, and I'm sure we'll meet again, God Bless you," said Laurette, holding back tears.

Standing at the open back door to her house, Laurette with tears in her eyes, watched Giselle mount the back seat of the motorcycle, and wrap her arms around Jacques' waist, as he throttled the motor, then took off into the darkness of the night.

Upon arrival at the village of Oradour-sur-Glane, Jacques found the village quiet, and its streets empty, due to the late hour. He followed the map's directions he'd memorized, and soon found the brick-and-stone house, which had a dim light overlooking its main entrance. He'd been told that an unused old tractor would be parked on the side of the house, as a landmark. Approaching the house, he saw the tractor, and stopped the engine of his motorcycle whose noise had awakened the occupants of the house.

Jacques and Giselle got off the motorcycle, and as they approached the entrance door, it was suddenly opened by a stocky middle-aged man facing them with a pistol in his hand hidden behind him.

"What do you want?" asked the man.

"We're looking for Monsieur Ernest Latreille," replied Jacques.

"And who might you be?" asked the man.

"My name is Jacques LeGrand, and this is my sister Giselle. I have this letter for you from Madame Laurette Bouchard," replied Jacques, handing him the envelope with letter.

The man opened the letter, read it, and then looked at these two teenagers with a smile.

"I'm Ernest Latreille. Come on in."

Inside the house, a light was turned on by his wife Danielle, curious about their visitors.

"Apparently, Fernand Bouchard is in trouble with the Gestapo. I've got to rendez-vous with him at the Place de Nergout, and bring him back here with Albert Auclair, and a Free French commando," said Ernest to his wife.

"Do you have anything to add to this letter?" asked Ernest to Jacques.

"Well, yes. Giselle and I saw several Gestapo officers on the beach where Monsieur Bouchard keeps his boat in a shed.

They were armed and talking to their neighbor who is German. Then the Gestapo officers hid behind the shed and in the bushes. I guess they were waiting for Monsieur Bouchard's return with the Free French Commando that had parachuted onto the lake. But Madame Bouchard radioed Monsieur Bouchard, and warned him in code not to return to the house, but to go to Pointe B, which is the Plage de Nergout. Madame Bouchard wants you or someone in the Maquis to meet Monsieur Bouchard at the Plage de Nergout, and bring him and his companions back to your house for safekeeping," said Jacques.

"We've been expecting the arrival of the Free French Commando. That's good. Thank you, Jacques, for that important information," said Ernest Latreille, who then turned to his wife.

"Cherie, you'd better wake up Roger. He'll have to come with me to the Plage de Nergout," said Ernest Latreille.

"You two must be tired. Let me find you a room for you to sleep," said Danielle Latreille.

"I'm going to move your motorcycle to the back of the house in our shed," said Ernest Latreille, "so when you wake up later, you won't think someone stole it."

It was late morning, when Jacques and Giselle got up from separate beds in the same room and were greeted by Danielle who showed them the bathroom, then invited them to have breakfast in the dining room with her younger son Jean-Pierre.

"Did you have trouble finding our house?" asked Jean-Pierre, who had just turned thirteen.

"No, I was given a map of the village and the location of your house by Madame Bouchard," said Jacques.

"This is a small village with no more than about 650 people where everyone knows everybody," said Jean-Pierre. "That gives us assurance we don't have any German spies or collaborators among us."

"That must be very reassuring," said Giselle.

"The fact that Madame Bouchard sent you here to deliver that important message is also very reassuring of your loyalty to France," said Jean-Pierre, obviously well indoctrinated by his parents, members of the Maquisard.

"So you're not going back to the Bouchard residence," said Danielle Latreille.

"No, it would not be safe. We're returning to our home at the LeGrand farm near Orleans," replied Jacques who considered himself a member of the family, since he was given the LeGrand surname.

"I hope you've been told to stay on the country roads, and avoid the main roads," said Danielle.

"Yes, Madame Bouchard gave us instructions," replied Jacques.

"Very well, then. I wish you both a safe trip home. Give my love to Roland and Madeleine for me," said Danielle.

"We will. Thank you for this delicious breakfast," said Giselle.

It took Jacques several hours to reach the LeGrand farm house, stopping once at a café and gas station, without incident. Upon arrival, they were greeted by Madeleine LeGrand, whose husband was off the farm on a meeting with Maquisard confederates.

Madeleine hugged and kissed her daughter Giselle and shook Jacques' hand warmly, then asked for the reason behind their early visit.

"There's lots to tell you, Maman. Let's go inside, I could use a cup of tea, and we'll bring you up to date," said Giselle.

Sitting around the kitchen table, Jacques and Giselle took turns recounting the events that led to their early return to the LeGrand farm.

"Good heavens, wait 'till Roland hears about this," said Madeleine.

"When is Monsieur LeGrand returning," asked Jacques.

"Sometime this evening. My son Etienne is with him," replied Madeleine. "So the three of us will have dinner in a little while, and then you can tell Roland what you told me when he comes in."

That evening, Roland and Etienne sat in the living room with Madeleine listening to Jacques and Giselle relating all of the events preceding their return to the LeGrand farm, with few interruptions.

"You two have become important members of the Maquisard in spite of your young age. I want you to know, Jacques, that you have earned your place as a member of this family," said Roland.

"Thank you Monsieur LeGrand," replied Jacques humbly.

"Regarding what happened at the Bouchard residence, I think that Fernand and Laurette are in serious danger as long as their German neighbor is loose, and for that matter, their daughter's SS Captain. But that's not something for you to concern yourself with. That a job for the Maquis," said Roland.

A couple of weeks passed without any Gestapo movement towards the Bouchard family and residence.

However, that did not deter the Maquis centrally located in the village of Oradour-sur-Glane near Limousin from taking action they believed was necessary to eliminate the threat posed by Franz Wagner and their frequent visitor SS Captain Johan Scholl. Both men were quietly kidnapped, and they disappeared after revealing invaluable information regarding the workings of the Gestapo in that area of France. Their disappearance alerted the Gestapo, who sent agents into the Limousin area to investigate. Missus Wagner and her daughter Ingrid related their suspicions of the Bouchard family, but no significant leads were ever developed. Nevertheless, the Gestapo decided to maintain a loose surveillance over the Bouchard residence and its activities.

CHAPTER XIV
The Search for Jacques

Two black cars and a truck suddenly arrived at the Lemagne family farm in Chambery. Several men exited the cars and carefully removed two wounded men from the rear of the truck. Not having a stretcher, the men formed a human stretcher transporting the patients to the entrance of the house where Monique was standing and calling for Andre and Christiane to come quickly to their aid.

"Bring them downstairs," said Andre, leading them to the large basement room equipped with several beds next to the operating room.

Andre quickly examined the two men, both nearly unconscious, to determine the extent of their wounds and apply emergency remedies before taking the most seriously wounded man into the operating room.

"OK! What are their names?" asked Andre, with Christiane standing next to him.

"The man with the chest wound is Albert and the other man with the shoulder wound is Luc," said Charles Lemagne.

"Bring Albert into the operating room. I must attend to his wound right away. I'll attend to Luc immediately afterwards," said Andre.

"Christiane, get the instruments sterilized and ready for surgery while I scrub, and then get the patient anesthetized," said Andre.

Four hours later, both patients lay asleep in beds next to the operating room.

"Was the surgery successful?" asked Lemagne.

"Yes, they both will recover, but it will be several weeks before they can return to their normal activities," replied Andre.

"On behalf of their families and the entire Maquis Resistance, I thank you and Christiane for the wonderful work you did for us today," said Lemagne, accompanied by his wife Monique and Francois Lucier.

"This is a list of medical supplies that I will need as soon as possible," said Andre to Lemagne.

"No problem. I will get those supplies to you within the next three days," replied Lemagne.

"I haven't asked you how these two men got those wounds, because the less I know the better, I guess," said Andre.

"I don't think there's any harm in you knowing that. We raided the railroad yard on the outskirts of Paris where munitions had been loaded onto two railroad cars to be transported to Germany. We blew up both cars, and in the process Albert and Luc got wounded in a firefight with the security guards," replied Lemagne.

"That's ammunition that won't be used against anyone," said Lucier.

"I suppose you're right, and it was worth the risk. I'm glad I was able to help you," replied Andre.

The next day, Christiane convinced Andre to ask Lemagne for permission to leave the farm and visit the Bon Secours Orphanage, in an effort to locate their son Jacques.

"I don't see how Monsieur Lemagne can refuse our request after we saved two of their men from dying," said Christiane.

"Yes, I guess the timing is right. I'll go ask him now," replied Andre.

"I'll go with you for moral support, and let's make sure Monique is present. As a mother, she'll understand my need to find Jacques, and she'll have a most positive influence on her husband in our search for Jacques in Paris and its environs," said Christiane.

"Alright, let's go find them," replied Andre.

Charles Lemagne and his wife Monique were sitting in the kitchen drinking coffee which offered the perfect setting for what Andre and Christiane had to do.

"May we join you?" asked Andre.

"Yes, of course. Would you like a cup of coffee?" asked Monique.

"That will surely hit the spot," said Andre, as he sat down with Christiane at the kitchen table.

"Now that Christiane and I are together, our thoughts are to find our son Jacques, who most likely is somewhere in Paris or its suburbs. We would like to take a few days or perhaps a week off to search for him, starting at the Bon Secours Orphanage where he was adopted by persons unknown," said Andre.

Charles looked at his wife for an answer to this difficult question, which Monique obliged.

"We can certainly understand your desire to find your son. But you must also understand the risks involved in traveling through Paris even with your forged documents," said Monique.

"Why don't you let us make inquiries which won't put you in jeopardy," said Charles.

"I think that if we dressed in our religious habits, we would be more productive, especially with the Sisters at the Bon Secours Orphanage and Hospital," said Andre.

"Also, I know how to recognize my son, if we should come across a boy of his approximate age," said Christiane.

"How would you recognize him from other boys?" asked Monique.

"Because I noticed that Jacques had a birth mark in the form of a butterfly on his right shoulder when they let me see him after his birth," replied Christiane.

"That's very interesting. I guess that, dressed in your religious habits, with such direct evidence of his identity, you stand the best chance of finding Jacques. However, I must insist that you carry a concealed pistol, Andre, because you and Christiane must not be apprehended and incarcerated for intensive interrogation which would reveal our location and identities," said Charles.

"Since I have already informed my Bishop at the Abbey in Madrid of my intention to resign from the order, I have no problem with arming myself under such circumstances in time of war, especially with the Nazis," said Charles, looking at Christiane for her reaction to his answer.

"If I had to choose between my son's life and that of a Nazi, my son would win hands down," said Christiane in support of Andre's decision to carry a concealed handgun.

"Alright, you may go and search for your son. However, I'm going to give you the name and address of someone in Paris who can help you in an emergency. You must commit this to memory and not have anything on your person that would reveal our identity and location, in the event you are arrested," said Charles Lemagne.

"We understand," replied Andre for the two of them.

Armed with a Modele 1935 semi-automatic pistol with a 7-round magazine containing 7.65mm cartridges carried in his trouser pocket under his habit, Andre boarded the Maquis' four-door black sedan with Christiane, for transportation to the center of Paris, where they were then left to their own devices in search of Jacques. Their first stop was at the Bon Secours Orphanage, where they were met by Mother Dominique, in charge of the orphanage.

"Mother Dominique, this is Father Andre from the Abbey of Jesuits in Madrid. As you may remember, I gave birth to a son named Jacques on the 10th of March 1930, and he has since been adopted. Father Andre and I are planning on leaving our religious orders in order to be married so we can raise our son together. For that reason, we're looking for our son Jacques, who I understand has been adopted. We would sincerely appreciate it if you could tell us who adopted him, and where we could find him," said Christiane.

"So you are Jacques' father, then," said Mother Dominique, addressing Father Andre.

"Yes, I am," replied Father Andre.

"You must know that I am not permitted by law to reveal the identity of the person or persons who adopted Jacques," said Mother Dominique.

"Yes, we understand, Mother Dominique, but these are special circumstances with Paris under the occupation of the Nazis. There's no telling what may have happened to Jacques and the people who adopted him," said Christiane.

"I do understand you plight, Sister Christiane, but nevertheless, I can't break the law, especially under the Nazi regime," replied Mother Dominique.

"Well, if you can't reveal their identity, perhaps you could direct us to someone who is in a position to give us that information?" said Father Andre.

"I'm afraid I can't help you, Father Andre. I'm so sorry," replied Mother Dominique.

"That's alright, we understand your difficult position," said Christiane, who then exited the orphanage with Andre, and an alternate source in mind.

"What have you got in mind, Christiane?" asked Andre.

"Let's go pay a visit to Mother Superior Lucille at the Congregation of the Sisters of Bon Secours, not far from here," replied Christiane.

Mother Lucille was ecstatically surprised to see Sister Christiane with whom she had an earnest friendship.

"Oh! My God, it's been such a long time since you've been gone, Sister Christiane. What are you doing in Paris?" asked Mother Lucille.

"Well, first I'd like to introduce you to Father Andre, from the Abbey of Jesuits in Madrid," said Christiane.

"You are a long way from home, Father," said Mother Lucille, looking at the two of them together, both stationed in countries outside Paris, yet together in Paris, arousing her suspicion regarding the unknown identity of the father of Christiane's illegitimate child put up for adoption shortly after his birth.

"Yes, Mother Lucille, your suspicion is correct, Father Andre is the father of my son Jacques, and we're here to find him," said Christiane, reading Lucille's mind.

"But that's impossible. You're both members of a religious order, which makes it doubly impossible for you to obtain custody of the child, even if the adoption parents agreed to release him to you," said Lucille.

"We both are planning on leaving our religious orders so we can marry and raise our son Jacques in America," said Christiane.

"Really...well, in that case, what can I do?" asked Mother Lucille.

"You could tell us who adopted Jacques, and where we could find him," replied Christiane with Andre smartly leaving the inquiry to Christiane, who used to work for Mother Lucille until Christiane got transferred to Belgium.

"Under the unusual circumstances surrounding this adoption where the child could be in serious danger, I feel morally justified in revealing the name of the adopting parents," said Mother Lucille.

"What unusual circumstances?" asked Christiane.

"Doctor Aaron Cohen delivered your son, Jacques if you remember. Well, Doctor Cohen and his wife Anna adopted Jacques, and of course Jacques was given Cohen's last name," replied Mother Lucille.

"My God, he was adopted by a Jewish couple, and the French Police, at the behest of the Gestapo, have been rounding up all the Jews in Paris for internment at Drancy, according to our sources," said Christiane.

"That's why I'm revealing their names to you. We haven't seen Doctor Cohen for some time. I believe his medical license was revoked by the Gestapo because he's Jewish," said Mother Lucille.

"What hospital did he work out of?" asked Father Andre.

"The Hopital Hotel Dieu, in Paris," replied Mother Lucille.

"I know where it is. That's a good place to start looking for him," said Christiane.

"Well, I hope you find him safe and in good health," said Mother Lucille.

"Thank you so much for your kind assistance, Mother Lucille, and God bless you," said Christiane, truly grateful for her help.

Christiane and Andre quickly found their way to the Hopital Hotel Dieu, where they were met by the nurse in charge of visitors to the hospital.

"We're looking for Doctor Aaron Cohen," said Father Andre.

"Doctor Cohen no longer works here. His privileges at this hospital were rescinded by the Gestapo Office of Jewish Affairs," said the nurse officiously.

"When was that?" asked Christiane.

"A few months ago," replied the nurse.

"Would you have his home address by any chance?" asked Andre.

"Yes, I can do that if you'll wait a moment while I check our records," replied the nurse.

While waiting for the nurse to search through her files, Andre looked at Christiane with a smile at their apparent progress. The nurse returned with a piece of paper.

"I've written his home address on this piece of paper," said the nurse, handing the note to Andre.

"Thank you very much for your help," said Christiane, pleased at the lead they now had in locating the Cohens, and hopefully their son, Jacques.

Upon arrival in the 17th Arrondissement of Paris, Andre and Christiane found Doctor Cohen's large home had two vehicles parked in the front entrance; one a Mercedes convertible and the other a Daimler-Benz sedan.

"Those cars are only driven by German officers," said Andre. "It looks like the Cohen family may have been evacuated from their home, and the Gestapo took over their house."

"Maybe the Cohens are just being visited by the Gestapo," replied Christiane.

"We won't know until we go over there and ring the doorbell," said Andre.

"I'm scared, Andre. Maybe we should just assume they've been interned at Drancy, and go over there instead, and inquire about their possible internment," said Christiane.

"Yeah! I think you're right. Why take a chance. Besides, if they're no longer residing in their home, then the only alternative is their interment at Drancy. So let's go there," replied Andre.

The Drancy internment camp was located in the northeastern suburb of Paris. The barracks and courtyard's perimeter were enclosed with barbed-wire fencing, and its access was only through a gate with a guard shack. Andre and Christiane, dressed in their religious habits, approached the guard shack and asked to be directed to the administration building without giving a reason for their request.

"It's on the first floor of the second building on the left," said the French security guard respectfully.

"Thank you, monsieur," replied Andre as they entered the camp.

"I can't believe he allowed us in so easily," said Christiane.

"That's because he's French and apparently still has some respect for people of the cloth," replied Andre.

Upon entry into the administration building, they were immediately asked for their identification by the male clerk, a Frenchman in the employ of the Gestapo in charge of the camp.

"Your papers are in order. What is the purpose of your visit?" asked the clerk.

"We believe that a Doctor Aaron Cohen, his wife Anna, and their son, Jacques were interned at Drancy. We would like to confirm this," said Andre.

"I don't understand why a member of the Catholic Church would be interested in the interment of Jews," said the clerk.

"Well, monsieur, we are particularly interested in their son, Jacques, who is a Christian, not a Jew and was adopted by the Cohens," said Christiane.

"Oh! I see. So you want to know if their son was also interned at this camp with his adopted parents," said the clerk.

"Yes, that is correct, monsieur," replied Andre.

"Very well, then. Do you have any idea when the Cohens would have been interned here?" asked the clerk.

"Perhaps about six months ago, but I would check as far back as the first round-up of Jews in Paris," said Andre.

The clerk went back to the rear of the large office and retrieved a large book with a dark green cover, which he brought back to the counter facing Andre and Christiane.

The clerk started leafing through the pages containing a list of names, their assigned barracks number, and the date of deportation and destination if applicable.

"Here it is. Aaron and Anna Cohen. Arrived at Drancy on 16 July 1942, and deported to Auschwitz, Poland on 27 August 1942. There's no record of their son being interned here at Drancy, or deported anywhere," said the clerk.

"Are you absolutely sure their son Jacques, or by any other name, was not interned here at Drancy, or anywhere else for that matter," said Christiane.

"Yes, I'm certain of that. We keep impeccable records. If anyone had accompanied Monsieur Cohen and his wife, there would be a record of it," said the clerk in a confident manner.

"Thank you very much for that information, monsieur," said Andre, satisfied and pleased with that information.

Sitting in a café, sipping a café-au-lait with a croissant, Andre and Christiane weighed the possibilities of Jacques' current location.

"Maybe the Cohens anticipated their eventual internment, and made arrangements with someone they trusted to shelter Jacques for the duration of the Nazi occupation. I can't think of any other explanation," said Andre.

"Neither can I. It makes perfect sense. The question is whom would the Cohens trust for such a dangerous obligation?" asked Christiane.

"You can be sure that whoever accepted that responsibility will be very cautious about revealing Jacques' location, and even members of the clergy will be suspect," said Andre.

"Well, I guess we've reached a dead end," said Christiane.

"For the time being, anyway. We'd better get back to the safety of the farm and provide what we've learned to Monsieur Lemagne, who then perhaps can use it in our search for Jacques," said Andre.

CHAPTER XV
Massacre at Oradour-sur-Glane

The news that Italy had surrendered to the allies on the 3rd of September 1943 emboldened the French Resistance throughout France and in particular, the Maquis cells in the Free Unoccupied Zone of France, notably in the Limousin area, where the Free French commando, Jean-Guy Boivin, brought his expertise in warfare and demolition.

In the ensuing months, the French police were becoming less cooperative in enforcing German laws, and supporting Wehrmacht decrees. The recruitment of French Resistance fighters increased dramatically with the news of German defeats in Russia, and the expected forthcoming allied invasion of France.

In March 1944, the 2nd SS Panzer Das Reich Division was assigned to the Southern French village of Valence-D'agen, not far from Limousin, where they were to await further orders. One of the Division Staff Commanders was SS Major Adolf Diekmann, Commander of the 1st Battalion.

On 6 June 1944, the largest armada of invasion forces the world had ever seen, occurred on the shores of Normandy, France. Three days later, Commander Diekmann learned that a Waffen-SS Officer from the Das Reich Division had been captured and was being held prisoner by the French Resistance in Oradour-sur-Glane, situated in the Haute-Vienne region, about 24 kilometers northwest of the city of Limoges.

Major Diekmann became enraged by this act of defiance by the French. He had learned the day before that SS Major-General Heinz-Bernhard Lammerding in response to an attack by the Maquisards had ordered his troops to purge the region of Clermont-Ferrand resulting in the hanging of more than 90 men from the village of Tulle. This brutal act of reprisal emboldened Major Diekmann to commit a purge of superior magnitude. The fact that allied forces were advancing from the shores of Normandy further incensed and increased Diekmann's sense of urgency.

Major Diekmann assembled his battalion the following day, the 10th of June 1944, and on that sunny Saturday afternoon, ordered his men to surround and seal-off the village of Oradour-sur-Glane. He then ordered everyone in the village to assemble in the town square to have their identity papers inspected. One of those families was Fernand Bouchard and his wife Laurette, visiting Ernest Latreille and his wife Danielle.

Surrounded by more than three hundred German soldiers, the inhabitants of the village surrendered peacefully to the Germans' orders, not expecting any violent actions against them.

"They're probably looking for the Waffen-SS Officer that our Maquisards kidnapped two-days ago," said Ernest Latreille to Fernand Bouchard.

"What happened to him?" asked Fernand.

"He's gone. They'll never find him," replied Ernest.

"I really don't like the looks of this. That SS Commander has hate in his eyes and a vengeful disposition," said Fernand, referring to SS Major Diekmann, giving orders to his troops.

"At least, my two sons are visiting cousins some distance from here, thank God," said Ernest.

The men were then separated from the women and children, and formed into two groups, arousing suspicions of foul play from the men and much anxiety from the women and their children. The women watched their men being marched away to a part of the village that had two empty barns and three garages. The men were ordered into them, and then were summarily sprayed with machinegun bullets, many of them in the legs, unable to move. The wounded were then killed with rifles, and all were subsequently doused with fuel and set on fire within earshot of their women and children being herded into the village church. However, in the first barn, one of the men, a mason by trade, managed to make a hole in the wall of the barn, and escaped with four other men before the rest lost their lives.

Of the 196 Frenchmen herded into those barns and garages, only 5 managed to escape. The remaining died and then doused with fuel by SS men who set the barns and garages on fire to obliterate the evidence of their crime.

The women and children numbering 452 were herded into the Oradour-sur-Glane Catholic Church. Having heard the loud noise of machinegun fire that lasted for several minutes, the women, including Laurette and Danielle now incarcerated in the church, had little doubt about the fate of their husbands.

"My God, Danielle, do you think they actually shot our husbands and all these men?" asked Laurette.

"I don't know. Maybe they're just trying to scare us into cooperating with them. I know it doesn't look too good, but being assembled in this church, I don't think they would harm us women and children, not in a church," said Danielle.

At that moment, two SS soldiers entered the church carrying a large box of explosives with some attached strings sticking out of the box. They laid the box on the church altar, lit the strings, and quickly exited the church, when suddenly the box exploded, ejecting thick black suffocating smoke. The half-choking women and children, screaming in terror, rushed to those parts of the church not yet contaminated, and many of them attempted to leave the church through windows and were shot to death. SS soldiers threw firewood, chairs and other flammable items into the church. Then several grenades were thrown through the church windows exploding amongst the women and children, eliciting horrible screams and cries of "maman" from children and sobbing from women as fire ignited inside the church. Some of the grenades exploded near a cache of ammunition hidden inside the church by the local French Maquisard, intensifying the inferno within the church. Several women and children attempted to escape through doors and windows, but were shot to death by machine gun fire. However, one woman in her mid-forties managed to escape through a rear window, followed by a young woman and child. All three were shot as they jumped from the window, but only the middle-aged woman made it to safety without fatal injury, hiding in nearby bushes overnight until she was found and liberated in the morning. She related her experience as a witness to the massacre by Major Diekmann and his SS troops.

While the massacre was taking place, SS soldiers vandalized the village, looting houses and buildings, then setting them on fire. The entire village was reduced to rubble, as if it had been through a bombing raid.

SS Major Diekmann stood in front of the burning church with a look of sadistic satisfaction as the village lay in ruins.

When the rest of France hears me coming, he thought, *they'll drop to their knees in fear. No one will dare resist me.*

It didn't take long for the news of the Oradour-sur-Glane massacre, numbering 648 French inhabitants, to travel to the far corners of France. This included the Charles Lemagne farm in Chambery, where Andre and Christiane were still providing their medical service for the French Resistance, and word of this atrocity also reached the LeGrand farm near Orleans, where Jacques and Giselle were again under the care and protection of Roland and Madeleine LeGrand.

CHAPTER XVI
End of Search—Family Reunion

News of the Oradour-sur-Glane massacre was especially hard to accept by Jacques and Giselle, who had recently stayed overnight at the Ernest Latreille residence with his wife Danielle. However, the discovery that Fernand Bouchard and his wife Laurette were also victims of the massacre, was more than Jacques could digest, remembering Laurette's piano lessons that endeared him to her, in an almost maternal relationship.

Jacques was having dinner with the Roland LeGrand family, including Giselle and her brother Etienne, when the reason for the massacre was raised by Etienne.

"There is no justifiable reason for such barbaric conduct," said Roland, the patriarch of the family, "and I don't think this subject should ever be raised at the dinner table, not now, not ever."

Everyone at the table remained silent at Roland's unexpected declaration, and then Jacques broke the silence.

"May I be excused?" asked Jacques, directing his question at Roland.

"Yes, you may, young man. Are you feeling alright?" asked Roland in an apologetic tone.

"I just need some time to myself, thank you," replied Jacques, who then got up from the table, went outside the house, and sat in a rocking chair on the porch. His thoughts were about the world he lived in, the constant cruelty and killing that surrounded him, which seemed to be ever increasing in ruthlessness and brutality. His hatred for Germany's Third Reich and its Gestapo was now at its height, bringing mixed emotions which needed to be acted upon or diffused. His intrinsic gentleness and sensitivity railed against any form of violence, yet his rage towards those who massacred innocent women and children, and especially Madame Laurette, after the loss of his own adopted parents, in his mind justified that desire for revenge. Feeling as he did, he hated to think what he might do, if faced with a German SS officer. He hoped those feelings would leave him before he came face-to-face with such an occurrence.

Giselle hurried her dinner and excused herself so she could join Jacques, who seemed distressed by the news of the Oradour-sur-Glane massacre. She didn't have far to look as she stepped onto the front porch.

"You mind if I join you, Jacques?" asked Giselle.

"No, I don't mind. I just don't understand how people can be so cruel. Is this the world we must grow up in?" said Jacques rhetorically.

"No, Jacques. It's just the war. The Germans are desperate because the allied forces are now in France, and the Germans know they're losing the war," replied Giselle.

"Even, so, Giselle, the war can't excuse the atrocities committed by the German Wehrmacht. If people can do that during wartime, then they have the capacity to do the same during peacetime if the opportunity is offered. To me it shows their innate character and moral standards," said Jacques.

"But in peacetime, those opportunities don't exist," replied Giselle.

"So if we didn't have law and order and a police force, we'd have complete anarchy. That's a terrible condemnation of the human race," replied Jacques.

"You're an idealist, Jacques. You're now only thirteen, but as you get older, you'll realize that people are not perfect, and the good people must outweigh the bad ones, which is what the allied forces are now doing," said Giselle.

"C'mon, Giselle, you're only one year older than me, so don't pontificate about my idealism and immaturity," replied Jacques.

"Oh! Jacques. I'm not criticizing your idealism. I just think you expect too much from people," said Giselle.

"Well, maybe so, but that's the way I feel and see things, at least right now," replied Jacques.

"Ok! Do we have a truce?" asked Giselle with a disarming smile.

"Of course, Giselle. I can never be angry with you. You're my best friend," replied Jacques.

"Oh! Jacques, I hope we'll always be best friends, at the very least…" replied Giselle, not finishing her sentence but wanting to reveal she loved him.

The following morning, Jacques went into the stable with Giselle to let the horses out into the pasture. Jacques stepped into one stall with Blackie, a very spirited horse, and as he walked behind him, Blackie must have been stung by an insect on its rear end because he suddenly kicked his left hind leg backwards hitting Jacques' left calf, fracturing the fibula bone. Jacques fell backwards and managed to crawl outside the stall in severe pain. Giselle ran over to him.

"What happened?" asked Giselle.

"Something disturbed Blackie which made him kick his hind leg hitting my lower left leg. I think the bone in my leg is broken," replied Jacques.

"Listen, Jacques. Don't move. I'm going to get some help," said Giselle.

Within a few minutes, Jacques was surrounded by Roland LeGrand, his wife Madeleine and Giselle. After examining Jacques' left leg, Madeleine opined to her husband and Jacques that his left leg was broken, and he needed a doctor.

"First let's fasten a splint around his leg to immobilize it. Then we can move him into the house," said Madeleine, the medicine woman of the family.

"The only place we can take him is to my cousin Charles Lemagne's farm. He has a doctor and also a nurse there, taking care of the Maquisards, and it's the only safe place Jacques can get medical attention," said Roland.

"Who's going to take him there?" asked Madeleine.

"Well, I can take him, but I'll have to use the truck so he can lie flat with that broken leg," said Roland.

"Can I go with you, Papa?" asked Giselle.

"I think she can stabilize him during the trip," said Madeleine, knowing her daughter's feelings for Jacques.

"OK! Let's get going. He needs immediate attention, or else he might lose his leg," said Roland.

Upon arrival at the Lemagne farm, Roland checked with Giselle on Jacques' condition lying in the back of the truck.

"He's in pain, Papa, but we made it, so he's alright," replied Giselle.

"Wait here. I'm going to get some help from my cousin," said Roland.

As Roland stepped onto the front porch of the large house, Monique opened the front door, with a surprised look at seeing Roland.

"Well Good Heavens, Roland, what are you doing here?" asked Monique, greeting him with a warm hug.

"I've got a boy with a broken leg that needs immediate attention," replied Roland.

"C'mon inside. Doctor Andre Duval, and his nurse Christiane, are downstairs cleaning up, after some surgery they did this morning on one of our Maquisards, who caught a bullet in the shoulder," said Monique.

"You remember my two sons, Julien and Maurice," said Monique, "they've grown into two strong young men."

"Yes, they have," replied Roland, shaking their hands.

"Well, you wait here, Roland, while I fetch the doctor," said Monique.

"I've got another patient for you, doctor," said Monique, addressing Andre with Christiane standing next to him.

"Really, another Maquis?" asked Andre.

"No, this is a young boy with a broken leg," replied Monique.

"What, a local boy?" asked Christiane.

"No, my cousin Roland Lemagne brought him here from his farm in Chambery," said Monique.

"Alright, let's go see him, and bring him here," said Andre.

Monique led the way, followed by Doctor Andre Duval, Christiane, Monique's two sons, and Roland.

"This is my daughter, Giselle," said Roland as they all stared at Jacques lying prone in back of the truck.

"You can come down now, Giselle. They're going to move him inside the house," said Roland.

"I see you've got his leg in a splint. That's good. We'll need a stretcher to bring him inside," said Andre.

"Julien, Maurice, go get the stretcher," said Monique to her two sons.

"Alright. Let's ease the boy onto the stretcher. Be careful you don't bend his leg," said Doctor Andre Duval.

In the basement of the farmhouse, where the surgical room had been set up, Jacques was stretched out on the operating table, and Christiane removed the splint covering his left leg.

"Let's get some information about our patient," said Andre.

"What's your name, young man?"

"Jacques LeGrand."

"What is your date of birth?"

"March 10th 1930,"

"And I assume your parents are Monsieur and Madame LeGrand," said Andre.

"Not really. I was initially adopted by Doctor Aaron Cohen and his wife Anna," replied Jacques.

Christiane looked at Andre, then they both looked at Jacques with incredulity.

"We're going to remove you shirt, Jacques, if you don't mind," said Christiane.

"No, I don't mind," replied Jacques.

With his shirt removed, Christiane looked at Jacques' right shoulder, and nearly fainted at the sight of a birthmark in the form of a butterfly.

"Did your adopted parents ever tell you the name of your mother?" asked Christiane.

"Just before they were taken away by the Gestapo, Monsieur Cohen told me that my mother was Sister Christiane from the Hopital de Bon Secours, who had to put me up for adoption, and Monsieur Cohen and his wife Anna adopted me. He also gave me a letter to be given to Doctor Michel LeGrand, which provided all that information to him. For my safety, Doctor LeGrand took me to his brother's farm and they gave me forged papers identifying me as Jacques LeGrand."

Standing next to Christiane, Andre gently put his arm around her.

"We've finally found our son," said Andre.

"I'm Sister Christiane, Jacques, I'm your mother. We've been searching for you for years, my dear. That butterfly birthmark on your right shoulder, and your date of birth is confirmation," said Christiane with tears in her eyes.

Christiane leaned over and embraced Jacques, careful not to cause pain from his injured leg.

"Maman," said Jacques softly with tears in his eyes, "who's my father?" asked Jacques.

"Your doctor, Andre, standing next to me. His last name, which will be your last name, is Duval. Your father is going to fix your fractured fibula. Now that we've found you, Jacques, we're never going to let you go. We're a family now. We've got lots to talk about, my darling, but right now, we're going to give you a sedative that will put you to sleep, so you won't feel any pain, when Andre performs surgery on your leg," said Christiane, kissing him on the forehead.

Jacques looked up at Christiane, studying her face for some similarities with his own facial features, but it was the kindness in her eyes that seized his heart and mind. He felt a peaceful love as he closed his tearful eyes, awaiting the injection of the sedative.

Christiane turned towards Andre. "I can't believe we've found him. We must thank God for that incredible miracle."

"Indeed, especially in view of our plan to leave our religious congregations in order to be married and adopt our son," replied Andre.

"Give him the sedative now, so he won't feel any pain, as we remove the clothing around his leg," said Andre.

Two hours later Jacques lay in a bed with his left leg in a plaster cast, fast asleep from the sedative.

Upstairs, Monique had been working hard preparing dinner for her family and guests. Around the dining table, sat Charles Lemagne, his sons, Julien and Maurice, their guests, Roland LeGrand and his daughter, Giselle, Doctor Andre

Duval, and Christiane Laurent. A chair next to Roland was reserved for his wife Monique, busy serving dinner.

"May I help you?" asked Giselle of Monique.

"Yes, you can help me serve some of the food," replied Monique.

Giselle's blond hair, usually tied in a ponytail, now loosely hung, touching her shoulders, gave her the allure of a healthy and attractive country girl with a purity seldom found in city girls, which did not go unnoticed by Christiane and Andre.

"How old is your daughter, Monsieur LeGrand?" asked Christiane.

"She just turned fifteen last month," replied Roland LeGrand.

"How long has Jacques been living at your farm?" asked Christiane.

"Since his adopted parents were taken by the French Police and interned at Drancy. That would be about two years ago," replied Roland.

"I suppose Jacques and Giselle have had time to become close friends, then," said Christiane.

"Yes, especially after Jacques saved her life," replied Roland.

"Really, what happened?" asked Andre, now entering the conversation.

"Jacques and Giselle, along with my son Etienne, were assigned to take photographs from a distance, with telephoto-lens, of people entering and leaving the Gestapo headquarters, situated across from a public park in the village of Creteil, a southeastern suburb of Paris. Etienne stationed himself behind the Gestapo building, and Jacques and Giselle took photos from an empty house in the middle of the park. Unfortunately, an SS Colonel taking a walk in the park got curious and entered the house. Seeing Jacques and Giselle with a camera with special telephoto-lens made him suspicious, and he arrested them at gunpoint. Jacques knew what would happen to Giselle in particular, which he couldn't accept, so he shot and killed the SS Colonel, and escaped with the camera containing valuable photos of a French collaborator," said Roland.

"What happened to your son Etienne?" asked Andre.

"He made it back to the farm without incident," replied Roland.

"That's quite a story. How did Jacques subsequently respond to the killing of that Colonel, considering his young age?" asked Andre.

"He seemed to have justified his shooting that SS Colonel because he showed no outward signs of emotional distress," replied Roland.

"Well, that's good. Thank God he won't have to experience any more killings," said Christiane.

"Actually, I hate to mention this, but as Jacques' parents, you must be told all such experiences, which I must emphasize, saved not only his life, but that of Giselle and the two Maquisards driving them to their new home at Fernand Bouchard's estate in Limousin," replied Roland.

Christiane looked at Andre with a surprise look on her face at Roland's revelation.

"Do you mean Jacques was involved in other killings?" asked Andre.

"I'm afraid so. It was not planned, I assure you. My two French Resistance confederates, while driving Jacques and Giselle to their new home, got a flat tire, and while they were replacing it, a car with a Gestapo agent and a French Policeman drove up and stopped. Upon seeing two teenagers being driven by two men, they became suspicious, especially since there was a reward posted for the arrest of two teenagers responsible for the killing of a visiting SS Colonel and Inspector from Berlin Headquarters. They arrested all of them at gunpoint, and while they were busy handcuffing our two Maquisards, Jacques shot both of them in order to save their lives," said Roland. "As far as I and the entire French Resistance are concerned, your son is a hero."

"How is he reacting to that latest... incident?" asked Christiane.

"Fine. Again, he apparently feels completely justified. He really had no choice, when you consider what happens to those who are arrested by the Gestapo, especially when they're from the French Resistance," said Roland.

"I now can see why Jacques and Giselle are close friends. I would be too, if someone had saved my life twice," said Christiane.

"This war has forced our children to grow up too fast," said Roland.

"According to the BBC radio, our allied forces have successfully landed in Normandy, and they're moving rapidly towards

Paris. I anticipate Paris will be liberated before September," said Charles Lemagne.

"Now that you've found your son, Jacques, what do you intend to do?" asked Monique, who had joined them at the dinner table.

"Well, the first thing we have to do is gather any documents that will establish Jacques' identity and relationship to me, his mother. One thing Jacques said to us that is important is that Doctor Cohen gave him a letter containing information about his birth, and the identity of his mother, which he gave to Doctor Michel LeGrand. I hope he kept that letter, because we will need it as evidence," said Christiane.

"I will take care of that. I will contact my brother Michel as soon as I get back to the farm," said Roland LeGrand.

"We'll also have to get a letter from Mother Superior Lucille, of the Congregation of the Sisters of Bon Secours in Paris, relating what she told me and Andre about Doctor Aaron Cohen delivering Jacques and identifying me as his mother. So we'll have to go back to Paris for that letter as soon as possible before anything happens to Mother Lucille," said Christiane.

"Yes, but even after you've acquired all those documents, you won't be able to take Jacques out of France until you've officially adopted him, and in order to do that you will have to get married, in France, and that, my dear Christiane, is something you won't be able to do until France is liberated from the Germans, and the French administration is back to normal," said Monique.

"I don't think we'll have to wait that long, with the allies moving so rapidly towards Berlin," said Andre.

"True, but when France is liberated, you'll have to select a church in which you wish to be married. Then you have to get four witnesses and post their names in the 'Publication des bans' announcing your forthcoming marriage, which has to be posted at the local Mairie for no less than ten days. Getting married in Paris is time consuming and requires a lot of documentation, and France does not recognize marriages performed within the Embassy or the American Consulate in France. Furthermore, marriages must be performed by a French civil authority before any religious ceremony can take place," said Charles Lemagne.

"You will both need to produce a birth certificate, a French residency permit, a medical certificate, a certificate of celibacy, and proof of domicile, and all of these documents must be authenticated and translated into French by an official French translator," said Roland LeGrand.

"My God, I didn't realize the French bureaucracy was so demanding. What is a certificate of celibacy?" asked Christiane.

"That's a certificate which assures you are legally free to marry," replied Roland.

"Well, I guess, we'd better get those birth certificates over here tout-de-suite," said Andre, meaning right away.

"You know, Andre, when I first got off the *SS Ile de France*, I was given a lift to Paris by Madame Claire Beaumont, who is married to an American Lawyer with a daughter named Madeleine. They have a home in Long Island, New York and one in Paris. She gave me her card with her address in Paris. I hope she's still living in Paris, but when I met her, we were not at war with Germany," said Christiane.

"It's certainly worth a try. With her husband being a lawyer in New York, he could be a great help to us," said Andre.

"Even if Madame Beaumont is still in Paris, getting mail from New York under Nazi occupation is next to zero. But with the liberation of Paris looming, it won't be long before you'll be able to communicate with your parents in New York and Montreal for those birth certificates," said Roland LeGrand.

"I agree. Our first step is to get those documents from Doctor Michel LeGrand and Mother Lucille," said Christiane.

"I can get Doctor Cohen's letter from my brother. But you must not take the risk of going into Paris to see Mother Lucille. Better yet, why don't you write her a letter requesting she write you back with all the information you need on an official letter from Bon Secours, which one of our couriers can pick-up," said Roland LeGrand.

"That sounds like the best and safest solution," said Charles Lemagne.

"I agree. An official letter from Bon Secours would be most convincing to French authorities," said Andre.

"Well, then. I guess I'd better get busy writing that letter to Mother Lucille," said Christiane.

"So, I presume you'll be returning to your farm in Orleans with your daughter Giselle, tomorrow, then," said Charles Lemagne.

"Yes, I do have to return home where there's a lot of work to be done, especially now that Jacques won't be available with no replacement," replied Roland LeGrand.

"But Papa, why can't I stay here with Jacques," asked Giselle, imploringly.

"Because, you're needed at the farm which is your home, ma Cherie," replied Roland.

"Jacques won't need our motorcycle, so if you want to use it, Giselle, you're welcome to it. You could use it to visit us on weekends, when you're not working at the farm," said Monique, knowing Giselle's infatuation with Jacques.

"Really! Oh, that would be wonderful. Thank you, Monique," replied Giselle, now looking at her father for approval.

"I suppose that if you do all of your chores faithfully during the week, I don't see why you can't visit Jacques on weekends as long as you're back home by Sunday evening," said Roland LeGrand.

"Thank you, Papa. Thank you," replied Giselle excitedly. "May I be excused? I want to tell Jacques the good news."

Giselle went downstairs where Jacques was recovering from his broken leg, still requiring immobilization.

"I have to return home tomorrow morning with my father, but I've been given permission to use the motorcycle to visit you on weekends," said Giselle.

"Hey! That's great. I'm glad you learned to drive the motorcycle. When you do come on weekends, and I'm able to walk, I'll show you how to do the maintenance on it, so it doesn't break down on your trips. I think you should carry your pistol with you on those trips. You never know," said Jacques.

"Yes, I will, Jacques. Don't worry, I can take care of myself," replied Giselle confidently.

"Yes, I'm sure you can," said Jacques.

"I'm sure going to miss you, Jacques. Those weekends are going to be very special times for me," said Giselle, already feeling sadness at the thought of being away from Jacques during those weekdays.

More than a week transpired when Monique Lemagne received a sealed letter from the Bon Secours Hospital, delivered by a Maquisard sent by Roland LeGrand. Monique saw that the letter was addressed to Sister Christiane, therefore, did not open the letter but waited for Christiane, who had gone horseback riding with Andre.

Upon her return, Christiane opened the letter in the presence of Andre and Monique.

"Well, it's all in here, all the documentation verifying my giving birth to Jacques at the Hopital de Bon Secours on the 10th of March 1930 with Doctor Aaron Cohen as the delivery doctor and person who adopted Jacques on the 2d of August 1930," said Christiane with a satisfied look on her face.

"Now that you also have the letter that Doctor Cohen gave to Michel LeGrand, all that's left is for you and Andre to be married," said Monique.

"Yes, but that also requires documentation, so we're not there yet," replied Andre.

That weekend, Giselle had a chance to go horseback riding with Christiane, and upon their return to the farm, Christiane decided to have a talk with Giselle to learn about her future intentions and continued relationship with Jacques, who would soon relocate to New York with his newly found parents.

"Tell me, Giselle, is this war preventing you from attending school?" asked Christiane.

"No, our schools are open as usual, with the exception that some of the things we're now taught are mere Nazi propaganda, which we just ignore," replied Giselle.

"Have you decided on any type of career, or do you just want to be a housewife on a farm or in the city?" asked Christiane.

"Actually, I want to be a nurse like you," replied Giselle.

"Really, when did you decide that?" asked Christiane.

"When I saw you assisting Doctor Andre in surgery. I thought you were so efficient, and I don't think the doctor could have performed the surgery without you," said Giselle.

"I think you're giving me too much credit, Giselle, but thank you for the compliment. When do you graduate from high school?"

"In another eighteen months," replied Giselle.

"Are you then going to enter a nursing school?" asked Christiane.

"Yes, I would like that, and there's a fine nursing school in Paris. I hope my father will approve my going there, although he does need me at the farm," said Giselle. "But I'm also concerned about Jacques going to school in New York, and me in Paris, never able to see each other again."

"Listen to me, Giselle. You can come and stay with us in Long Island, each and every summer, and also during the Christmas holidays, at our expense, so your father doesn't have to worry about the cost of your travel. How does that sound?" said Christiane.

"Really…do you mean that?"

"Yes, of course," replied Christiane, smiling at Giselle's innocence.

"Oh! Wait 'till Jacques hears that. I know he was also worried about our long separation, but now our future looks so very bright. Why are you so good to me, Christiane?" asked Giselle.

"Because you're a nice person, and you love my son," replied Christiane.

"Oh! I do love him so much, but sometimes it scares me," replied Giselle, eliciting a laugh from Christiane who had those feelings when she was her age.

"Don't let it scare you, Giselle. Just enjoy the feeling, because it's the most precious thing life has to offer," replied Christiane, who spoke from experience.

CHAPTER XVII
The Liberation of Paris

The allied armies were steadily advancing towards Paris. They consisted of the United States Third Army and the French 2nd Armored Division, supported by the 9th Armored Company, manned primarily by veterans of the Spanish Civil War, armed with American tanks and trucks from the United States. The FFI (French Forces of the Interior) decided it was time to gather all of its resistance fighters, including the Maquisard, for a full, organized attack on the occupying German Wehrmacht, including sabotage, in an effort to assist the allied armies liberating Paris.

The FFI under the command of Henri Rol-Tanguy, initiated an uprising of its Parisians commencing with a strike by its railroad workers, followed by the Gendarmerie and French Police deserting the streets of Paris. More than fifteen thousand French Resistance Fighters participated in the erection of barricades in the city streets, armed with rifles and handguns mostly stolen from the German occupiers. Posters were spread all over Paris calling on all Parisians to mobilize and join the battle against the German aggressors and their collaborators. The Red Cross, true to its humanitarian mission, moved its mobile medical units into the city of Paris to care for the injured French and German combatants.

At the Lemagne farm, an emergency meeting was held by Charles with several FFI leaders from nearby French Resistance cells, including Roland LeGrand and his son Etienne. Giselle was brought along to assist Andre and Christiane, also in attendance.

"We've been commanded by Colonel Tangy of the FFI to join and assist his forces in the liberation of Paris. In that regard, I've been asked by the Director of the Red Cross for you, Doctor Andre, and Nurse Christiane, to join them in treating the French and German wounded. They expect hundreds of casualties, and they simply don't have enough doctors and nurses to treat all those injured," said Charles Lemagne.

"Well, I'll gladly volunteer my services as a nurse for members of the French Resistance, but I won't treat those German murderers of women and children. No way," said Christiane, remembering the rape and murder of her Sister friend in Belgium and the massacre at the village of Oradour-sur-Glane.

"I understand your reluctance to treat wounded Germans, but the Red Cross can make no distinction between friend and foe. They are duty bound to treat all wounded patients with equal care, regardless of nationality and military connection," said Charles Lemagne.

"My position on this matter is non-negotiable. If the Red Cross wants my assistance, they can separate the Germans from the rest of their patients and assign me to treat the non-Germans," replied Christiane.

"I don't know if the Red Cross is going to accept that," said Charles.

"Is that your position too, Doctor Andre?" asked Charles.

"Let me have a private talk with Christiane, and then I'll get back to you with my answer," replied Andre.

Having stepped out of the room, Andre faced Christiane with a question on his face.

"I know what you're thinking, Andre. That I may have shed my habit but not my religion, which requires I love my enemies. However, when God made that statement, he never envisioned the likes of an SS Commander or soldier murdering women and children, and the torture of innocent victims," said Christiane.

"I must admit, that you're reasoning is most compelling. Frankly, I don't have any argument against your decision, so I'm going to support your decision although myself, as a doctor who took an oath of impartiality, I will have to treat all patients alike. I hope you will understand my position and support my decision," replied Andre.

"Thank you for your support, Andre. I understand your position as a doctor, and I'm sorry I won't be able to assist you when you treat a German soldier. I just can't forgive and forget their barbarism," said Christiane.

Andre and Christiane re-entered the conference room, with solemn looks on their faces, as they confronted the FFI leaders.

"I fully support Christiane's decision to nurse only non-German patients. I'm totally satisfied with her reasoning for making that difficult decision. However, as a medical doctor, I took the Hippocratic oath, obligating me to treat all patients equally, regardless of their political or military affiliations;

therefore, I will fulfill that obligation to the best of my ability," said Andre.

"Very well, then. I will inform the director of the Red Cross of Christiane's conditional acceptance, and your unconditional acceptance, Doctor Andre," said Charles Lemagne.

"I would like to mention, Monsieur LeGrand, that your daughter Giselle wishes to be a nurse and is planning to attend nursing school after graduation from high school. In that regard, she asked me if she could be my assistant while working for the Red Cross in order to gain some real-life experience, and I told her I would be glad to have her as my assistant with your permission, of course," said Christiane.

"That is news to me. I don't know if she should be placed in such a dangerous environment at her age," replied Roland LeGrand.

"I don't think Giselle would be in any real danger working in the hospices of the Red Cross, especially as Christiane's assistant, who will most likely be assigned to one of the hospitals rather than in one of their mobile medical units in the combat zones because non-German patients are segregated in the hospitals," said Andre.

"Since Giselle wants to be a nurse, why not give her this opportunity to work with an experienced nurse under real-life conditions, Roland," said his cousin Charles.

"Well, I suppose you're right. I'm sure Madeleine will agree," said Roland, giving Giselle a look of approval.

"Thank you, Monsieur Roland. I'll take good care of your daughter as if she was my own," replied Christiane.

The director of the Red Cross wasted no time in recruiting Doctor Andre Duval, Nurse Christiane Laurent and assistant nurse Giselle LeGrand into the Red Cross, whose headquarters were temporarily located at Hopital Pitie-Salpetriere in Paris.

Charles Lemagne personally delivered Andre, Christiane and Giselle to the Hopital Pitie-Salpetriere, after they had said their goodbyes to Jacques, now confined to a wheel-chair at the Lemagne farm house, recovering from his fractured leg.

The Red Cross director, Madame Marguerite Boucher, a middle-aged woman with a strong presence and personality, received the three recruits with a warm welcome.

"You must be Doctor Andre Duval, and you must be Nurse Christiane Laurent," said Boucher, now looking at Giselle whose young age betrayed her role as Christiane's assistant nurse in training.

"So you want to be a nurse, huh!" said Boucher to Giselle. "Well, you're going to get a lot of on-the-job training here, my dear."

"I do have a contract for you all to read and sign, which is routine for all personnel employed by the Red Cross. Afterwards, I will give you your assigned posts and quarters," said Boucher.

"Doctor Duval, as an experienced surgeon, you are being assigned to one of our mobile medical units, number 5, covering Paris in section number 2, which is shown on the map you will be given. You will have a registered nurse and a practical nurse assigned to you. Further instructions will be given to you after you've settled into your quarters," said Boucher.

"Mademoiselle Laurent, as an experienced registered nurse, you will be assigned to Hopital Saint-Louis, in Paris, along with Giselle LeGrand, whom I understand, volunteered to be your assistant in order to learn nursing," said Boucher.

"I was hoping to be assigned as the registered nurse assisting Doctor Duval, with Giselle LeGrand as my assistant," said Christiane.

"I was informed that your employment with the Red Cross was on the condition you would not have to treat German patients. For that reason, you have been assigned to Hopital Saint-Louis, which has only non-German patients. German patients are considered prisoners of war, therefore are housed in a separate, secure facility," replied Boucher.

"I see. Well, it does make sense. Thank you for that explanation," replied Christiane.

That evening, Christiane wondered whether she had made the right choice. She realized that her hatred of Germans had transformed her into a vengeful, dogmatic xenophobic, contrary to her innate goodness and kindness to all living things. This vengeful curse was separating her from the man she loved, who needed her nursing experience in this time of emergency to save patients' lives, and for God to judge their souls. Enlightened by this self-revelation, Christiane immediately contacted Director Boucher that same evening to inform her she had changed her mind and wished to assist Doctor Andre Duval without reservations regarding a patient's military affiliations.

"I'm so glad you changed your mind, Christiane. May I call you Christiane?" asked Boucher.

"Yes, please do," replied Christiane.

"Your nursing experience is much needed, and I'm sure Doctor Duval will be delighted to have you as his assistant. I will inform him of this change right away," said Boucher.

"I assume Giselle LeGrand will come with me as my assistant," said Christiane inquiringly.

"Yes, of course. You three came as a package that must not be undone," replied Boucher with a broad smile.

"You've been most patient and understanding. I promise I won't disappoint you," said Christiane with gratitude.

"I'm sure you won't, and you'll make a fine team," said Boucher.

The next morning, the Duval team was introduced to their mobile unit driver, Gabriel Marais, a young man in his mid-twenties, a university drop-out from the German invasion. His dark eyes immediately focused on Giselle, only fifteen, but well developed for her age, which did not go unnoticed by Christiane, who would serve as her protector.

The mobile medical unit, consisting of a large box-framed van, contained a compact, but full surgical facility, with a double bed capacity for post-surgery patients needing transfer to a hospital. Its exterior had a large red cross painted on its roof and sides, alerting observers of its neutrality under the Geneva Convention.

Barricades were erected by the French Resistance, with the assistance of French residents, now heartened by the approach of allied forces. Unfortunately, some of the blocked streets caused Doctor Andre's Red Cross mobile unit to take several detours, before reaching its destination, not far from the center of Paris, where the action was taking place.

Parked a reasonable distance from a street barricade to avoid being hit by flying projectiles, it didn't take long for the wounded to appear at the mobile medical unit to be treated.

While Doctor Andre attended to the wounded, so far, ambulatory and non-critical, Christiane examined those awaiting treatment to determine which ones needed immediate attention, while Giselle stood by her, to retrieve medication and bandages when required. That day and evening, Andre and Christiane treated some twenty-four patients, but none of them required major surgery and hospitalization. However, the following day, in mid-afternoon, a Maquisard officer approached the mobile medical unit, with two of his confederates, carrying a semi-conscious uniformed SS Major, suffering from a gunshot wound to his abdomen. Addressing Doctor Andre, with Christiane and Giselle at his side, the Maquisard identified himself as Captain Jean Battieux of the FFI.

"Doctor, it is imperative that this SS Major be treated immediately to save his life. He was the SS officer in charge of the transfer of works of art recently stolen from the Arts Museum in Paris, and he knows where they were taken and hidden. We believe they're still within the Paris environs," said Battieux.

"Very well, bring him inside the van."

Andre, with Christiane's help, undressed the Major, revealing an entry wound in the abdomen, with no visible exit wound, indicating the bullet was still lodged in the Major, and needed to be extracted.

"What's this SS Major's name?" asked Andre of Captain Battieux.

"Major Max Schumacher apparently assigned to the Paris SS Garrison," replied Battieux.

"We'll do our best to save him, Captain. Now you'll have to step outside while we do our job," said Andre.

"Well, Christiane, this is a test of your resolve to uphold what has now become 'our' oath," said Andre.

"Don't worry, I'll keep my end of the bargain, especially in view of the benefits in saving his life," replied Christiane, with a winning smile, shared by Giselle.

Two hours later, with the bullet removed, and SS Major Schumacher sutured, bandaged and resting asleep on one of the double bunks in the van, Andre stepped out of the van, and advised Captain Battieux that the patient had survived the surgery, and was resting until he could be transported to a hospital for recovery.

"That won't be necessary, Doctor. We have a hearse ready to transport him to a secure area for his recovery and interrogation," said Battieux.

"A hearse...were you expecting a corpse?" asked Andre, humorously.

"No, but that's truly what he deserves, were it not for his value as a prisoner of war," replied Battieux.

"What makes you think the Major will tell you where the art work is hidden?" asked Andre.

"Because he will have two choices, execution as a war criminal or a prison term as a thief. Which would you prefer?" asked Battieux.

"I see your point. As always, the victor makes the rules. Do you want him now?" asked Andre.

"Yes. Is there any reason why we can't move him into the hearse, which allows him the same comfort as an ambulance," said Battieux.

"No, I guess not. You may use our stretcher," said Andre.

In the meantime, the French Resistance became aware of a recent order by Adolf Hitler, for General Dietrich von Choltitz, commander of the Paris garrison, to destroy the city of Paris. Alarmed at the prospect of such destruction of their capital city, the leaders of the French Resistance persuaded Raoul Nordling, the Swedish Counsul-General in Paris, to negotiate with General Choltitz, and on the 19th of August 1944, Nordling and Choltitz reached an agreement for a truce that saved Paris from destruction which resulted in an indefinite ceasefire. Columns of German tanks, trucks and vehicles carrying troops moved out of Paris, heading northeast to Germany.

On the evening of 24 August 1944, some units of General Philippe Leclerc's 2d French Armored Division entered Paris and rested at the Hotel de Ville. The following morning, the full measure of the 2d French Armored Division, supported by the United States 4th Infantry Division, entered the city of Paris, amid rousing jubilation by Parisians. That same day, General Choltitz, commander of the German garrison and military governor of Paris, surrendered at the Hotel Meurice, the newly established headquarters of General Leclerc.

With the entry into Paris of the French and American armed forces, and its liberation, came acts of vengeance by Parisians and members of the FFI against French collaborators with the Nazis. Women in particular had their heads publically shaved, and some were also beaten. Many Parisians felt that most of that anger should have been directed at their government, which had failed to protect them from German invasion and occupation.

Another week transpired before the Red Cross mobile medical units at designated combat zones in Paris were withdrawn for assignment elsewhere. It was now time for Andre, Christiane and Giselle, to return to the Lemagne farm, where Jacques was waiting for news of their activities in Paris, and its liberation.

Upon arrival at the Lemagne farm, Jacques could be seen moving around in a wheel chair as if he'd been born in it.

"When do you think I can have this cast removed from my leg?" asked Jacques of Doctor Andre.

"In about two weeks, but take it easy. You don't want to re-fracture your leg. It's still healing," replied Andre.

The following evening, while having dinner at the Lemagne farm, the discussion quickly turned to the resumption of normal affairs and activities in Paris and France.

"I think it's safe now for us to visit Paris, and while there, pay a visit to Madame Claire Beaumont," said Christiane.

"It's been about sixteen years since you've seen her. Do you think she's still residing at that address, and in Paris?" asked Andre.

"Well, it's been a long time, but we won't know until we visit Paris," replied Christiane.

"Actually, I'm thinking of sending a telegram to my father for him to send me some funds and my birth certificate. It might be a good idea, Christiane, if you also send your folks a telegram asking them to send your birth certificate," said Andre.

"You could use this address for your folks to send the mail now that we've been liberated. But I don't think you're going to find any telegram service in Paris or anywhere else in France at this time," said Charles Lemagne. "However, I heard that last week, on the 8th of September, the American Embassy in Paris reopened. Maybe they can help you."

"That's good news, indeed. That will be our first stop after we've visited Madame Beaumont," said Andre, looking at Christiane for confirmation.

"I think that's an excellent idea. They can tell us about the status of the Canadian Embassy or Legation as well," replied Christiane.

"As a matter of fact, the American Embassy can tell us exactly what will be needed to have Jacques issued an American passport," said Andre.

"Looks like you'll be going to New York sooner than expected," said Monique, with Giselle sitting next to her in silent agony at the thought of Jacques leaving for New York.

Almost two weeks to the day predicted by Doctor Andre, Jacques's plaster cast was removed, and he carefully started walking, at first with a cane, which he chucked after a week to go fishing along the creek. At first, he instinctively looked for the motorcycle, then remembered that Roland LeGrand had loaded it onto the back of his pick-up truck for Giselle to use when visiting him on weekends.

Andre and Christiane borrowed one of the old cars owned by Roland Lemagne that had been used by members of the Maquis to go to Paris and see Madame Claire Beaumont, but more importantly, to visit the newly reopened American Embassy. They also made sure they had the documents verifying Jacques' identity and ancestry, so they took him along, with Giselle, who was on a week's vacation and familiar with Paris.

Armed with a map of Paris and with the card given to Christiane by Madame Beaumont, containing her name and address, they finally found the house located on one of the main streets of Paris. It was a two-and-a-half story brick house, set deep inside a large lawn, surrounded by a black metal fence with wide gate, opening onto a circular driveway to the house entrance. The house appeared to be abandoned, and the gate was wide open. Yet a German flag still flew above the entrance doorway. Hesitantly, Andre and Christiane, accompanied by Jacques and Giselle, drove onto the driveway, and parked the car in front of the house entrance. Andre used the door knocker, and banged on the door several times, not expecting any response, when suddenly someone opened the door.

"Who are you looking for?" asked the old lady.

"I'm looking for Madame Claire Beaumont," said Christiane.

The old lady looked at Christiane, then at Andre, Jacques and Giselle, realizing they were not from the Gestapo, hence not a threat.

"Are you a friend of Madame Beaumont?" asked the old lady.

"I met Madame Beaumont and her daughter Madeleine in 1929, when we arrived at the Port de Saint-Nazaire aboard the *SS Ile de France*. She gave me this card, and invited me to visit her, but events beyond my control prevented me from visiting her until now. My name is Christiane and this is Andre and my son Jacques and his friend Giselle," said Christiane.

"Please come in," said the old lady. "Please excuse my appearance. I've been cleaning the house, after the mess those Gestapo officers made while removing anything of value as they vacated the house on their retreat back to Germany. My name is Gertrude Menard. I've been Madame Beaumont's housekeeper since she and her husband bought the house shortly after they were married," said Menard.

"I presume Madame Beaumont is not here at the present time. Do you know when she'll be back?" asked Christiane.

"Oh! My God. I guess you haven't heard. Madame Beaumont was betrayed by one of her friends as a Jew to the Gestapo during the round-up of Jews in 1942. Luckily, her daughter Madeleine was in New York with her father at that time. The Gestapo took over this house. I was only the housekeeper, so they let me stay upstairs in the loft, and I was allowed to remain here as their housekeeper. However, a few weeks ago, they left in a hurry, when they heard the American forces were approaching Paris," said Menard.

"Do you know where Madame Beaumont was taken by the Gestapo?" asked Christiane.

"At that time they took all the Jews in the round-up to the Drancy Internment Camp and from there to Auschwitz," said Menard.

"So you haven't heard anything more about her?" asked Christiane.

"No, I'm afraid Madame Beaumont, who was a kind and generous lady, was betrayed by one of her closest friends and ended her life at Auschwitz," replied Menard.

"Well, thank you, Gertrude, for that information. I'm glad you survived the German occupation of Paris. God Bless you, Madame," said Christiane.

While they were talking, Jacques noticed a grand piano prominently located in the living room. He hadn't had a chance to practice since his sudden departure from the Bouchard estate in Limousin, where he received piano instructions from Laurette Bouchard, herself an accomplished concert pianist and piano teacher.

"Excuse me, Madame Menard. I see you have a grand piano. Who in the Beaumont family played the piano?" asked Jacques.

"Oh! That was Madeleine's toy. Madame Beaumont wanted her daughter to become a concert pianist, something she herself was not able to attain. Unfortunately, Madeleine was not musically inclined, and preferred the medical profession. So the piano has remained silent for many years," said Menard.

"It is such a grand piano. May I play something?" asked Jacques.

"Yes, of course," replied Menard, surprised at his request, but not as surprised as Andre and Christiane, who were never told of Jacques' musical talent.

"When did you learn to play the piano, Jacques?" asked Christiane.

"Anna Cohen was a music teacher, and she taught me to play the piano since I was a child," replied Jacques, who then turned towards the piano, and lifted the cover to the keyboard, then sat down examining it lightly with his fingers.

"Jacques, please play Claude Debussy's 'Clair de Lune,'" said Giselle.

"You mean you knew he could play the piano," said Christiane to Giselle.

"Yes. My folks have an old out-of-tune piano that Jacques once played. My uncle does not have a piano. But when Jacques and I went to stay at the Bouchard estate in Limousin, that's when I heard Jacques really play on a grand piano, and Laurette Bouchard, who's a music teacher, thought Jacques was good enough to play at the Paris Music Hall," said Giselle proudly.

Jacques began softly touching the keys, creating a wistful atmosphere of a traditional song into a melody of pure love, which transcended earthly aspirations into a heavenly rendition of Claude Debussy's musical poem. Jacques' performance held his limited audience in a state of wonderment for a boy of his tender age.

"I can't believe it," said Christiane, with tears in her eyes, "that our son has such musical talent."

"I can't either. For sure we're going to have a grand piano in our house in New York," said Andre, looking at Jacques with admiration.

"You haven't heard anything yet. Wait 'till you hear him play Tchaikovsky's Swan Lake," said Giselle.

"Would you play 'Swan Lake,' Jacques," asked Giselle.

"If you don't mind, Giselle, I'd like to play Rachmaninov's piano concerto number 2 for Andre and Christiane. It's really my favorite," replied Jacques, who did not wait for an answer and began playing this most moving piano piece.

During Jacques' performance, even Gertrude Menard, moved by the music, had tears in her eyes. As the music gained crescendo, it seized the heart and soul of every listener with a power that temporarily elevated their spirit into a heavenly place they wished would never end. Andre and Christiane were left in absolute awe, and Giselle hopelessly in love with Jacques and his musical talent.

Madame Menard thanked Jacques for his performance, and said goodbye to her guests, knowing they would never meet again.

Inside the car, as they were driving away from the house, Christiane, again congratulated Jacques on his incredible performance, and Andre renewed his promise to have a grand piano in their home in New York for him to practice, and play to his heart's content. But then Christiane regained the reality of their current situation, as she recalled the news of Madame Beaumont's extermination by the Nazis.

"Can you believe what happened to Madame Beaumont. She was one of the nicest persons I had ever met. She gave me a ride in her chauffeured limousine from the Port de Saint-Nazaire to Paris, and we had a wonderful conversation about her family in New York. I hope that person who betrayed her rots in hell," said Christiane.

"There was a lot of betrayal during the occupation, and there will be a lot of finger pointing and reprisals," said Andre, with Jacques listening attentively, recording everything into his young timeless memory.

Finally, Andre located the building that housed the American Embassy, on the northwest corner of the Place de la Concorde. It was an imposing building, now flying the American flag.

"That's the American Flag representing the United States of America, Jacques, and this is the American Embassy," said Andre, proudly.

CHAPTER XVIII
The marriage, adoption and return to America

Parked in front of the American Embassy, Andre explained to Giselle the reason she could not accompany them into the Embassy.

"Giselle, I'm afraid you'll have to stay in the car. Our passports only cover Christiane and me, and a passport for Jacques is the reason for coming to the Embassy, you understand?" said Andre.

"Yes, of course. I'll be alright. I'll wait here for you," replied Giselle.

"It shouldn't take too long, Giselle," said Christiane.

Two United States marines guarded the gate entrance to the American Embassy, and as customary, they requested identification from Andre and Christiane.

"This is our son, Jacques," said Andre, after showing his United States passport, and Christiane's Canadian passport.

"Our son needs a passport. That's why we're here, to see the Ambassador or one of his representatives."

"Very well, sir, once inside, you'll be directed to the proper person," said the marine.

After presenting their passports again to the receptionist at the front desk, Andre, Christiane, and Jacques were directed to room 106 on the first floor to see Mister William Anderson.

"I'm Bill Anderson. What can I do for you folks today?"

"I'm Andre Duval, this is my fiancée Christiane Laurent, and our son, Jacques," said Andre, handing Anderson his passport and that of Christiane.

"So you are an American citizen, Mister Duval, and you are a Canadian citizen, Miss Laurent. I'm sure you'll have a reasonable explanation for claiming Jacques as your son."

"It's complicated, but let me explain," said Andre.

"Christiane and I were on the SS *Ile de France* from New York City to the Port de Saint-Nazaire. I was a Jesuit priest and medical doctor, and Christiane a sister and nurse for the Hopital de Bon Secours, both assigned for duty in Paris. Aboard the ship, we fell in love. About six weeks later, Christiane realized she was pregnant, and attempted to contact me. However, I had already been reassigned to Madrid, Spain. She elected to spare me the shame and responsibility by agreeing with the Bon Secours Mother Principal that her only choice was to put her child up for adoption. Her only request was for her child to be named Jacques, which was granted. Christiane was then transferred to a Bon Secours hospital in Brussels, Belgium. Within a few months, Doctor Aaron Cohen, who had delivered Jacques on the 10th of March 1930, and his wife Anna, adopted Jacques and gave him their family name of Cohen. All went well until the Nazis invaded France and occupied Paris. They rounded up Jewish families, including the Cohens, but not Jacques, who was hidden in the attic of their house. The Cohens were incarcerated at Drancy Internment Camp and then transported to Auschwitz for extermination. Doctor Cohen had made arrangements with a friend, Doctor Michel

LeGrand, at the Hopital Hotel Dieu for him to hide and care for Jacques. Michel LeGrand turned Jacques over to his brother Roland LeGrand, and his wife Madeleine, at their farm near Orleans, where he was accepted as a member of the LeGrand family. When Jacques hid in the attic, he had in his possession a letter written by Doctor Cohen, providing details regarding Jacques' birth and adoption, to be given to Doctor Michel LeGrand. I managed to obtain that letter from Doctor LeGrand. I also have an official letter from Mother Superior Lucille of the Congregation of the Sisters of Bon Secours in Paris, attesting to the birth and adoption of Jacques by Doctor Aaron Cohen," said Andre, handing Anderson the documents.

"Are you both still in your religious orders?" asked Anderson, observing Andre and Christiane were both dressed in civilian clothes.

"No, we submitted our resignations, and plan on getting married here in Paris, as soon as the French administration is able to process our request for a marriage permit," said Andre, speaking for Christiane as well.

"Looking through these documents, it's evident that Jacques is your son, Miss Laurent, and we can presume that the Cohens are deceased, leaving Jacques an orphan, eligible to be adopted by you, after you've been legally married by a French magistrate. Once that is accomplished, I would highly recommend that you, Miss Laurent, become an American citizen, to facilitate the issuance of a U.S. Passport to your son Jacques," said Anderson.

"Christiane and I have already discussed the matter of citizenship, and she has agreed that it would be the best course of action for this family," said Andre.

"Very well, then. May I make a copy of these documents, and you can retain the originals, until you return for the final ceremony," said Anderson.

"Yes, of course. But there is another matter of importance that I need to discuss with you, sir," said Andre.

"What is that?" asked Anderson.

"At the present time, we're unable to contact our parents to obtain authenticated birth certificates, required by the French administration for marriage. I also need to contact my father, also a medical doctor, in New York City, for him to send me five thousand US dollars, to cover expenses while we're still in France. Is there any way you can assist us in obtaining those birth certificates and money from my father?" asked Andre.

"Well, these are extraordinary times and circumstances. If you will provide me with two addressed letters to your parents, each requesting the desired information, I'll get them posted for you. In turn, instruct your parents to post their return letter to my attention at this embassy in Paris, and upon receipt, I will notify you. So please use my office to write those letters, while I have my secretary get some coffee for you. How do you take your coffee?" asked Anderson.

"Both of us like it with cream and two sugars, thank you," replied Andre, who then looked at Jacques to see if he wanted coffee.

"No thank you. I don't want any coffee," said Jacques.

Having written their letters, and addressed the provided envelopes, Andre wrote his name and address at the Roland LeGrand farm in Orleans, for notification from Anderson, when the return letters arrived.

"You've been most helpful, Mister Anderson, well beyond my expectations. I can't wait for our son Jacques to see New York, thanks to you and the American Embassy," said Andre.

"You are most welcome. I'm looking forward to seeing you again as Mister and Missus Duval, and you too, Jacques Duval," replied Anderson with a big smile.

Back at the Lemagne farm, Doctor Andre Duval and Christiane Laurent's medical services were temporarily not needed, due primarily by the entry of the Red Cross into the areas of Paris still under combat with remaining Nazis. Andre sought an opportunity to get acquainted with his newly discovered son Jacques by inviting him to go fishing in the farm's nearby creek where Jacques had often fished.

"I borrowed Mister Lemagne's fishing rod and tackle. Would you like to go fishing with me at the creek, Jacques?"

"Sure, I'd like that. The creek's got carp, pike, and I'm told by Julien that there's even trout in the creek although I've never seen any," said Jacques.

"What have you been using for bait?" asked Andre.

"I was using worms, but then Julien gave me some lures which I've been using with great results. Do you have any lures in that tackle box?" asked Jacques.

"Yes, a few. So how about going fishing now?" asked Andre.

"OK, I'll get my rod and tackle box, and be with you in a minute," replied Jacques, who had never used the word 'father' or 'dad' in his conversations with Andre because it connoted an intimate relationship, not yet established, which Andre intuitively understood and accepted.

They sat next to each other, a few feet apart, on the east side of the creek with their lures floating on the surface of the water waiting for a strike from a fish which invited a tête-à-tête conversation.

"I guess finding out I was a Jesuit Priest, and your mother a Sister Nurse when we met on the *SS Ile de France*, was a bit of a shock," said Andre, testing the waters so to speak.

"Well, yes, I was surprised, but I can tell you and my mother are in love, and that's what really matters," replied Jacques.

"I suspect your understanding comes from your relationship with Giselle, and you're correct, love is what really matters, Jacques, and I'm glad you recognize that, and also that you are my son," said Andre.

"After our meeting at the American Embassy, I asked my mother about the Jesuits, and she told me that Jesuits are the intellectuals and teachers of the Roman Catholic Church. Is that right?" asked Jacques.

"Well, that's a bit of exaggeration. However, we have been known to teach theology," replied Andre.

"Maybe you can explain something to me because I don't understand how an almighty God can allow these Nazis to commit such horrendous crimes against humanity," said Jacques.

"When God created us humans, he gave us free will. Therefore, we are responsible for our actions, and God will not interfere. He can influence those who seek his help to do the right thing, but he won't obstruct our actions. We are here on this earth to earn our way into heaven, where God awaits us. However, in order to enter heaven, we must have gained the wisdom of pure love and complete rejection of hatred. Then we have attained enlightenment. Until that is accomplished, our spirit is doomed to return to earth upon our physical death as a reincarnated human being at the moral level we had reached when we died. So, you may view your efforts to do good and reach enlightenment as steps on a ladder to heaven. When you do reach enlightenment, you will enter heaven and never return to earth," said Andre.

"When I studied the Jewish Faith with Doctor Cohen and Anna, I understood that reincarnation was only taught and believed in Asian religions, such as Hinduism, Jainism, Buddhism and Sikhism, which arose in India. Since you are of the Christian faith, how come you believe in reincarnation?" asked Jacques, somewhat confused.

"Numerous bibles and sacred writings have been published with various theories about the human soul and how we attain the required requisite for immortality in a place commonly known as heaven. I believe all of these religions have something to contribute to the understanding of how we should live our life. The Asian theosophy dictates that our actions in this life decide our fate in future existences, which is known as Karma. Christians believe that there will be a final judgment day when God will decide the fate of our souls. I have studied most aspects of religious philosophy and have come to the conclusion that reincarnation is a most valid theosophy," said Andre. "The final judgment day belief is compatible with karma and reincarnation; they both require us to observe God's commandments for entry into heaven."

"Then what will happen to criminals like Mussolini and Hitler, responsible for the deaths of millions of people. Will they be forever reincarnated without ever entering heaven?" asked Jacques.

"Criminals like that will not escape final judgment day, and I have to believe they will never attain enlightenment because of their own diabolical choice; therefore, I believe they will never enter heaven," replied Andre.

"I'm glad we had this talk, father. You've renewed my faith that those bad people will pay for their actions, and good people will be rewarded for their faith in God," replied Jacques, whose use of the word 'father' gave Andre a much sought-after feeling of acceptance as Jacques' father.

A fortnight later, two letters, one addressed to Andre, and the other to Christiane, were delivered to the Lemagne farm, compliments of the American Embassy.

"My father says that he and my mother are most supportive of my leaving the Jesuit order, and upon my return to New York, I can join his medical group in Long Island. He's enclosed my birth certificate and a Bank of New York money order for five thousand dollars. Did you get your birth certificate?" asked Andre of Christiane.

"Yes, I have it. My mother wrote the letter on behalf of herself and my father. They congratulate me on my decision to get married, and hope I'll visit them soon afterwards. I'm sure they wished I'd married someone from Montreal, where they would be able to visit their grandchildren, but they also understand that love has no geographical boundary, and New York is not that far away from Montreal," said Christiane.

"I agree, sweetheart. We'll be able to visit them and vice versa, that's no problem. I've got to visit the Banque de France, and find out if the French currency at the present time is and will continue to be honored before I deposit my money order," said Andre. "You want to accompany me to Paris?"

"Not if it's just a visit to the Bank," replied Christiane.

"Well, if the bank accepts my money order, then I can afford to take you to a fine restaurant. But that depends on the value of the French currency," said Andre.

"Why don't I wait until you return with results of your trip," said Christiane.

Upon his return two days later, Andre had some disappointing news.

"I spoke to the manager at the Banque de France, and he advised me to wait until Germany had officially surrendered because the new 4th Republic of France may issue new currency, which will secure my deposit. He said Germany is on the brink of defeat and surrender," replied Andre.

"Well, we do have some money left, but I hope it lasts until the war ends," said Christiane.

"I will have a talk with Charles and show him my Bank of New York money order. That will reassure him of my ability and intention to repay him for the support he's given us, including Jacques, during our stay here," replied Andre.

"Yes, that's an excellent idea," said Christiane.

The Christmas holidays were celebrated by the Duval family at the Lemagne farm with joy and optimism for the forthcoming year when expectations of the war's end appeared to be near, judging from the allied armies' success against the German Army.

The welcome news arrived in the L'Aube French newspaper announcing the suicide of Adolf Hitler and Eva Anna Paula Hitler, nee Braun, his wife of one day, on the 30th of April 1945. A week later, on the 7th of May 1945, German Marshal Alfred Jodl signed the unconditional surrender of the German Army in Reims, France.

Andre, Christiane, and Jacques celebrated the end of the war with Germany, along with the Lemagne family which had also invited Giselle to join them.

"Well, it's just a matter of time, perhaps a few weeks before the French administration gets its house in order, and you're able to get your marriage license," said Charles to Andre and Christiane sitting at the dinner table with the rest of the family.

"Yes, and I'm anxious to see the new French currency in circulation," said Andre.

"I'm sure that will be a priority 'cause the economy depends on it," replied Charles.

Three months later, Andre and Christiane were married in the Notre Dame Cathedral with Jacques and Giselle in attendance, along with several Maquisard leaders and members of the French Resistance, some of them thankful former patients. Afterwards, a luxurious reception was held at the Hotel Crillon, overlooking the Place de la Concorde, which in the past had kings and many celebrities as guests. Andre's recent loan from his father was most timely for the occasion.

Mister William Anderson of the American Embassy officially sanctioned the adoption of Jacques by Andre and Christiane Duval, and in the process, Jacques and Christiane became United States Citizens and were issued passports for entry into the United States.

It was on the eve of the Duval family's departure for New York aboard the *RMS Queen Mary* ocean liner due to depart from the Port of Le Havre that Giselle was provided an opportunity by Christiane and Madeleine, Giselle's mother, to spend the last hour of the evening with Jacques in the garden of the Hotel Crillon, knowing it would be some time before they would see each other again.

"I'm going to miss you, terribly, Jacques. Who knows when I will see you again," said Giselle with tears in her eyes.

"My mother assured me she'll send you airplane tickets for you to spend Christmas and New Years with us. So it won't be long before we'll be together again," replied Jacques, holding her hands.

"I hope so. I'm entering nursing school in two months.

What about you. What school are you going to be attending?" asked Giselle.

"My father said I was going to enter Forest Hills High School on Long Island, which has a great music department," said Jacques.

"Are you going to make music your career?" asked Giselle.

"I don't know. I'd like to, but can I earn a living at it is a good question. Perhaps I should become a medical doctor like my father, who knows," replied Jacques.

"Whatever you do, Jacques, you'll be a great success, I'm sure," replied Giselle.

"Thanks for your vote of confidence Giselle. I'm sure you'll make a great nurse, and hopefully I'll be your favorite patient," said Jacques.

"Jacques, you won't be my patient, you'll be my lifetime lover," replied Giselle, moving close enough to Jacques for him to kiss her, which he did for several seconds, seemingly an eternity for the both of them.

"My parents are driving us back to the farm tonight, so I won't be seeing you off tomorrow morning, when you leave for the Port of Le Havre," said Giselle sadly.

"It had to happen, we knew that, but cheer up, it won't be long before you're in New York for the Christmas holidays. In the meantime, you'll be busy in nursing school, making friends, and learning your new vocation," said Jacques, attempting to raise her spirits.

"Yes, you're right, Jacques. We must keep a positive attitude. Patience is not one of my virtues, but I'll learn to master it," replied Giselle.

"That's my girl. I'll always love you, Giselle. Please remember that, and you'll overcome all obstacles," said Jacques.

It was on the seventh day of their voyage aboard the *RMS Queen Mary* when they sailed past the Statue of Liberty on a small island in Upper New York Bay and the New York harbor.

"You know, Jacques, that Statue of Liberty monument was given to us by France," said Andre, looking at it from the port side of the ship with Jacques and Christiane.

"When was it given to the United States?" asked Jacques.

"I believe it was in October 1886," replied Andre.

"Even I didn't know that," said Christiane. "You're a walking history book."

"History always fascinated me, especially since it seems to repeat itself," said Andre.

"I guess we're hard-pressed to learn from our mistakes," replied Christiane.

"Amen!" said Andre.

"Where are we going to live in New York?" asked Jacques.

"We're staying temporarily at my parents' house in Oceanside, Long Island, while we look for a house in that area. My father has already hired a real estate agent to find us a house," replied Andre.

"Is that far from New York City?" asked Jacques.

"No, it's only about a half-hour subway ride. You're going to like Oceanside. It's about a half hour drive to Jones Beach or Far Rockaway Beach overlooking the Atlantic Ocean," said Andre.

"And Forest Hill High School, where you'll be matriculated, has the best music department of any high school on Long Island," said Christiane from her discussions with Andre.

"I hope my limited English won't hold me back. I had only one hour of English a day in school in Paris, as a secondary language. Doctor Cohen and Anna would often talk to me in English because they thought it was important for my future," said Jacques.

"They never realized how prophetic their advice would be," replied Christiane.

"I owe them so much," said Jacques, holding back tears.

"You can be sure, they're being amply rewarded in heaven, my dear," said Christiane.

CHAPTER XIX
Jacques' assimilation and Giselle's visits to New York

Upon arrival in New York, the Duval family got a taxi taking them to the Duval residence in Oceanside, where they were warmly received by Andre's parents, Doctor Robert Duval and his wife Marilyn.

After embracing their son Andre, Marilyn embraced Christiane, welcoming her to the family and then turned her attention to Jacques.

"My goodness. So, you're my grandson, and you're so tall. How old are you, Jacques?"

"Sixteen."

"Well, you're taller than me, so you'll have to give me a hug," said Marilyn, with a hearty laugh, as she embraced him.

"You know, Jacques, you're my only grandson, so don't be embarrassed if I spoil you," said Marilyn.

Robert Duval shook Jacques' hand and then embraced him.

"You're home now, Jacques, and you have your own room here, even after you move to your new house," said Robert, immediately taking a liking to his grandson, in whom he saw some resemblance to Andre.

Later that night when Robert lay in bed with his wife Marilyn, they compared notes on their impressions of their daughter-in-law and grandson.

"Well, what did you think of Christiane," asked Robert.

"She's very attractive and intelligent, but most of all, she truly loves our son, that's quite obvious," replied Marilyn.

"Yes, I agree. What about Jacques?" asked Robert.

"I couldn't believe how tall he is for his age. He takes after Andre. But what struck me most of all about him was his pensiveness as he evaluated us. That boy is a thinker but with a big heart once he knows he can trust you," said Marilyn.

"I got the same impression. I guess we've been together so long we think alike. Andre did mention in his letters that Jacques is an exceptional pianist with a great future. Too bad we don't have a piano," said Robert.

"Yes, but we could arrange for the five of us to visit our dear friends, Bill and Cheryl McGuire, who do have a baby grand piano that their granddaughter Vivian uses for her piano lessons. It's only natural that we introduce our family to our closest friends, don't you think?" said Marilyn with a knowing smile.

"Yes, you're absolutely right. Why don't you make the arrangements," replied Robert.

The following Saturday, all five members of the Duval family arrived at the expansive home of the McGuires on the southern end of Oceanside overlooking Middle Bay, and from its third story tower, Long Beach and the Atlantic Ocean.

There were several cars in the parking area next to the circular driveway indicating the McGuires had invited several of their friends besides the Duvals, who were not aware that it was their granddaughter Vivian's birthday. The McGuires were using this occasion to celebrate their granddaughter's sixteenth birthday and display her talent as a pianist, in the presence of her music teacher, Missus Margaret Holden. Also invited was Vivian's best school friend, Alice Tanner, whose father, John Tanner, a prominent real estate developer, was also in attendance with his wife Dorothy. Several other affluent couples were there, but none familiar to Andre except for the McGuires, due to his long absence as a Jesuit priest.

Andre had taken Jacques to his tailor earlier that week to get him a dark suit, and also a dark-blue blazer with silver buttons to be worn over light blue dress trousers and of course the traditional white shirt with solid-color ties. Jacques wished he could have been accompanied by Giselle to this swanky party but contented himself with the thought that eventually she would be there with him this forthcoming Christmas holiday.

The usual introductions were made by the hosts Mister and Missus McGuire. Two tuxedoed waiters and a waitress mingled with the guests carrying trays of hors d'oeuvres and alcoholic drinks for their consumption. There was easy-listening music coming from a cabinet containing a turntable playing 78 rpm records with emphasis on string instruments rather than piano. Andre later concluded it was cleverly intended to avoid eclipsing their daughter's piano performance.

It didn't take long for Vivian and her girlfriend Alice to zero in on Jacques, the only boy in attendance.

"I'm Vivian and this is my friend Alice. You must be Jacques, who just arrived from Paris."

"Yes, I am," replied Jacques, a bit shy from Vivian's forwardness.

"It must have been awful with the war over there in France. I'll bet you're glad to be out of there," said Vivian.

"I'm glad the war is over, and I'm sure Paris will recover, and still be the city of lights," replied Jacques.

"Well, wait 'till you see New York City. There's no place like it in the world," said Vivian proudly.

"Where will you be attending school?" asked Alice.

"Forest Hills High School," replied Jacques.

"Really. That's where we go. You'll like it there. It's a big school with more than four thousand students," said Alice.

"I'm sure I will. I've been told that the school has the best music department of all the Long Island schools," said Jacques.

"You got that right. I'm the lead pianist in the school's orchestra," said Vivian.

"You'll see why this evening when Vivian gives us a recital," said Alice.

"Really, what will you play for us?" asked Jacques.

"That will be a surprise," replied Vivian.

"I'm looking forward to it," said Jacques, not mentioning his own talent as a pianist.

As the evening progressed, Robert Duval and his wife Marilyn got into conversation with Bill and Cheryl McGuire.

"We didn't know it was your granddaughter Vivian's birthday you were celebrating this evening. When we learned that our grandson Jacques was a gifted pianist, we immediately thought of your baby grand piano, but with all these people here, I don't think this is the right time for him to show us what may be an embarrassing performance," said Robert.

"I agree with Robert, the poor boy has just arrived in the United States. He doesn't need that kind of pressure. He'll have plenty of time at the Forest Hills High School music department to show his skill as a pianist," said Marilyn.

"Well, he's welcome to use our piano whenever he wants. I'm sure my granddaughter will be glad to have someone here with the same musical interest," said Bill McGuire.

"As a matter of fact, Vivian will be playing a couple of numbers for us this evening," said Cheryl McGuire.

"We're looking forward to her presentation," replied Robert with his wife Marilyn nodding in agreement.

A few minutes later, Cheryl stood in front of the piano, and called everyone's attention.

"May I have your attention, please," said Cheryl.

"My granddaughter Vivian, in celebration of her birthday, is going to play two beautiful melodies on the piano. The first one by Strauss is 'The Beautiful Blue Danube.' The second melody will be Georges Bizet's 'Habanera' from *Carmen*," said Cheryl, turning towards Vivian, now seated in front of the keyboard ready to commence her recital.

Jacques stood to the side where he could see Vivian's fingers moving across the keyboard. He was familiar with the melody and thought that Vivian's rendition had a mechanical, easy-piano-tutorial flair. Bizet's 'Habanera' demanded a full excursion of the keyboard, but Vivian's execution was a simple, mechanical interpretation of a vivacious melody. Everyone applauded, including Jacques, who realized that Vivian had just turned sixteen years old, with room to grow. Furthermore, she may not be motivated to spend the long hours of practice required to attain professional status.

"May I have your attention, please," said Cheryl.

"I just learned that Bob and Marilyn's grandson, Jacques, who just arrived from Paris, is a gifted pianist. I think we should give him a big hand of encouragement to play us one of his favorite piano pieces," said Cheryl, clapping her hands as a signal for the audience to do likewise, ensuring his participation.

"I wish she hadn't done that," said Marilyn to her husband Robert.

"She thinks her daughter is a piano prodigy, and Jacques's lesser performance will raise her status," said Robert.

"Sometimes, I'd like to strangle Cheryl. Let's hope Jacques' performance hits the mark," said Marilyn.

Andre and Christiane walked over to Jacques.

"Give them the performance of your life, Jacques. Play Rachmaninov's piano concerto #2. That will blow their socks off," said Christiane.

Jacques walked up to the piano and turned to Vivian.

"That was a very nice recital, Vivian," said Jacques, who then without announcing the melody he was about to play, started with Rachmaninov's piano concerto. It soon became apparent to Missus Margaret Holden, Vivian's music teacher, that Jacques' mastery of the keyboard and his interpretation of Rachmaninov's composition was extraordinary, especially for a teenager. She yearned to make his acquaintance and learn more about him. His performance mesmerized the audience. It also made Vivian feel her performance was amateurish. She didn't know whether she should admire or hate Jacques for making her feel so inferior. On the other hand, Cheryl McGuire felt nothing but envy and regret for allowing Jacques's musical talent to eclipse her daughter's performance. However, their long-standing friendship would not be affected by Cheryl's faux pas, as a lesson learned, not to be repeated.

Jacques left the piano and joined his parents standing nearby. They were soon approached by Missus Margaret Holden.

"That was quite a performance, young man. I'm truly impressed. Where did you learn to play the piano so well?" asked Holden.

"In Paris, from my adopted mother, who was a music teacher," replied Jacques.

"Vivian told me you were entering Forest Hills High School this Fall. They have a wonderful music department, and its director, Doctor Carl Sebastian, is also the conductor of their orchestra, which has performed at very exclusive theatres. I will tell him about you, because I believe you have great music potential," said Holden.

"I'm Christiane, Jacques' mother, and this Andre, his father. We appreciate your kind comments, and I'm sure Jacques will live up to Doctor Sebastian's expectations."

"Well, if you need any assistance, Jacques, do not hesitate to contact me. I am one of the music teachers at Forest Hills High School," said Holden.

Vivian finally got up the courage to approach Jacques, congratulating him on his performance.

"I had no idea you could play the piano," said Vivian.

"Oh, something I picked up in Paris," replied Jacques, in good humor.

"Oh, yeah. What else did you pick up in Paris?" asked Vivian, sarcastically.

"Humility and a sense of humor," replied Jacques, who was then interrupted by his grandfather Robert Duval.

"Excuse me, Vivian. Jacques, I would like you to meet someone who's interested in your experiences in France during the occupation," said Robert, who tactfully led him away.

"Grandpa, I'm really not anxious to talk about my experiences in France. If you don't mind, Grandpa, can we skip it?" asked Jacques.

"Well, if that's how you feel, Jacques, then let's skip it," replied Robert, who was then accosted by his wife Marilyn, along with Andre and Christiane.

"I see you'll be starting school this Monday, huh!" said Marilyn.

"Yes, and I'm looking forward to it," replied Jacques.

"Don't forget to contact Doctor Sebastian in the music department," said Robert.

"I won't forget," replied Jacques, feeling tired and wishing to go home, which Christiane perceived and suggested they return to the Grandparents' residence, herself wishing they were returning to their own house.

On the drive back to the Duval residence, the conversation dwelved on Vivian's performance.

"Maman, where were Vivian's parents, I only saw her grandparents," said Jacques.

"Oh! I should have told you. Vivian's parents were both killed in an airplane accident when she was very young. Her grandparents, Bob and Cheryl, took over and raised her as their own child. Vivian inherited a fortune, which is managed by her grandparents, but she can't have access to it until she's twenty-one," said Christiane.

"She's worth more than twenty million, and she's the sole heir to her grandparents' estate. That girl will never want for anything," said Robert.

It took several days for Jacques to get matriculated into Forest Hills High School. He didn't get a chance to see Doctor Sebastian, until he reported for a music class, instructed by Missus Holden, who had him stay after class.

"I see you haven't yet met with Doctor Sebastian, so why don't we go over to the music hall, where Doctor Sebastian is rehearsing with the orchestra on a new musical," said Holden.

"Alright," replied Jacques with nonchalance.

The music hall was actually an amphitheater with a large stage accommodating a full orchestra composed of high school students majoring in music.

Upon seeing Missus Holden with Jacques, Doctor Sebastian gave the orchestra a break, and walked over to greet Holden and Jacques.

"Doctor Sebastian, I would like you to meet Jacques Duval, the boy I told you about. He just matriculated into the school this week," said Holden.

"Welcome to Forest Hill High School, young man. Missus Holden told me you are a very gifted pianist, well beyond your age. I think there's no time like the present while we have the orchestra on hand to determine your level of musical talent. So why don't we step over to the piano, and let's see what music you wish to play that our orchestra is familiar with," said Sebastian.

Jacques noticed Vivian McGuire sitting at the grand piano as he approached it.

"Hello, Vivian," said Jacques, somewhat embarrassed at having to take her place at the piano.

"Hi! Jacques. Nice to see you again," replied Vivian.

"You two know each other?" asked Sebastian.

"Yes, our parents are close friends," replied Vivian.

"Very well, Vivian. Jacques is going to use the piano and play a melody for us," said Sebastian. "What would you like to play, Jacques?"

"I'm familiar with some of the works by Debussy, Tchaikovsky, Rachmaninov, Shubert, Mozart, Chopin, and Barroso," replied Jacques.

"How old are you?" asked Sebastian, astonished by Jacques' reply.

"Sixteen, sir," said Jacques.

"This is a high school orchestra; therefore, my students have not yet had sufficient experience to master all of the works you mentioned. So tell me, which of Debussy's melodies you would like to play?" asked Sebastian.

"'Claire de Lune' or 'Arabesques No.1' or 'Reverie,'" replied Jacques.

"'Claire de Lune' is a very popular number. Let's do that," said Sebastian, who then informed members of his orchestra, they were to play 'Claire de Lune.'

Jacques sat at the keyboard of this magnificent grand piano and looked up at Doctor Sebastian standing on a pedestal with his conductor baton for direction.

By this time, several students, and some members of the faculty had gathered in the front seats of the near empty amphitheater. Vivian sat in one of the few empty seats in the orchestra not far from the piano where she could observe Jacques' performance at close range.

The music began with Jacques' fingers traveling deftly over the keyboard in concert with the sound of the orchestra's instruments with such sensitivity to Debussy's theme that Sebastian realized he was conducting a prodigious pianist. At the conclusion of the concert, members of the orchestra applauded Jacques' performance. They were then dismissed, but Vivian stood behind, hopeful she would connect with Jacques.

"Jacques, don't leave yet. I would like to talk to you," said Sebastian.

"You mentioned you were familiar with Ary Barroso's work. Which ones?" asked Sebastian.

"Only one so far. I was captivated by its energy. It's called 'Acuarela do Brasil,'" said Jacques.

"Really. That's a most difficult number. I don't know that our orchestra would be up to it,'" said Sebastian.

"Well, one number I really like is Sergey Rachmaninov's piano concerto number 2. Could your orchestra play that one?" asked Jacques.

"Yes, actually they did perform that number last season, but our pianist graduated, and Vivian, our current pianist, is doing well, but struggling with some of our more complex numbers. But with you at the piano, I'm sure our orchestra will fully support you," said Sebastian, whose words were unfortunately overheard by Vivian.

"Does that mean, you'll have me play for you and your orchestra?" asked Jacques.

"After this demonstration, consider yourself a member of this orchestra, with Vivian, of course, effective today. Here's a schedule of our classes and practice sessions," said Sebastian.

As Jacques was leaving the amphitheater, Vivian accosted him.

"Well, I see we're now piano partners in the orchestra," said Vivian, smiling with approval at this turn of events.

"I guess so. How does this work. Do we take turns at the piano, or do we play together?" asked Jacques in good humor.

"We take turns, of course, at the direction of Doctor Sebastian," said Vivian. "I think this gives us an opportunity to practice at my house."

"Yes, but I don't drive, and your house is quite a distance from my house," replied Jacques.

"I'm sixteen now, and I'm getting my driver's permit. My granddad is taking me to a Cadillac dealership to pick out a new car, and I already know which one I want," said Vivian.

"Oh! Yeah! Which one are you going to pick?' asked Jacques.

"A cream, 1947 Cadillac, Series 62, 2-door convertible," replied Vivian proudly.

"Wow! That's an expensive car," replied Jacques.

"So what, I can afford it," replied Vivian.

Jacques then remembered the automobile conversation he had with his grandparents regarding Vivian's inheritance and wealth.

"Well, that's nice," replied Jacques.

"That means I'll be able to pick you up, and drive you to wherever we want to go, for piano practice, of course," said Vivian with other ideas in mind.

Jacques mentioned to his parents he was now eligible for a driver's permit, and if he got a car, they wouldn't have to drive him to school.

"That certainly would be a relief for us, and it would give you freedom and independence from those who wish to quarantine you," said Christiane, who had Vivian in mind.

"I think you can get a nice used car at a reasonable price. I'll give you a budget of two thousand dollars to work with. So, shop around and see what's available, then get back to me. How does that sound?" asked Andre.

"That sounds just great, Dad. Thanks a million. I'll get right on it," replied Jacques, who was becoming Americanized, and for the first time, called his father *Dad*.

It didn't take long for Jacques to get his driver's permit after taking the required classes. He then visited a couple of dealerships that had used cars as trade-ins and found one to his liking. It was a 1932 MG Midget convertible with a sky-blue body. Jacques returned to the dealership with Andre, who had the original price reduced to fourteen hundred dollars. Jacques drove his MG Midget off the lot with ecstatic joy and that evening wrote a letter to Giselle to tell her of his new toy.

The Christmas holiday arrived, and on the 22nd of December, Jacques met Giselle at Idlewild International Airport in New York.

Giselle, dressed in winter clothing, sporting a camel hair overcoat, and knee-high brown boots, walked towards Jacques. The moment she saw him she quickened her pace, and releasing her wheeled luggage, jumped into his arms with an uninhibited embrace that drew nearby people's attention and envy.

"How was your flight?" asked Jacques as he pulled her wheeled suitcase towards the escalator.

"I had never flown before, but I like it, especially the service, and the fact it was bringing me to New York to be with you," said Giselle, grabbing and holding him by the arm, with a big, happy smile.

"Wait 'till you see our new house in Oceanside, and you'll have your own room with bath," said Jacques proudly.

"Wow! I won't want to go home," replied Giselle with a laugh.

"We celebrate Christmas and New Year big time," said Jacques. "Of course, being winter, traveling is limited, and we can't go to the beach, but there are plenty of other things to do."

Upon arrival at the two-story brick house, consisting of five bedrooms, four full-baths and a half-bath, a large back yard, and shed, Giselle was greeted with a warm and loving embrace by Christiane, who then led her upstairs to her bedroom so she could unload her suitcase. They then returned to the downstairs area where she was given a tour of the house and its yard. Eventually, Andre came home from work at the hospital and greeted Giselle like his own daughter, reminiscent of old times. A large Christmas tree adorned the living room with several presents underneath it, two of them for Giselle.

On Christmas Eve, Andre, Christiane, Jacques, and Giselle, all attended midnight mass at Saint Patrick's Roman Catholic Church and upon their return opened all their presents from under the Christmas tree. Needless to say, they all expressed their gratitude and love for each other on that Christmas day.

The Forest Hills High School had a Christmas Holiday concert scheduled for the 28th of December at the school amphitheater and expected a packed audience. Jacques was scheduled to be their pianist, and Rachmaninov's piano concerto, which they had fervently practiced, was on the program for that evening.

"Oh! God. I wouldn't miss that for anything. That's a great piece of music, and you bring it to life, Jacques," said Giselle.

"You're biased, Giselle, but thanks for the compliment," replied Jacques. "Andre had a tuxedo tailored for me for the occasion. I suggested he just rent one for me, but he said that he expects me to be using it regularly as I progress into the music profession."

"Really, is that the profession you've chosen?" asked Giselle.

"Well, that's what I like to do, and as the old saying goes, if you choose a job you love, then you never have to work," said Jacques.

"As a pianist, where would you work?" asked Giselle.

"I don't know. I suppose I could do like Doctor Sebastian, be a director of a music department at a high school or university, or give piano recitals at concerts throughout the United States and even around the world. Who knows?" said Jacques.

"That doesn't provide for much of a home life, does it," said Giselle.

"Ah! Gee, honey. I don't know that I'll be doing any traveling. Not if I'm director of a music department of a school with my own school orchestra. Doctor Sebastian has a family with four children, and his work time is devoted to Forest Hills High School and his home," said Jacques, attempting to diffuse Giselle's anxious concern.

"I suppose you're right. Besides, who knows what the future holds for us. Why worry about something that hasn't happened," replied Giselle, rationalizing a worrisome situation.

On the evening of the scheduled concert at the school amphitheater, Jacques, dressed in his tuxedo, looked very mature for his age as he sat at the grand piano with the full orchestra behind him. Doctor Sebastian, also dressed in a tuxedo, stood on the small pedestal with baton, ready to start the concert, with the amphitheater filled to capacity.

The Duval family, with Giselle, was seated in the same row of the amphitheater with the McGuire family, including

Vivian, who had surrendered her role as the orchestra's pianist to Jacques for that evening. Sergey Rachmaninov's piano concerto number 2, began softly, with its melody capturing the listener's soul on a journey so melodious, it begged never to end. Jacques' piano rendition was superb, and the applause deafening, with a standing ovation, which included Doctor Paul Parmentier, director of the Eastman School of Music at the University of Rochester in New York.

The audience slowly exited the amphitheater with many entering the hall next door for refreshments and social gathering with parents, friends and faculty members.

"I see you made it, Paul," said Carl Sebastian.

"Yes, and I'm glad I did. You were right when you said you had a piano prodigy in your orchestra. Is there any possibility I might meet this young man this evening," said Paul Parmentier. "By the way, this is my wife Camile."

"It is a pleasure meeting you, Camile. Our prodigy's name is Jacques Duval, and his parents were in the audience. I hope they're still here and in this hall. Let me see if I can find him. I'll be right back," said Sebastian.

A few minutes later, Sebastian returned with Jacques, accompanied by his parents and Giselle.

"This is Paul Parmentier, the Director of the Eastman School of Music at the University of Rochester, Jacques," said Sebastian.

"I was very impressed with your performance this evening, and I would like to invite you to play as a guest pianist at one of our concerts this summer," said Parmentier.

Jacques looked at his parents for approval.

"I think it would be an excellent opportunity for you to expand your musical experience, Jacques," said Andre, with Christiane nodding her approval.

"Yes, sir, it would be my pleasure to play with your orchestra," replied Jacques, a bit intimidated by the offer.

"Well, I'll send you information about our School of Music, and we'll be in touch many times before your scheduled performance," said Parmentier.

While Andre drove his family and Giselle home in Oceanside, Christiane commented on the offer by Parmentier.

"You know what Doctor Parmentier's offer means, Jacques. It means you'll be offered a scholarship by the University of Rochester to attend their School of Music at their expense," said Christiane.

"Their School of Music has produced some world-famous musicians and composers. This is just the beginning. Other offers will be made, Jacques," said Andre.

Giselle listened attentively to the conversation which made her feel insecure at the thought of Jacques becoming so famous; she would lose him to women of high social status.

She remained quiet in her thoughts, afraid her anxiety would betray her insecurity.

Five days later, Giselle boarded her flight back to Paris, France, as scheduled, with Jacques' promise to write to her at least once a week and telephone her frequently. He also assured her of his love for her which she needed to hear badly.

During the several months that followed, Vivian made sure her time with Jacques at music rehearsals kept him from engaging in social activities with other female students. Having her driver's license and Cadillac convertible at her disposal, Vivian made herself available and oftentimes dropped by his house unannounced to lure him away to some private place such as a restaurant. However, on one occasion, Vivian took Jacques to an expensive restaurant which he couldn't afford, and she insisted on paying the bill. He felt humiliated and told her that he was still in school, and not employed, therefore not in a position to take her to lavish restaurants, and he could not accept her charity.

"Oh! Jacques, you're so bourgeois. So I'm rich, so what. If I can afford it, why not use it. That's just your male ego talking, I swear," said Vivian.

"Look, Vivian, you start paying for everything, and you'll feel you own me, and that ain't going to happen. So, if you want to date me, you'll have to get used to hamburgers and hot dogs, Cherie," said Jacques.

"Alright, I got the message. No more ritzy restaurants. I'll just invite you to my house for dinner more often, that's all," replied Vivian.

The Spring of 1948 was now nearly over, and the school semester ended with summer plans in the making. Jacques expected Giselle to notify him in one of her weekly letters of her itinerary and flight reservations from Paris to New York. She was to spend the summer at the Duval residence in Oceanside.

Finally the letter from Giselle arrived with news that her mother had contracted amyotrophic lateral sclerosis, a disease subsequently named after Lou Gehrig, a famous baseball player for the New York Yankees whose career was ended by the disease. As a nurse and her only daughter, she had no choice but to care for her mother which prevented her from visiting Jacques in New York for the summer, and the debilitating effects of the disease required her constant care for an undetermined period of time. She begged his understanding, and promised she would continue writing him weekly letters and for him not to abandon her as she loved him unconditionally, and as soon as the crisis was over, she would fly to New York to be with him.

Jacques read and reread Giselle's letter with a heavy heart longing for her presence. He wrote her a letter of understanding regarding her plight and responsibility for the care of her mother and offered his support and that of his father with whom he had discussed her situation knowing her family's limited resources.

Giselle wrote back, stating her mother's medical coverage was not an issue, and she thanked God for giving her the nursing skills she needed to take care of her mother. She also thanked Jacques for standing by her in her time of need for his love and support. Jacques found Giselle's letter most comforting with the assurance their cherished relationship was unaffected by this temporary separation.

Vivian took advantage of Giselle's absence that summer, by inviting him to beach parties and other social functions, hoping an intimate relationship would develop. However, Jacques' newfound interest and active participation in the High School baseball team as one of their pitchers severely limited his availability to Vivian and her social activities. Having to share him with other female students in the school stadium's bleachers proved most challenging as Jacques became more popular with his colleagues. Undaunted, she managed to get him to attend one of her beach parties at her house overlooking Middle Bay. Only this time, it was a party-for-two.

A fire had been lit in a stone pit in the sandy beach not far from the house patio. Vivian brought a cooler stocked with cans of beer, and stacked on a low-slung beach table lay a bag of marshmallows and several sticks, to cook them over the fire. Being a Saturday, Vivian's parents were conveniently out for the evening.

"Is anybody else coming to this beach party?" asked Jacques.

"No. I thought it would be nice if we could be alone, just the two of us, Jacques. You've been so busy and unattainable that I wondered if I would ever get to see you. You know how much I care for you," said Vivian.

"No, I didn't. Besides, I'm busy with baseball, and also piano practice for the coming concert in the Fall," replied Jacques.

"What concert in the Fall?" asked Vivian.

"Oh! I guess you haven't heard. I've been invited by the Director of the Eastman Music School to be one of three pianists to play Claude Debussy's 'La Mer' for Three Pianos, this September," replied Jacques.

"Really, who are the other two pianists?" asked Vivian, feeling left out.

"Two pianists from their own orchestras, I presume," replied Jacques.

"So, you'll have to go to Rochester, New York, then," said Vivian.

"That's right. I'll be traveling with my Mom and Dad, who want to see the concert," said Jacques.

"Will you let me know the date when the concert will take place," asked Vivian.

"Yeah! Sure, it's no big deal," replied Jacques casually, which irritated Vivian, who felt left out of his busy life.

It was on a mid-September evening that the concert at the Eastman Music School amphitheater took place before a packed audience that had looked forward to this much advertised concert performed by a piano trio that promised exceptional entertainment.

Sitting in the audience, not far from the orchestra, Andre and Christiane discussed the list of melodies on the program.

"I see that in addition to Debussy's 'La Mer' by the Piano Trio, each pianist will individually play other melodies, and Jacques is scheduled to play Debussy's 'Clair de Lune' and also Tchaikovsky's *piano concerto Number* 1," said Christiane.

"Yes, they listed the other two pianists as Anthony Pucceli and George Palmer. They'll be playing Debussy's 'Reverie' and Beethoven's *Emperor piano concerto*," said Andre.

"That's a full and very ambitious concert," replied Christiane.

Sitting several rows back from the Duvals, Vivian quietly observed them discussing the program, her stalking presence unknown to them. She had never experienced such an obsession over anyone, and wondered whether it was his unavailability, his musical talent, or his looks that attracted her so desperately and concluded it was all of them.

The concert was a complete success, and the Duvals were invited to a reception for Jacques, members of the orchestra, and their families at the nearby restaurant 'Margo' reserved specifically for that occasion.

Vivian made sure she was not noticed by the Duvals or Jacques as she watched them join the group of revelers on their way to the reception. She felt isolated and regretted attending the concert, promising herself she would either become one of the family or else avoid further contact with Jacques although her parents were close friends with the Duvals. Upon her return to Long Island, Vivian made certain her presence at social events which Jacques attended was favorably noted by surrounding herself with popular suitors, hoping it would arouse his attention, jealousy, and desire for her. While it succeeded in getting Jacques to accept some of her invitations to escort her to some social events, she failed to obtain exclusive rights to his personal datebook. But that did not discourage her. In fact, the challenge made her more determined to conquer and tame him like a wild horse.

Having been awarded a full scholarship from the Eastman School of Music at the University of Rochester, New York, Jacques made new friends at the fraternity house where he resided while attending school. Doctor Carl Sebastian, the Director of the Eastman School of Music, who was largely responsible for Jacques' scholarship, was especially interested in his progress and challenged him to more advanced musical compositions, and piano performances than his other students which did not disappoint him.

At Oceanside, Long Island, Vivian had an opportunity to see Jacques when he came home from Rochester to celebrate his mother Christiane's birthday on the 4th of October 1950. Although his visit was for only three days attached to a weekend, Vivian managed to lure Jacques away from his parents for a full day with the intention of seducing him into an intimate relationship. She drove him in her Cadillac convertible to the Yankee stadium as a surprise, knowing his love for baseball.

"I know how you love baseball, and today is the second game in the World Series between the New York Yankees and the Philadelphia Phillies. What's more, I got two Field MVP seats in row 15," said Vivian with a big smile.

"Wow! How did you manage to get those MVP seats?" asked Jacques, visibly surprised.

"My Dad got them for me. I told him you were home, and I wanted to give you something for you to remember," replied Vivian.

"Hey! That's great. Let's go inside and join the crowd. By the way, who are you going to root for?" asked Jacques.

"The Yankees of course, what about you?" asked Vivian.

"The Yankees. If I said the Phillies, you'd probably tear up my ticket, and have me walk home," replied Jacques, laughing.

"You got that right, pal. Only Yankee fans ride in my car," replied Vivian in good humor.

Once in their seats in row 15, Vivian decided she was hungry for the stadium's famous hot dogs.

"Let's get a hot dog and a coke," said Vivian.

"Good idea, let's do it before the game starts." replied Jacques.

Back in their seats, eating their delicious hot dog with savory soft drink, Jacques looked at the program.

"Who's pitching for the Yankees?" asked Vivian.

"Allie Reynolds, and for the Phillies it's Robin Roberts," replied Jacques.

The game was a very tight one with both pitchers doing an outstanding job of keeping the scores low. The game ended with the Yankees winning by a score of 2 to 1. Jacques' enthusiasm was most contagious, and Vivian could not remember when she had enjoyed such a spirited and exciting afternoon, which she attributed to Jacques' unfettered and buoyant personality. She had given much thought to where to have dinner with him, remembering his previous admonishment about going to expensive restaurants he couldn't afford. Therefore, in view of her parents' absence, vacationing in Florida, she decided to have dinner at her home, where she could show him her culinary skills.

"Where are we going?" asked Jacques, as they were leaving the stadium in Vivian's Cadillac convertible.

"I'm taking you to dinner, where the food is great, the atmosphere is romantic, and the price is right," said Vivian.

"Really, where is that?" asked Jacques.

"At my house of course. My folks are vacationing in Florida, and we have the house all to ourselves," replied Vivian.

"I hope your culinary talents are as good as your presentation," said Jacques.

"Never fear, my dear. We're having New York Strip steaks on the outside grill; that'll be your department, and I'll take care of the rest with a bottle of red wine to celebrate the Yankees' win over the Phillies," replied Vivian.

"I must admit, you planned the whole day perfectly," said Jacques.

"Well, it's not often I get a chance to have you all to myself," replied Vivian.

"Yes, I guess I've been pretty busy and not very accessible, being in Rochester," replied Jacques.

"You know, Jacques, Rochester is a nine-to-ten-hour drive from here, and flying is no picnic either, not to mention having to book a hotel room, and then having to rent a car to get around. It's very discouraging," said Vivian.

"I know, Vivian. I'm not blaming you for your reluctance to come up to Rochester to see me. My school schedule prevents me from leaving Rochester, except on national holidays," said Jacques.

"When will you graduate from Eastman School of Music?" asked Vivian.

"Next year in June. I completed a lot of work last summer, which moved my graduation to that earlier date," replied Jacques.

"What will you do then," asked Vivian.

"Well, Doctor Sebastian told me that I should sign-up with a talent agent who will arrange for me to perform at concerts throughout the United States and foreign countries as the demand arises. In short, he will be my entertainment manager," said Jacques.

"You know, Jacques, next year, I will turn twenty-one, and I'll be in a financial position to really help you. I could be your manager with the funds to get you started in a big way. You'd be saving a good twenty-to-twenty-five percent of a manager's commission by having me as your agent. Furthermore, you'd be my only client; therefore, all of my energy, devotion and wealth would be focused on promoting you and your talent as a concert pianist. I could also finance the recording of your piano concerts for world-wide distribution, and that could bring you unsurpassed recognition and much wealth. Well, what do you think?" said Vivian.

"You most certainly present a valid and lucrative proposal. I'm not there yet, but you've given me a lot to think about. In the meantime, let's get dinner started," replied Jacques, wanting to put the subject on a back burner.

Vivian expected a more enthusiastic response from Jacques and decided that a more persuasive method needed to be implemented.

After dinner ending with a glass of red wine, Vivian invited Jacques to join her in the third floor tower which had a panoramic view of the bay area. Earlier that day she had brought a record player to the tower with several mood music records which she now turned on, starting with 'Moonlight Serenade.'

"May I have the pleasure of this dance?" asked Vivian, alluringly.

"Mais Oui, Cherie," replied Jacques in French.

Vivian gently pressed her entire body against Jacques, then her right cheek against his as they slowly danced to Glenn Miller's romantic melody. She then looked directly into his eyes, and whispered "I love you, Jacques."

He didn't answer, so she kissed him on the lips, at first gently, then passionately, moving her right hand down to his buttocks, feeling its round firmness and arousing her sexual passion. Her back was near the couch, so she pulled him back on top of her as she fell on the couch facing him, with her skirt up, revealing her naked torso sans panties.

"Make love to me, Jacques," she said in a low, sexy voice.

"I'm sorry, I can't do that, not now," replied Jacques getting off of her and standing up.

"Why not, don't you find me attractive?" asked Vivian.

"Of course, but I'm not going to engage in sexual intercourse with anyone until I'm married to a woman who loves me as much as I love her," replied Jacques.

"Well, if it's marriage you want, Jacques, you just name the date," replied Vivian.

"Not so fast, Vivian. I'm not ready for that commitment, and I certainly don't know you well enough to make that vow," said Jacques, not mentioning it would be a betrayal of his love for Giselle.

"What's wrong with making love now. How else you gonna know what you're getting. There's an old saying that time is what life is made of, so don't waste it," replied Vivian.

"There's an older saying; Don't rush in where angels fear to tread," replied Jacques.

"You're the only man I know whose verbal fencing equals mine," replied Vivian with laughter.

"Well, aside from my moral standards, Vivian, it wouldn't be beyond a woman's desire to get pregnant, in order to land a husband, present company excepted, but accidents do happen," said Jacques.

"Oh! Jacques, don't you trust me. I'm wearing a diaphragm," replied Vivian, who was not wearing any protection with the intent to get pregnant as her alternative method.

"Vivian, please. If you truly love me, then you'll respect my moral standards and wait for that day at the altar when you take your vows to love me in sickness and in health until death do us part," said Jacques, not realizing the significance and prophecy of his statement.

"Well, I didn't know you felt so strongly about that. Of course I will wait until you're ready, if that's what you want," replied Vivian.

"That's what I want. Thank you for your understanding," said Jacques, who then descended from the tower with a disappointed Vivian.

Jacques had just celebrated his 21st birthday on the 10th of March, when he received a letter from Giselle revealing that her ill mother had died five days before, and she just returned from her mother's burial at the Saint Denis cemetery. Her father was in a state of depression over her death, and her presence and care of him at this time was necessary. But soon she would be able to visit him in New York. At least now, Jacques thought, she is free to resume her career and life.

Three months later, Jacques graduated from Eastman Music School and immediately received an invitation to play Tchaikovsky's piano concerto Number 1, at the Palacio de Bellas Artes in Mexico City on the 22nd of June, compliments of Doctor Carl Sebastian, as his graduation gift. Jacques was elated at this wonderful opportunity, and his parents, unable to attend, wished him a safe flight and much success. Vivian was less enthused, feeling somewhat rejected but not discouraged, knowing he would only be spending two days in Mexico, and upon his return, she would apply a new strategy for his conquest.

On the morning of the 23rd of June, Christiane received a long distance call from a doctor at the General Hospital in Mexico City.

"May I speak to Doctor Andre Duval?" asked the Mexican Doctor.

"One moment please, I'll get him for you," replied Christiane.

"This is Doctor Andre Duval, what can I do for you?" asked Andre.

"I'm Doctor Fernandez at the Hospital General de Mexico. Your business card was found inside the wallet of a patient named Jacques Duval, who was involved in a vehicle accident."

"Jacques Duval is my son. You said he's a patient in your hospital. What was his injury?" asked Andre.

"He suffered a severe concussion from the collision of the taxi he was riding with another vehicle. He did not suffer any other physical injuries except for some minor bruises. However, he is blind, hopefully only a temporary condition," said Doctor Fernandez.

"I am a doctor and surgeon. I am taking the next available flight to Mexico City, and I'll be in your hospital, hopefully tomorrow afternoon. What is your hospital's address?" asked Andre, with Christiane now standing by his side.

Andre recited the address given to him by Doctor Fernandez to Christiane standing next to him with pen and paper.

"Thank you for that information, Doctor Fernandez," said Andre.

"I'm looking forward to meeting with you, Doctor Duval. I assure you your son is being well taken care of. Upon your arrival, please ask for me, and if I'm not available, please ask for Doctor Martinez," said Doctor Fernandez, ending the telephone call.

"I overheard you say Jacques is blind," said Christiane, anxiously.

"He suffered a severe concussion in a car accident, and he's blind, hopefully a temporary condition, said the doctor," replied Andre. "I have to book a flight to Mexico City right away. I'm going to call Doctor Munson at the hospital and tell him of my emergency and flight to Mexico, so he can cover my absence. Listen, Christiane, please don't tell anyone of Jacques' blindness, only that he suffered a concussion, that's all."

"Alright, I understand. Oh! God. I'm going to pray hard that his blindness is only temporary. I wish I was going with you, but I understand you're the doctor in the family and will know what medical action needs to be taken," said Christiane, with a worried look on her face.

After booking his flight for the following morning, Andre called a friend, an ophthalmologist, for information regarding Jacques' condition and blindness. He was told that a cerebral angiography should provide the necessary information to form a diagnosis and treatment.

Upon arrival at the Hospital in Mexico City, Andre was met by Doctor Fernandez, who informed him that a cerebral angiography was conducted, and he was given diuretics to excrete fluids and alleviate pressure buildup and swelling in the brain. He was of the opinion that Jacques' blindness was only temporary and would last from a couple of weeks to as long as two months. However, he should be looked at by an ophthalmologist upon his return to the United States. He would then send him his medical records including the results of the cerebral angiography. Jacques remained in the Mexican hospital for another two days, then was released in the care of Andre for return to the United States. Andre dutifully called Christiane to inform her of Jacques' condition and prognosis which she found encouraging.

While Andre and Jacques were still in Mexico City, Vivian pulled up to the Duval residence in her Cadillac convertible, expecting to find Jacques.

"Jacques is not here, Vivian. He's still in Mexico City," said Christiane.

"He was supposed to return yesterday," said Vivian.

"Well, he was the victim of a car accident in Mexico City, and Andre had to fly there to evaluate his injuries and then bring him home," said Christiane.

"Injuries? What kind of injuries?" asked Vivian, alarmed at the thought of him being mangled.

"He suffered a severe concussion, but that's all we know right now. So, I'll let you know when Jacques is back, OK?" replied Christiane.

"Yes, I'm so sorry to hear of Jacques' accident. Please let me know the minute he gets back," replied Vivian, with genuine sincerity.

At the Hospital General de Mexico, Andre sat next to Jacques lying on the hospital bed still suffering from blindness.

"I looked at the cerebral angiography, and I also discussed your condition, not only with Doctor Fernandez, but also with Doctor Munson, an ophthalmologist and friend of mine in Long Island, and we've all come to the conclusion that your blindness is only temporary, and your eyesight could return in full measure as soon as a couple of weeks but most probably in a month or two," said Andre.

"That is good news, Dad. You don't realize how important your eyesight is until you lose it," said Jacques.

"I know that you've been romantically pursued by two very desirable women, and you're probably being pressured into matrimony. Am I correct?" asked Andre with a big grin, that unfortunately could not be seen by Jacques.

"Yeah! Vivian has been very active in that department, but Giselle has been too busy taking care of her sick mother, to broach the subject," said Jacques.

"I'm going to give you some very wise advice which I hope you will follow because marriage is the most serious decision you make in your entire life, and a mistake of choice can be disastrous for you and the person you marry," said Andre.

"Right now, I can use all the advice you can give me, Dad, so I'm listening," replied Jacques.

"In choosing the woman you're going to marry, make sure you love her, but make *absolutely* sure she loves you. Now, your temporary blindness gives you a unique opportunity to find out which of the two women you love and contemplate marrying, loves you truly and unconditionally, for richer or poorer, in sickness and in health, in accordance with the vows you will take in church at your wedding. So, when we return to New York, you will not tell anyone, especially Vivian and Giselle that your blindness is only temporary. They must believe your blindness is permanent, so that you will then find out who truly loves you unconditionally and without reservations," said Andre.

"Wow! You really thought this all out, and I think it's a great idea, but when will I reveal my recovery?" asked Jacques.

"OK! As soon as you've decided who you want to marry, make the wedding arrangements right away, but continue to appear blind even if you've recovered your eyesight because I've got a plan that General George Patton would be proud of, but it must remain a secret between you, me and Christiane," said Andre.

CHAPTER XX
A Marriage Made in Heaven

Christiane stood among other people waiting behind the security gate where airline passengers exit at Idlewild International Airport. After more than a half hour, passengers from the flight arriving from Mexico City began to appear and pass through the exit gate. Finally, she saw Andre guiding Jacques, who was holding a white cane that alerted people to his blindness. As soon as they passed through the exit gate, Christiane walked up to Jacques and hugged him with a deep embrace.

"Welcome home, Jacques, we're gonna take good care of you," said Christiane, now linking her arm with his arm, while Jacques walked between his parents to the baggage area and then the ride home.

Christiane was informed by Andre of his plan to have everyone believe Jacques' blindness was permanent, and she readily agreed with the plan. Christiane then called Vivian and informed her of Jacques' arrival home. She was asked if she wished to visit Jacques, and Vivian agreed to see Jacques that afternoon.

Upon arrival at the Duval residence, Vivian was greeted by Christiane whose husband was at work at the hospital.

"Vivian, before I take you into the living room to see Jacques, there's something I must tell you. Jacques is blind, and there's little hope of recovery. He's having a hard time dealing with it, so please don't ask him any questions about his condition. Now let's go see him," said Christiane.

Upon entering the living room, Vivian's sight immediately focused on the white cane Jacques was holding by its handle, erect from the floor, while sitting in a stuffed chair.

"Jacques, Vivian is here," said Christiane.

Jacques immediately stood up, holding his cane for stability.

"Hello, Vivian, It's so nice of you to visit me. Please excuse my awkward greeting, but I'm sure you've been told the circumstances of my physical condition," said Jacques.

"Oh! Jacques, you don't need to apologize," replied Vivian, walking up to him and then carefully embracing him. Seeing his lifeless eyes staring straight ahead frightened her with the thought of spending the rest of her life with a blind man. She wanted to know if his blindness was permanent, but knew it would be an inappropriate question to ask him, hence it would wait until she could talk to Christiane alone.

"How did the concert go?" asked Vivian.

"It went very well indeed. The director was most pleased with the performance and said he would invite me again," replied Jacques.

"That's very encouraging. I'm sure your medical condition is only temporary, and you'll be performing again, soon," said Vivian in an attempt to determine his chance of recovering his sight. However, she received no response from Jacques or Christiane.

Standing in the vestibule ready to exit the Duval residence, Vivian turned to Christiane with a final question.

"What's the prognosis on Jacques' eyesight? What are his chances of recovery?" asked Vivian.

"Not very good, I'm afraid, Vivian," replied Christiane.

Vivian left the premises with serious doubts about her future with Jacques.

That evening Christiane had a talk with Andre, without Jacques's presence, pertaining to Vivian's visit that afternoon.

"I got the distinct feeling that Vivian was horrified by Jacques' blindness and realized her inability to cope with his medical condition, especially in the long term as his wife," said Christiane.

"I figured that much. She's now a wealthy woman who does not want her social activities restricted by a blind husband. I don't think she'll be visiting Jacques any time soon, not unless she discovers his blindness is temporary," said Andre.

"Let's now invite Giselle and her father to visit us," said Christiane.

"Why the father at this time?" asked Andre.

"Because if she's the one Jacques decides to marry, her father will have to be here to give the bride away at the wedding," said Christiane.

"I can always count on you for those details," replied Andre.

"Let's send Giselle a letter by priority mail, informing her of Jacques' accident and blindness, and invite her to come and visit us as soon as possible. Also we would like her father to come with her, as it would make a nice family reunion for old times' sake," said Christiane.

"Good idea. That will invite an immediate response from Giselle. I'll get that done right away," said Andre.

A fortnight later, Christiane received a letter from Giselle, offering her deep sympathy for Jacques' medical condition. She also provided her flight itinerary for herself and her father, with much appreciation for the kind invitation.

It had been nearly a month since Vivian had visited Jacques, without any subsequent inquiry, and Giselle was about to arrive in New York with her father that afternoon.

Roland LeGrand, dressed in a conservative gray suit, still sporting a full head of gray hair, arrived at Idlewild International Airport with his daughter, Giselle, wearing a long maroon dress with mandarin collar that flattered her ballerina figure. They were greeted at the airport by Andre, while Christiane remained home with Jacques.

"Welcome to New York. I hope you had an enjoyable flight," said Andre, greeting Roland and Giselle with a warm handshake and embrace.

"Oh! Yes. Isn't Jacques with you?" asked Giselle in French, in deference to her father who understood but was not fluent in English.

"No, he stayed at home with Christiane. But you will see them shortly when we get to the house. Let's get your luggage," said Andre, guiding them downstairs to the baggage section.

While waiting for the luggage to appear on the baggage conveyor system, Giselle could not contain her curiosity over Jacques' medical condition.

"How is Jacques doing. Are his eyes getting better?" asked Giselle.

"No, and his condition may be permanent. But we pray for a miracle," replied Andre.

"Is he still playing the piano?" asked Giselle.

"Not since his accident. He has to allow the swelling in the brain to recede; therefore, he must refrain from physical activity for a while," said Andre.

"But eventually, he will be able to play the piano from memory, and if he learns Braille, he'll be able to read music sheets," said Giselle, optimistically.

"Unfortunately, Braille reading requires the use of one's fingers, which he needs to play the keyboard," replied Andre.

"Of course, why didn't I think of that," replied Giselle.

"Ah! Here comes the luggage," said Andre.

Upon arrival at the Duval residence, Christiane immediately embraced Giselle and Roland, whom she hadn't seen since her departure from France. Without delay, she brought Giselle and Roland into the living room where Jacques sat in his usual stuffed chair with white cane, and upon hearing their voices, stood up to greet them.

"Jacques, it's me Giselle," she said embracing him eagerly.

"My father Roland is here too," said Giselle.

"It is very nice meeting you again, Jacques. I am very sorry for your accident," said Roland, in French.

"I'm glad you could make it. I wish I was able to show you New York, but I'm sure Andre and Christiane will make up for my disability," replied Jacques in French although he knew Roland understood English. Furthermore, they were all fluent in French.

"Let me show you your rooms upstairs where you can unpack, then come down for dinner," said Christiane.

During dinner, chicken was served with assorted vegetables, preceded by a salad, followed by French red wine for the occasion.

"We're very sorry about the death of Madeleine, and hope she didn't suffer and her passing was peaceful," said Andre.

"Yes, she died in her sleep, and I'm sure she was well received by God in Heaven," replied Giselle.

"Madeleine's illness required a lot of your time and nursing. Did that interfere much with your studies and attendance at nursing school?" asked Christiane.

"The director of the nursing school was very understanding, and allowed me much flexibility and home study, so that I was able to graduate on time this past June," said Giselle with unusual humility.

"Well, that's wonderful. So, you're now a registered nurse in France, and I'm sure also acceptable in the U.S." said Christiane, also a nurse.

"Yes, I suppose it would be acceptable here in the United States," replied Giselle.

"Perhaps you could be Jacques' nurse," said Christiane, probingly.

"I would love nothing better than to be Jacques' nurse if the opportunity offered itself," replied Giselle.

"That's good to know. You can never tell what the future holds for any of us," said Andre.

"You've been very quiet, Jacques. What do you think of Giselle being your nurse?" asked Christiane.

"I couldn't think of a better and kinder nurse," replied Jacques.

"Well, I hope you will stay with us long enough for Jacques to find out just how wonderful a nurse you really are," said Christiane with a gentle smile of approval.

During the days that followed, Andre went to work at the hospital, and Christiane would take Roland for a drive to the market place and other stores while Giselle got acquainted with Jacques, and they grew closer to each other with the remembrance of their love and affection while in France. It seemed as if Jacques' blindness had increased Giselle's love with an empathy that made it boundless. Jacques felt her sincere affection and realized that she truly loved him, regardless of his medical condition and decided that he would ask her to marry him after he discussed it with Andre and Christiane, for their valued opinion.

Under the pretext of taking Jacques for an eye examination by Doctor Munson, Christiane took Jacques for a drive, leaving Roland and Giselle at home. However, Christiane drove Jacques to the hospital where Andre worked, for a family conference outside the ears of their two guests.

"Mom, Dad. I've decided that Giselle is the woman I want to marry. We've had long talks since she's been here, and I'm convinced she truly loves me, unconditionally. She believes

I'm permanently blind, yet that just makes her more loving and caring. On the other hand, I haven't heard from Vivian in a month. Obviously, my disability is more than she can handle. But I think it goes deeper than that. I believe Vivian is a very selfish person, who cannot put any other person above her own interest, which true love demands," said Jacques.

"You know, Jacques, you have matured well beyond your age. Your mother and I both agree with your decision. Furthermore, the fact that Giselle is a registered nurse indicates an empathic personality towards other human beings. However, in case you should recover your eyesight before the wedding date, I think you should refrain from revealing it to Giselle until you're at the altar and have been declared husband and wife. That way, there can be no doubt in anyone's mind about the sincerity of her declaration of love," said Andre.

"Yes, I agree with your father, Jacques. I think it's a good idea to wait until you're married before revealing your recovery," said Christiane.

"Well, if I recover my eyesight before then, I will tell her the good news when I kiss her at the altar," replied Jacques with a mischievous grin.

The date of the wedding was set and its announcement published in the local newspapers which did not escape Vivian and her parents' attention.

"Well, what do you know? Jacques is getting married to that French girl Giselle," said Vivian to her parents.

"She didn't waste any time, did she?" replied her mother, Cheryl

"Well, it's a good thing she's a nurse, because he's gonna need one for the rest of his life," said Vivian.

"I do feel sorry for that young man. He's such a talented pianist. But you got out in time, Vivian. I don't think you would have been happy being married to a blind man," said Robert McGuire, who knew only too well his granddaughter's human frailties but was a close friend of Doctor Andre Duval.

"I'm sure we'll be invited to the wedding. Bob and I don't think that under the circumstances, we can refuse to attend," said Cheryl, inquisitively.

"Yes, we'll have to attend. After all, we've been close friends with the Duval family for decades. You'll have to join us, Vivian, no exceptions my dear," said Robert, whose patriarchal authority Vivian would never question.

At the Duval residence, plans for the wedding were being executed with excitement. Christiane had taken Giselle to an upscale shop for a white wedding dress with all of the usual paraphernalia while Andre took Roland to his tailor for a black suit, shoes, white shirt and tie, so he could escort his daughter down the church aisle in style and dignity. A surprise wedding gift from Jacques' grandparents was the purchase and significant deposit on a beautiful house in Oceanside for the newlyweds, whose keys were to be given to them only at the reception following the wedding as is the custom for wedding gifts.

Saint Patrick's Church in Long Island City was quickly filling up with worshippers as the hour of Jacques and Giselle's wedding approached.

Jacques, still using his white cane, accompanied by Andre, arrived at the rear of the church, and made his way into the rectory connected to the rear of the church, where they met with Father McLaughlin.

"You're early, that's good. This is a big day for you, young man," said Father McLaughlin.

"Yes, father, it is, and I've been looking forward to it for some time," replied Jacques.

"It's an event you'll remember for the rest of your life," said Father McLaughlin. "If you have any doubts, now's the time to tell us."

"No, Father, I have no doubts," replied Jacques.

"That's good. I think it's time for us to go into the church and for you two to take your position. When you hear the organ playing 'Amazing Grace' that's when you take your place in front of the altar to receive the bride from her father," said Father McLaughlin.

"I thought Giselle had chosen 'Ave Maria'" said Jacques.

"Well, whichever song is played, that's when you take your position. I presume you have the rings," said Father McLaughlin.

"Yes, I have the rings," replied Andre, handing them to Jacques, who placed them in his jacket pocket.

As Jacques stood with Andre, near and to the side of the altar, Jacques whispered in a low voice to Andre.

"By the way, Dad, I recovered my eyesight yesterday evening. So, when we get up to the altar, remain by my side, so I can give you my cane when Father McLaughlin pronounces us man and wife," said Jacques.

"Good grief, now you tell me. You just hope she doesn't faint when you tell her the news," replied Andre.

"Don't worry, I'll be ready to catch her if she does faint," replied Jacques.

"Just remember that the cameras are rolling and recording for posterity," said Andre.

"Here they come," said Andre. "Let me guide you to the front of the altar."

Giselle, dressed in a splendid white wedding gown, escorted by her father, dressed in a black suit, white shirt and maroon tie, slowly walked down the aisle to 'Amazing Grace.'

Giselle's beauty and poise were noticed and remarked by Robert and Cheryl McGuire, but Vivian remained silent, wondering what compelling attribute she missed that won Jacques' heart.

Giselle and her father finally arrived at the altar facing Jacques and Andre. Roland delivered his daughter to Jacques still holding his cane and pretending to be blind but instinctively held out his elbow for Giselle to grab and turn towards Father McLaughlin. Andre remained only a few feet away from them ready to accept Jacques' cane.

Father McLaughlin began the ceremony.

"Since it is your intention to enter into the covenant of Holy Matrimony, join your hands and declare your consent before God and his Church," said Father McLaughlin.

"I, Jacques Duval, take you, Giselle LeGrand, to be my wife. I promise to be true to you in good times, and in bad, in sickness and in health. I will love you and honor you all the days of my life."

"I, Giselle LeGrand, take you, Jacques Duval, to be my husband. I promise to be faithful to you in good times and in bad, in sickness and in health. I will love you and honor you all the days of my life."

"Jacques Duval, do you take this woman to be your wife? Do you promise to be faithful to her in good times and in bad, in sickness and in health, to love her and to honor her all the days of your life?" asked Father McLaughlin.

"I do," replied Jacques.

"Giselle LeGrand, do you take Jacques Duval to be your husband? Do you promise to be faithful to him in good times and in bad, through sickness and in health, to love him and to honor him all the days of your life?" asked Father McLaughlin.

"I do," replied Giselle.

Father McLaughlin verbally acknowledged that Jacques and Giselle have declared their consent to be married and openly prayed for God's blessing on them, declaring:

"What God has joined, let no one put asunder."

Jacques produced the wedding rings which Father McLaughlin blessed, then he ordered the exchange of the rings.

Jacques placed the wedding ring on Giselle's ring finger.

"I, Giselle LeGrand, receive this ring as a sign of my love and fidelity. In the name of the Father, and of the Son, and of the Holy Spirit."

Giselle then placed the wedding ring on Jacques's ring finger.

"I, Jacques Duval, receive this ring as a sign of my love and fidelity. In the name of the Father, and of the Son, and of the Holy Spirit."

"I now pronounce you Man and Wife," said Father McLaughlin.

Jacques turned towards Andre and handed him the cane, then turned towards Giselle, and with a big smile, embraced her on the lips, as Father McLaughlin watched with a puzzled look on his face.

Recovering from the embrace, Giselle looked into Jacques' eyes with bewilderment.

"Yes, Giselle, I have recovered my eyesight. Our wedding gift from God," said Jacques, who then winked at Father McLaughlin, then held out his right elbow for Giselle to grab, escorting her up the church aisle towards the exit. Vivian McGuire was not amongst the many parishioners wondering if they had witnessed a miracle, figuring Jacques had cleverly manipulated his accident into a test which she obviously failed.

Entering the limousine that would take the newlyweds to the reception, Giselle could not contain her curiosity.

"When did you recover your eyesight?" asked Giselle.

"Yesterday afternoon, just in time for our wedding," replied Jacques.

"Maybe it was a miracle after all," said Giselle thoughtfully.

THE END

EPILOGUE

The story in this novel is fictional. However, its locale, mostly in France during the Second World War, provided historical events that shocked the sensibilities of even the most cynical skeptic, when irrefutable evidence of its war crimes was eventually discovered.

In 1937, a drug known as Pervitin, subsequently identified as methamphetamine or crystal meth, was made available to the German public without a prescription, and marketed as a mood enhancer pill to alleviate stress, fatigue, and create feelings of euphoria. The benefits of Pervitin soon became known to the leaders of the Wehrmacht Armed Forces, and in 1939, during the invasion of Poland, the Nazi leadership recognized Pervitin's value as a stimulant in combat, which kept them awake, feeling exhilarated and invincible. The Wehrmacht subsequently ordered 35 million Pervitin tablets for its armed forces in preparation for its invasion of France in 1940. However, Pervitin's negative effects on its users eventually became apparent, but too late to prevent its continued use. One of the sinister properties of Pervitin was its sociopathic effect, stripping its user of all empathy, insensitive to the pain and suffering of the user's victims, as evidenced by the massacre at Oradour-sur-Glane in Limousin, France, where the inhabitants of the entire village, numbering six hundred and forty-two men, women and children, were executed, and the town looted and destroyed by a Wehrmacht Battalion, commanded by a Nazi Major.

In the history of the world, the Second World War has no doubt caused the greatest blemish on humanity's soul.

www.ingramcontent.com/pod-product-compliance
Lightning Source LLC
Chambersburg PA
CBHW070314260626
47160CB00003B/841